HARD KNOX

(Havenwood #3)

by
RILEY HART

Cover Design by Sleepy Fox Studio
Cover Photography by LUKEography
Edited by Keren Reed Editing
Proofread by Judy's Proofreading and Lyrical Lines Proofreading

Blurb

Callum

A gay guy walks into a straight bar and notices the hottest man he's ever seen.

Why am I not surprised my life sounds like the beginning of a bad joke? First, my ex cheated on me, and I went running to Havenwood and the mom I have a complicated relationship with. Then, there's Knox, the gorgeous lumberjack I don't stand a chance with. To top it off, he's more than just a pretty face, and I start to fall for him. Knox is kind, funny, honorable, quickly becoming my best friend, and unfortunately, straight with a capital *S*.

Knox

My life has taken a few unexpected turns lately. First, the new guy in town, Callum, has me strangely confused. Then my son, Logan, comes to live with me. He connects with Callum instantly, and I do too. Before we know it, he's become a daily fixture in our lives, making us laugh, calling me his lumberjack and making this foreign warmth spread inside me.

It doesn't matter that I've never been with a guy before—one kiss from Cal, and it's clear I'm bi. He turns me upside down. With every laugh, every conversation, every touch and exploration, I fall harder. Sneaking around isn't ideal, but there's a lot for us to consider. All I know is I need him. Life has a funny way of throwing a wrench into your plans, though, and things become a mess. But then I'm reminded that while nothing in life is guaranteed, not even love, what Callum and I have built is worth fighting for.

Special Thanks

Special thanks to Jaclyn Quinn for the help with all things asthma related! Any mistakes are my own.

CHAPTER ONE

Callum

O H, WOW.

If I had known there were so many pretty, rugged boys in Mom's hometown, I would have come here a lot sooner.

I always had a thing for rugged, even though most of the guys I dated weren't that. Not that they weren't out there, but I'd been in Los Angeles for years, and they felt different from this home-grown, small-town kind of guy. At least it did in my head.

And I didn't want to think about LA. California led me to thoughts about Stan, and I didn't want to go there. At all. Ever.

It was my first time at *Griff's*—even the name was sexy. I'd just gotten into Havenwood, reserved my hotel room, then came here. It had been a long trip, and I was second-guessing myself like crazy. When things crashed and burned with Stan, I realized how tired I was of the whole LA scene. I needed something new, so I'd started the process to get my Virginia work licensing taken care of—I was a nurse practitioner—then quit my job, sold my condo, and got on the road.

I scanned the bar again. It wasn't a large space—counter to the left, pool tables and darts to the right, and oh shit, a Pride flag in a straight bar? That was a first and not something I'd have expected from small-town Virginia. Maybe that was a good sign. I could use one.

My eyes found their way back to the group at the far end of the bar. A pretty, dark-haired guy sat on a blond's lap, so again, looked like Griff's was queer friendly. They were chatting with two women, and next to them stood a super-sexy guy with chocolate-brown hair, thick arms, and a Marilyn Monroe beauty mark. Definitely dude-bro but gorgeous.

The bartender had black hair, scruff along his jaw, and a kind smile. He had that whole rugged thing going on too, but my eyes skimmed past him to the knockout with the blond curls and the ginger on his arm—damn, two queer couples—before they landed on the last guy again. It was him I couldn't look away from.

Black, messy hair, long-ish. He had it pushed back, but it fell into his face when he moved, which was really hot. Nice, kissable mouth, his lips not too thin but not too plump either. Black beard. But it was his eyes that really got me. They were this crisp, sparkling, almost translucent green…and they were looking at me like, *Who in the fuck is this guy?* And not, *I want to bang the hell out of this guy.*

Probably straight.

As I made my way through the space, I got a few strange looks. The people here might be gay friendly, but I was new, and wore eyeliner sometimes, so I assumed they were wondering what city I came from.

I made sure to give them all my best smile, because that was the way I worked. I got some frowns in return, and there were some whispers, but I held my head high and kept going.

There was an empty spot at the counter beside the blond with the twink on his lap.

The bartender approached me as I sat down. "Welcome to Griff's. Can I getcha something?"

It was cute how he welcomed me. I was sure people knew every face in this town, except mine now, obviously. "Yes, please. I'd love a beer. What have you got on tap?"

He told me and I chose, watching as he filled the mug. I could feel eyes on me from the group. It probably wasn't often eyeliner-wearing men showed up in

Havenwood, so I got it, but it was still a little weird.

"You passing through?" Bartender asked.

"Nope," I replied, not offering anything else. I definitely wasn't telling him my boyfriend cheated on me and I came running to mommy—a mom I haven't been close with in a long time. Oh, and who had no idea I was moving here.

"I'm Griffin," he said, but I could tell it wasn't in a flirty way, just a polite one.

"Callum," I replied.

"Callum?" a guy asked from my right. I looked over to see blond curls. And wait. Was that…

"Are you Remington Monroe?"

Blond Curls tensed. Oh, someone was protective of his boy.

The redhead nodded.

"Wow…I feel like I stepped into Oz or something, but the good kind? I mean, I haven't been attacked by an evil witch yet, and there are queer boys and pride flags in straight bars and a famous musician." I dropped my head back. "Oh shit."

"What?" Lap Twink asked.

"Did I get into a car accident and I'm dead? And here I thought I'd landed in a pretty-boy oasis. Fuck. Of course I'm dead."

Griffin handed the beer over. A few of the guys laughed. My rugged lumberjack looked at me like I was an alien.

"You're Callum?" Blond Curls asked again. "Mary Beth's son?"

Wow. So Mom had been talking about me? I was surprised…yet not. Our relationship was complicated. "Yeah, and you are?" I took a drink of my beer.

"I'm Lawson. I own the café she works at—Sunrise. Your mom, she's great. I'm surprised she didn't tell me you were coming."

"Oh, that's probably because she doesn't know yet. Surprise!" They all looked at me like I was crazy. Except Lap Twink. I think he got me. It was him who recovered first.

"I'm Kellan, by the way. The grumpy bartender is my brother—"

"Hey, I'm not grumpy. I introduced myself before the rest of you," Griffin said. Kellan ignored him.

"This sexy guy is my boyfriend, Chase. The dude-bro is my bestie Josh."

"Oh my God. I called him the same thing in my head. Dude-bro, that is, not Josh, because obviously, I didn't know his name."

"What the fuck?" Josh said. Kellan ignored him too.

I liked Kellan.

"The ladies are Cynthia and Becca. My other bestie Natalie is working." He pointed to Blond Curls—Lawson—and said, "You know Law and Remy. Crazy, right? Remington fucking Monroe in Havenwood. He writes songs about Law and came out professing his love for him on TV."

I remembered that story, but I had no idea they lived in Mom's hometown and she worked for the dude who snagged Remington. Who would have thought?

"Jesus Christ." Lawson shook his head.

Chase laughed. "Can you stop acting like you're surprised at anything he says and does? This is Kellan, and we love him for it."

"Thanks, baby," Kellan said to him. "At the end of the counter we have Knox, who methinks you noticed." He lowered his voice. "Sorry, he's straight."

I shrugged. I wasn't going to deny I'd been interested. "Nice to meet you guys." The flag made more sense now. Griffin was clearly supportive of his brother and friends.

"Are you planning on telling Mary Beth you're here?" Lawson asked, studying me strangely. I was assuming he was close with my mom and maybe she had shared some things about me. He was staring like he knew more about me than just any random guy who employed my mom would.

"Of course. It was a spur-of-the-moment decision." Yet, I'd found time to get my work license, hadn't I? That was beside the point, though. I shifted on my stool, suddenly feeling like the worst son in the world. What did this guy know? "I'm going to go see her tomorrow. I drove out here from LA and I needed a drink, and now a bed, so if you'll excuse me." I grabbed my mug, finished the beer in long swallow after long swallow before asking Griffin, "What do I owe you?"

I was being a bit of a dick, and I knew it. I was prickly. My whole life had been turned upside down, and now I felt judged on top of it.

"On the house," Griffin said.

"No. I can't do that." I tossed a ten on the countertop, looked to my right, and saw Remington fucking Monroe talking with his boyfriend. What the fuck universe was I in? Maybe this really wasn't reality. I'd gotten into a car accident and was in a coma in a hospital in some random town where no one knew who I was, and they would never find me because, I don't know, my wallet caught on fire or something.

"I was just curious," Lawson said, but he didn't seem to mean it. "No judgment. Only, Mary Beth means a lot to me."

"It's fine." I waved him off, suddenly wanting to be alone. And maybe, maybe part of me was jealous of this man I didn't know, because he apparently had a strong relationship with my mom.

Without another word, I walked out of the bar. The hotel was down the street, so I made the quick walk, went to my room, and wondered if I'd made a huge mistake.

Like trusting Stan. That had been a mistake.

What in the hell was I doing in Havenwood, show-ing up to see a mom I hadn't been very close with in years, with no set place to stay and no job? If worst came to worst, I could live off the money I made selling my condo, but still.

The truth was, I couldn't even blame this on Stan. We'd broken up two months ago, and that's when I started planning the move, and I still hadn't told her.

Lawson was right. I was a dick.

Yet I knew I wouldn't leave.

THE MATTRESS IN this hotel room sucked.

Even if I could ignore the ugly, floral bedding, I

couldn't overlook the lumps, one of which seemed to follow me no matter where I moved. How a lump did that, I had no idea, but then, if there was someone who was going to be followed by a bed bulge, it would be me. I much preferred bulges of the male kind.

With a sigh, I got out of bed. I'd basically spent the last forty-eight hours in this room. I was being a coward by not going to see my mom, and hoping Blond Curls—*Lawson*—hadn't told her I was in town. If he had, Mom likely would have called. Since she hadn't, I could only assume he didn't get involved.

But I did have a rental to look at today and a job interview later this week, so I needed to get my shit together. I was lucky to even have gotten the interview this soon. It was a newer clinic, and they had a NP spot to fill.

The shower was hot, which was nice. I spent more time than needed in there, letting the hot water pelt my sore back muscles. When I got out, I dressed, brushed my teeth, took my meds—fiber and PrEP—before shoving my phone into my back pocket, grabbing my keys, and heading out.

First stop, coffee. Real coffee, not hotel-room coffee, which tasted like crap.

After that I typed Mom's address into my GPS because I was a shitty son who had never even seen his mom's house or been to her hometown until now.

I smiled when I pulled up in front of the small yellow home with white shutters. It looked quaint, comfortable, and *so* my mom and absolutely nothing like my dad. I never understood their relationship, and still didn't to this day. Yeah, they were divorced and had moved their separate ways—he and I had nothing to do with each other—but I didn't ever remember my parents appearing in love with each other. I didn't remember them smiling at each other and laughing with each other. On the surface, they had probably looked to others like they had things in common, but they hadn't. Mom had always had simpler tastes than him. She had never been flashy, or intent on appearances, or strict, which was why it had been so hard to handle when she found out I was gay and told me to deny myself. If Mom couldn't accept me, how could anyone? That had sent me into a spiral of depression and denial that had taken me a long time to shake. I was out now, had been for years, and she'd changed her tune, but things had never been the same between us. It probably made me an asshole, but I couldn't make myself forget.

"You got this, Callum," I told myself, turning off the car and getting out. As soon as I did, I saw her. She had her back to me, and was sitting on the grass with her hands in the dirt. The fence had prevented me from seeing her from the car.

Mom had always loved flowers and would spend hours a day out in the garden. Sometimes dinner would be late because she'd lose track of time, and Dad would get annoyed. *"You don't have anything to do all day, and you can't get dinner done on time?"*

Fuck, I hated him. Would always hate him. He wasn't abusive, but he was an asshole. No matter how hard I'd tried, I'd never been good enough for him.

"Like this, Cal. See, you need to dig the hole a bit deeper." Mom's voice flooded my head, and I smiled at the memory. I'd forgotten how much I'd liked gardening with her. How could I have forgotten that?

Suddenly I saw Mom's shoulders stiffen, like she knew someone was watching her. She turned slowly, and the moment her eyes landed on me, they widened in surprise. "Callum?"

I stood there, not sure what to say. Then I shrugged, kept standing on the sidewalk, looking at my mom over the small white fence. "Surprise."

"Callum," she said again, this time stronger, steadier, and shoved to her feet. We both moved toward the open gate, and then she threw her arms around me and held me. "You're here. I can't believe you're here. Is everything okay? Good God, are you okay?"

"Yeah, Mom." I pulled back a little, looked at her. "I'm all right. I…" Missed you…needed my mom.

"It's okay. As long as you're fine, it doesn't matter why you're here. I'm just glad you are. Oh God, I got dirt all over you." She tried to wipe the brown from my shirt.

"I don't care," I told her, and pulled her into my arms again.

CHAPTER TWO

Knox

MY CELL RANG, and I looked over at where it sat on my workbench to see my daughter's name on the screen. Charlotte was only ten, and while that was young for a cell phone, I'd wanted her to have one so she could get in touch with me anytime she wanted. Carol, my ex-wife, had moved back to Colorado after the divorce a few years ago to be close to her family, and it was hard being so far away from my kids, only seeing them over the summer and every other major holiday. So this way, Charlotte and Logan, my son, could at least call me anytime, anywhere. Both my kids knew that no matter what, I'd always pick up.

"Hey, Charlie-girl," I said the moment I answered. She was my fierce, bubbly, blunt little one. Charlie loved working with me, building things with me, but wanted to do so with a pretty manicure and nice hair. She was stubborn, tough as nails, and she wouldn't let you forget it, which Carol always said was just like me.

"Hey, Daddy."

"How are you?" I asked, and she rambled a few minutes about friends at school, gymnastics lessons, and this "super hard" math they were doing at school. It was the beginning of spring, and I couldn't wait for summer when they'd be spending some time with me. "How are you?" she asked when she finished.

"I'm better now. I miss you."

"I know. I miss you too. Mama and Logan are fighting again. I swear they're always fighting."

I frowned. Logan was twelve, and Carol had mentioned he'd been a little more difficult lately. Nothing big. He wasn't getting into trouble or anything like that, but he had been a bit more defiant. He was talking back to his mom, not wanting to go to school, which made no sense. Logan was smart. His brain constantly amazed me. Even if he didn't get something right away, he always caught on. He loved learning. He'd never been much into the social part of classes—friends had never come easily to him—but he was in sixth grade now, and we'd hoped middle school would be better in that respect.

"How's your brother been with you?"

"Okay, I guess. He still calls me buttface, and I call him four eyes."

I shook my head and smiled a little. Crazy as it sounded, I even missed hearing my kids argue. "I'll talk to Logan. But you need to be nice to him too. It's not okay to call him four eyes." We spoke for a little while longer before Charlotte said one of her friends was calling. That was much more important than talking to me, so I told her I loved her and we got off the phone.

Logan and I had always been different. He was small for his age, something he hated. He had asthma, and he wasn't into sports, or building and fixing things—none of the stuff that came naturally to me. He was quiet, artsy, liked video games, but I always made it a point to try and get into the things he was into. I tried his games, even though I wasn't good at them. I tried reading with him, never pushed him to get involved in things I liked. I wanted him to know I loved him the way he was.

I made an attempt to get back into my carving, but I couldn't focus on it.

Woodworking was something my dad used to do, and I followed in his footsteps. We hadn't been what I'd call close. I'd lost my mom when I was young, so it had just been him and me, before he passed about ten years ago. We might not have spent a lot of time talking, but he taught me to work with my hands. He'd been the silent type, built construction, never found anything he couldn't fix. Just like Carol said Charlie was like me, she used to tell me I was just like my dad, and she hadn't been wrong. I wasn't good at talking about all the emotional stuff, not when it came to myself, at least.

Setting down my carving knife, I picked up my phone again. Carol answered on the second ring. "Hey, you," she said softly.

"You were crying?" I could hear the sadness in her voice.

"Yeah, I got into it with Logan again. I don't know what's going on, Knox. He's failing one of his classes. You know that's not like him."

My heart spiked, and my hand tightened on my cell. "Why didn't you tell me?"

"I just found out! I don't know why I wasn't notified. I don't know what to do." Her crying filled the silence between us.

Bracing my elbow on the counter, I rested my forehead in my hand. "I hate being so far away. I feel helpless."

"I know you do. No matter what happened between us, you know I love you. You're the best man I've ever known and a great father. I—"

"Is that Dad?" Logan's voice came from the background.

16

"Yeah, sweetie. It's your father. Do you want to talk to him?"

There was rustling on the line, and then Logan said, "I want to live with you. I don't like it here anymore. Can I come and live with you?"

Carol gasped, and shock landed in my chest. Logan wanted to live with me? I would take my kids in a second, but from the beginning, as a family, we'd all decided it would be best for them to live with Carol. At the time the kids had agreed.

"I'm sorry, Mom. It's not you. I love you. I just...I wanna move in with Dad. Please, can I move in with Dad?"

My heart dropped at the pain in his voice. Clearly this was something he'd been thinking about but hadn't wanted to bring up. My mind raced through everything that could have gone wrong. Had we missed something? Had someone hurt him?

He started breathing too fast, trying to get air that wasn't coming to him. A wheeze came through the line, and I shoved to my feet, like I could do something from half a country away. "Logan, calm down, buddy. Breathe." My voice trembled as I paced the shop.

I heard Carol say something, and then she was back on the phone. "I gave him his inhaler. Listen, I gotta go.

Let me take care of Logan."

"Okay, but if he wants to come here—"

"I know, Knox. I know. Let me get him to calm down, and I'll call you back." She hung up without another word.

My hands were shaking, my pulse racing. It killed me when he had an asthma attack. I hated being so far away, being helpless. I should be there with him. "Fuck!" I shouted into an empty workshop, then forced myself to calm down. Losing my shit wasn't going to change anything.

A couple of hours later, Carol called me back.

"How is he?" I asked.

"He's resting. I guess…I guess he's been wanting to come stay with you for a while, but he was afraid to tell me. He didn't want to hurt my feelings. He says he has no friends. His buddy from elementary school moved, but I didn't realize there was no one else. He'd mentioned names before. I didn't know, Knox. How could I not have known that? I'm his mother. I should have seen it."

"Hey. Shh. It's okay. We'll figure it out. It's not your fault. Middle school is hard. There are all sorts of things going on around and inside him. You're not a superhero, so don't beat yourself up."

She sniffed, then blew her nose. When Carol and I divorced, we decided that no matter what, our kids came first. They were the most important thing, and I knew we were on the same page with that. "I know this is hard, but if he really wants to move here, we have to let him."

"I know," she said softly. "He's been missing you a lot. He talks about you all the time."

"He never calls. Half the time he doesn't answer when I call him." That should have been a stronger clue to me that something was wrong. I'd always had a different relationship with Logan—he'd never wanted to spend as much time with me as Charlie did—but until recently, he'd always take my calls. "I should have known."

"Hey, if I can't beat myself up, you can't either." She was quiet for a moment, then said, "I can't believe I might lose my boy."

"You're not going to lose him. Have I lost our kids now?"

"You're right. I'm sorry."

I sighed. "Listen, we don't have to figure it out right this second. Let him rest, then talk to him. The three of us can video-call and figure out what's going on, if that's really what he wants. But I can't...I won't turn my back on him if he wants to come and live with me."

"I know you won't. I wouldn't have loved you as much as I did if you were the kind of man who would turn away from his son."

The next day the three of us video-chatted. As soon as we got off the call, I booked a flight to Colorado.

CHAPTER THREE

Callum

I SMILED AS I looked up at the sign for Sunrise Café, where my mom was a waitress.

I'd been in Havenwood for a week now. Things were going well with Mom. We hadn't talked about anything important, like the past or my shithead ex. The fact that I was there was all she cared about. That was the mom I remembered. The one who would do anything for me and wanted me happy. That's what made her reaction when she had found out I was gay even harder to take. When she told me I could hide who I was, that I could change.

I shoved those thoughts from my head. It wasn't what I wanted to be thinking about then.

The house I went to look at hadn't been what I was looking for. Mom told me not to rush, that she'd love it if I stayed with her, and surprisingly, I accepted. I told myself it was because I didn't want to get into a house I didn't like, and what if I discovered Havenwood wasn't for me? But if that were the case, the job interview I just nailed didn't make sense. I knew I was staying with her because I wanted to.

The thing with Stan had fucked with my head, made me realize that even before he thought it was a good idea to fuck numerous guys behind my back, I hadn't been happy for a while. I wasn't sad or anything like that. I knew the signs of depression. Been there, done that, kept an eye out for it like a motherfucker, because you never knew if it would attack again. But I hadn't been *happy*. I was missing something, and I didn't know what that was or how in the hell I planned to find it in a small town in Virginia, but hey, a guy had to start somewhere.

Deciding I probably looked like a crazy person staring at a sign while standing on the sidewalk of a town that looked like a postcard, I pulled the door open and walked inside.

The place was pretty full. The white walls were filled with photography—mountains, beaches, and other nature scenes. Eyes darted my way—mostly, I assumed, because I was a new face and no one knew me. I wasn't wearing eyeliner, but I looked pretty damn good, if I did say so myself, in black slacks and a button-up shirt, the sleeves rolled up to my elbows. It was my interviewing outfit.

Mom looked up as she finished talking to people at one of the tables. Her eyes landed on me and widened with joy. I'd noticed that happen every time she turned my way since I'd been there. I'd catch her staring at me sometimes, watching me as if she couldn't believe I was there.

"Cal! Hey! I didn't expect you," she said as she approached me. I hated the name Cal. It was so *country*, but I didn't tell her that. She was the only one who used it for me. Anyone else who tried, I always asked them to call me Callum.

"I thought I'd come see where you worked."

"And…?" Mom prompted.

"I got the job! You're looking at the new Family Nurse Practitioner at Havenwood Clinic." Well, as long as my background checked out, which I knew it would.

"That's great news! I'm so happy for you. Here, come sit down. Lunch is on me."

"You don't have to do that," I said, following her to a small two-person table near the back.

"I know. I want to."

"Okay, but I'm buying dinner."

"Deal." I sat down, and she handed me a menu. "Do you want anything to drink other than water?" she asked, and I realized how strange this was, sitting at the café where my mom worked and having her serve me.

"Is it okay that I'm here? At Sunrise, I mean?" I'd come because I'd wanted to share the news about my job with her. I didn't know why that was so hard for me to say. Why I couldn't tell her how important it was for me to talk to her about it.

"Yes! Of course. I'm glad you're here. I love Sunrise. It…makes me happy, and Law is great."

I could see it in the sparkle in her eyes, how happy she was here—not just at Sunrise, but in Havenwood. My dad would have lost his shit if they were married and she wanted to be a waitress in a café, but it worked for her. It fit. "I can see that. That you're happy, I mean. And I'm glad for you, Mom. Seriously." Her eyes misted a bit, but she shook it off. "Just water," I added. I hated that I struggled to show my emotions with her. I wanted to get over it, but I didn't know how.

"I'll be right back."

By the time Mom returned, I'd already settled on a chicken Caesar salad for lunch. She gave me my water before disappearing to do her job again. Every few minutes, I'd find myself watching her as she hurried around the restaurant. She laughed and chatted with customers and the other employees. Everyone seemed to know and like her, and it hit me that I'd never seen this side of my mom. She had never been this confident and settled with my dad. It was incredible to witness.

She brought my salad not long later, and I wanted to tell her she looked more at ease than I'd ever seen her. That Havenwood fit her, that I felt a little uncomfortable in my own skin too, and that I hoped Havenwood would fit me as well. The words didn't come out, so I thanked her instead and devoured my salad because it was good as hell.

I was about done when Blond Curls came out—I really needed to stop calling him that. He talked to customers and joked with my mom, before the two of them ended up at my table together.

"Lawson, I'd like you to meet my son, Callum. Cal, I mean, Callum—I know you don't like that—this is Lawson," Mom said. My eyes caught his, and I nodded, somehow reading his question.

Lawson said, "We actually met the other night at Griff's. I didn't tell you because he said you didn't know he was home yet. I apologize about that."

"Oh, don't you worry. That's fine, Lawson Grant," Mom replied, and he smiled, giving her a one-arm hug. Jealousy wrapped a fist around my heart. It was stupid. I knew it was. She was my mom, and she loved me, but again, I saw that she and Lawson had a relationship we didn't have anymore, one I desperately wanted back but was afraid of at the same time.

"That, um…salad was good. Are you sure you don't want me to pay? I should probably head out." I wiped my face with my napkin before setting it down.

Mom frowned. "No, not at all. You're not paying."

"Okay. Dinner, then," I said again.

"The restaurant closes at two, and then after we clean up around here, I have to run to the hardware store to pick up a few things. Knox has put them aside for me. I'm going to build some new flower boxes."

"I'll pick it up for you," I told her, and it really had nothing to do with the lumberjack, even though it wouldn't be bad on the eyes to see him again.

"Are you sure you don't mind?" Things were obviously slightly stilted between us.

"Absolutely."

Lawson nodded at me weirdly, and then Mom and I said this awkward goodbye where we almost hugged but didn't. It wasn't until I was outside that I realized I had no fucking clue where the hardware store was or what it was called.

One Google search later, I had my answer. Knox's Hardware. I jumped into my car and put my sunglasses on, for what turned out to literally be a three-minute drive. Small towns were weird. I parked along the side of the natural-wood building that looked like it belonged in a Wild West movie. Ugh. It was cute. I didn't know why I thought it was cute. Maybe because I knew there was a bearded lumberjack inside.

I headed in, and the second I did, I spotted Knox saying goodbye to a customer. There was another worker stocking shelves.

"Do you wear flannel?" I asked Knox, pushing my sunglasses on top of my head.

He shook his dark hair out of his face, his brows pinched together. "Huh?"

"Flannel. Do you wear it?" I'd never been real big on it, but I could imagine Knox wearing it. I'd probably think that was hot.

I could see when he understood where I was going with this. He frowned and crossed his arms, which made the sleeves of his shirt tighten against the muscles there. Oh, he had great arms and nice hands. I loved hands. *Straight, straight, straight. Kellan said he's straight.*

"What is it with the lumberjack thing?" he asked, and I chuckled.

"So I'm not the first to ask?"

"No. Law just—You know what? Never mind.

27

You're the first person who's asked me if I wear flannel. I put two and two together when you asked because calling me a lumberjack isn't new." He rubbed a hand over his face. "Can I help you with something?"

There were so many things I wished I could say to that, but I wouldn't, because I didn't know him and he apparently didn't do men. Such a shame. "Yeah, I'm here to pick up Mary Beth's order."

"Oh yeah. I can check you out, and we'll get the stuff out to your vehicle."

Don't say anything about checking me out, don't say anything about checking me out. "Deal," I replied because I didn't trust myself to say more than one word without making a joke.

"She called to pay over the phone," the dude stocking the shelves said.

I rolled my eyes. Damn it. I'd wanted to take care of that for her.

"Thanks, Hank. I swear I'm all over the place today."

"It's to be expected," Hank replied. Obviously, I was curious what they were talking about, but it wasn't like Knox knew me. I had no reason to be all up in his business.

"I'm going to take this stuff out to his car, and then I'm heading out. Thanks for closing for me today," Knox told Hank.

"No problem."

Knox began to walk toward the back of the store, and I followed, saying, "Oh, hey, Callum, right this way. Come with me. Okay, Knox, no worries."

He stopped suddenly, and I slammed into his back with an *umpf*.

"Your brake lights are out," I joked. A tease of a smile curled his lips before he evened them out again. Knox didn't want to think I was funny, but he did.

"Sorry, like I told Hank. Crazy day." He began walking again.

"Is everything okay? I mean, I know we don't know each other, but when I actually shut up, I'm a pretty good ear."

He looked over at me, and this time he did smile, before rubbing his beard with his hand and covering it. "Yeah, it's okay. My son, he lives in Colorado with his mom. He's been having some trouble, and I'm flying out today to pick him up. He asked to come and live with me."

Oh, wow. Definitely should have seen the whole ex-wife thing coming. "Yet you're working?"

"Keeps my mind off stuff."

I could see that. Knox didn't seem the asshole-workaholic type the way my father had been. "Well…I think it's great that you're going to get him and letting

29

him stay with you. Not all parents would. I know that had mine divorced when I was still a minor, my dad sure as shit wouldn't have wanted the responsibility of me living with him. So it's okay to be nervous. Sounds like the permanent-single-dad thing will be new. But your son clearly knows he can depend on you if he asked to live with you. Being a kid can suck. I hope everything works out. You're a great dad." I was pretty sure that covered everything.

Knox stood there staring at me. It was what I would say to a patient if they were worried about being a single parent—well, if I thought it was true, at least. Which I did with Knox. There was something about him.

I could see the wheels turning in his head, the appreciation in those strangely icy-green eyes of his. "Thank you. I think I needed to hear that from someone other than my ex-wife or my best friend. They have to say shit like that."

"Well, I read it in a fortune cookie, so…" I teased. A laugh jumped out of Knox's mouth, husky and deep. It obviously surprised him because he sobered quickly.

"Where did you get it? I might need to buy a few to get me through this."

"I think you'll do okay." I placed my hand on his arm in support. Heat radiated from Knox's arm to mine, with this sort of static electricity, making me pull back sharply.

"Sorry. I think I shocked you."

"Yeah," I replied dumbly, feeling like I was looking at him with a dopey expression I didn't understand. "I don't know when your flight is, but we should maybe go...?" I added when neither of us spoke.

"Shit. Yeah, let's do this. Well, you can wait here, and I'll get it."

I nodded. Knox left, and a couple of minutes later he came out with a flat cart holding wood and a few other supplies. Leave it to my mom to build something like this herself rather than buy it. She was pretty badass like that.

"I'll take it out to your car for you," Knox said, and we went out. We had to lay the back seat down and put the supplies through the trunk and into the car, so they would fit. When we finished, he closed the trunk, paused. "Thanks again for the pep talk."

"Looks like I'm gonna be here for a while, so if you ever need another one, you let me know."

I smiled, put my sunglasses on, and got back in my car. As I started driving, my eyes found their way to the rearview mirror, where I saw Knox with his arms crossed, watching my car pull away.

CHAPTER FOUR

Knox

"I'T'LL BE A big adjustment, being at a new school this late in the year," I told Logan as we drove from the airport in Richmond back to Havenwood. We'd spent a couple of days at home with Carol and Charlotte. We'd sat down and had a conversation with Logan to make sure this was what he really wanted and trying to figure out what was going on with him, but he didn't want to talk to us about it. It was strange having my son keep something like that from me. Even with the divorce, I'd always been close with them, and I hated that Logan was going through something he didn't want to share with me. It made me feel like a failure as a dad. *But he does want to live with me. He has to trust me, right?* I tried to remind myself of what Callum had said. Why his words were the ones I recalled rather than Carol's or Law's, I didn't know.

"School's always hard, Dad. This isn't going to be

any different," Logan finally replied, making a sharp pain stab my chest. The last thing I ever wanted was for my kids to suffer, to hurt in any way.

"Do people pick on you?"

"I don't want to talk about it."

"I know it doesn't seem like it, but sharing helps. We can't help you fix something if we don't know what's broken." The same thing had been said to me more than once.

"Don't. Please. It's fine. I just…want a fresh start."

I reached over and patted his shoulder. "Well, you'll have that in Havenwood, and I might not like the circumstances that brought you here, but I'm glad to have you with me, Logan. I think it'll be good for both of us. I miss you, ya know?"

He dropped his head so his chin rested on his chest. "I missed you too." Logan turned to look at me after that. "I was thinking maybe we can start doing some other kinds of stuff together…like maybe you could teach me how to carve like you do or fix stuff. Or like…work out or something? You have that room with all the exercise stuff in it."

I frowned. Not that I didn't want to do those kinds of things with my son, but he'd never shown any interest in it before. In fact, he did everything in his power to keep from woodcarving, working on cars with me, or working out. "Absolutely. I'd love that, but you know you don't have to do those kinds of things with me if you don't want to, right? I don't want you to feel obligated or like those are things you *should* want to do."

He looked out the window, giving me the back of his head. "I want to."

His response wasn't sitting right in my chest, but if I was wrong, I didn't want it to look as if I wasn't interested in doing those activities with him. "Then we'll do it. And you can teach me to do some of the stuff you like that I don't know about. I was also thinking maybe we could get a puppy. We can—"

"Oh my God! Are you serious?" he cut me off. Warmth flooded my chest.

"Yep. I've been doing some research. We'll have to make sure whatever we choose doesn't bother your asthma, of course, but yeah."

The smile slid off his face.

"Hey, what is it?"

"Nothing." Logan shook his head. "Thanks, Dad. You're awesome. I wish I could be more like you."

"Well, I think you're pretty awesome. You're the smartest person I know. And you're kind and funny and—"

"*Stoooop.* Dude. You don't have to give me compliments like that. Parents are so weird."

That was more like it. Logan and I had always been able to joke around with each other. "You said I'm awesome and now I'm weird? I might have to give you some extra chores for that."

"Chores? What are those? Cleaning *bothers my asthma.*" It was said playfully, but I could read between the lines. His breathing disorder was the source of some of his anger right now.

"You wish. Why don't you look up hypoallergenic dogs? We'll look through them and figure out what kind of dog you want. We'll have to talk to the doctor and everything too."

"Okay," he replied, pulling his phone out of his pocket. "Thanks, Dad…for everything."

"You have nothing to thank me for, kiddo. I'm glad you're here."

We were quiet the rest of the ride. Logan put his earbuds in, which I took as a hint for me to leave him alone. Christ, I hoped I knew what I was doing. It was clear something was going on with him, something he didn't want to share, and I didn't know how much to push him. While Logan and I were different in a lot of ways, we were the same in that neither of us responded well to feeling cornered, which was the last thing I wanted to do to him.

When we pulled down the driveway, Logan took his earbuds out. "Mom says she doesn't know how you live in a place like this."

It was a large, two-story, farmhouse-style cabin. Having a place like this was my dream, always had been.

"Yeah, your mama likes having neighbors right next door and subdivisions. I like my space." It was one of the many differences between us.

"I think I do too—like my space, I mean. It's nice to have somewhere to go home to where you feel like you have your own little world, ya know?"

I killed the engine. "Yeah, I do know. We don't have to worry about anyone else out here, and town is only a few minutes away."

"Dad…Havenwood is hardly a town."

"Oh, I see how you are." I ruffled his dark hair and almost knocked his glasses off. "Sorry."

"It's fine." He got out, and we grabbed his things.

Logan and Charlotte each had a room in my house for when they came to visit. They were on the second floor, along with the exercise room, but the master bedroom was on the ground floor.

I unlocked the door, and Logan stumbled inside. The

house had hardwood floors and only a few rugs through-out, to be easier on his asthma. He had his nebulizer for when we needed it, his rescue inhaler, plus his daily inhaler and medication, as well as a peak flow monitor to check his oxygen.

I had leftover chili in the fridge, which was what we had for dinner, and after that we watched a movie.

I took the next day off work to get Logan settled in with a doctor and registered for school.

It was a Friday night, and we decided to hit up a pizza place for dinner.

We were sitting at the table, waiting for our food to arrive, when I heard, "Fancy seeing you here."

I looked up to see Callum with his mom, Mary Beth. His short black hair was styled, with this messy, fingered look. He had the black stuff around his eyes like he had the first time I'd seen him at Griff's.

Before I could reply, he looked at Logan. "You must be Knox's son. He was so excited to have you come and stay with him. I'm Callum, and this is my mom, Ms. Price. I just moved here too."

Logan's eyes darted from Callum to me, then back to Callum, as if he wasn't sure what to say. "Yeah, I'm Logan. It's great to meet you." Callum held his hand out for Logan, who shook it. My son looked at Mary Beth next. "Nice to meet you, ma'am."

"You can call me Mary Beth, if that's okay with your daddy. I'm not much for the miss stuff."

Callum turned to me. "Well, I guess hello to you too."

He was…different. I couldn't put my finger on what it was about him, but he was interesting to me. He was obviously a good guy and good with kids. There was more there, though, something underneath the surface that I couldn't quite figure out, but I could sense something there. "I guess hello to you too," I replied. "Good to see you, Mary Beth."

"How are you liking it here so far?" Callum asked Logan.

"It's good, but I've just been hanging out with Dad. I start school on Monday, which I'm not stoked about."

"I hear ya. I was never super fond of school until college. When I was younger I had to pretend I was someone I wasn't. It was exhausting."

I was surprised when there was a spark in Logan's eyes. "You had to pretend to be someone you weren't?"

"Yep. Like this eyeliner; I wanted to wear stuff like that and couldn't."

"That sucks," Logan replied.

"It does, but now no one can stop me from doing anything because I don't care what they think." He smiled. "I start a new job on Monday, so I'm nervous but also excited because I know I'll be great…and you will too, so have confidence and focus on the great part."

"You think?"

"I do. I'm a fab judge of character, and I wouldn't lie to you. It's all about knowing you're awesome and owning it."

Logan pushed his glasses up his nose and leaned back. "Yeah, I guess."

My brain was spinning. Callum had said all the right things, and Logan was responding to him. Did he feel similar? Did he have to pretend he was someone he wasn't?

"You'll see," Callum told him as the waitress approached with our pizza. Callum and Mary Beth moved out of the way as she set down an extra-large pizza, half pepperoni, half pepperoni and mushroom. "Oh my God. I love mushrooms. I'm definitely getting mushrooms on our pizza."

"I love them too!" Logan replied.

"Gross," I added.

"Whatever. You don't know what's good, Dad."

"I'm Team Logan." Callum smiled. "Anyway, we don't want to interrupt your meal. I wanted to meet the kid Knox was raving about. You guys have a good one."

We said our goodbyes, and Callum and Mary Beth walked away. Logan piled four pieces of pizza on his plate. The kid was tiny, but it wasn't for lack of eating. "Who was that?" he asked without looking at me.

"I don't know him well. He only got to Havenwood a week or so before you."

"But you were talking to him about me?"

"He came into the store, and I was excited you were moving here."

"He seems…nice."

I couldn't help glancing around the room, looking Callum's direction. "Yeah. Yeah, he does."

When my gaze found Logan again, he was staring toward the other side of the restaurant, where Callum and Mary Beth sat. "I wish I could be like that," he said softly.

I paused for a moment, questions swirling in my head as my pulse raced. Was that what had been bothering Logan? Was he gay?

"Like what, kiddo? You know that no matter what, we'll always love you, right? You have nothing to worry about with your mom and me. We just want you to be happy. That's all we care about."

Logan frowned, confusion set in his features. "Huh? I know that."

"Then what did you mean?"

"Nothing." He shook his head and took a bite of pizza. Clearly, the conversation was over.

CHAPTER FIVE

Callum

I REALLY NEEDED to get my ass out of the house.

Things were going well so far in my sleepy little town. Mom and I built flower boxes together and watched movies together. And it was nice. We talked a lot about random things, neatly ignoring the past between us that we had never actually dealt with.

I'd started work at the clinic. I didn't have much of a patient load yet, but I was doing some urgent-care stuff in that side of the practice.

What I missed was being social. While eating popcorn and watching movies night after night with your mom was fun and all, I was used to going out—hitting up bars and clubs with my friends and dancing the night away with my ex, who was a dick, and nope, I didn't want to think about him.

"I think I might go have a beer…at that bar, Griff's?" I told Mom before realizing I'd worded it like a question.

"Oh." She nodded. "Okay."

"I don't have to. If you wanted to hang out or—"

"No, of course not. You're an adult. You don't have to sit at home with me every night." Guilt teased at my brain, and I almost said I'd stay in before she added, "Callum, go out. Have fun. I want you to make a life here, meet friends and all that. I want you to be happy."

There was a plea in both her voice and her eyes. She was trying to say more than she was, maybe that she had always wanted me to be happy, but she didn't let those words escape.

"Okay. I won't be out late."

I pushed off the couch and went into the room I was staying in. There was no bathroom attached, so I grabbed my clothes and went back out to take a shower. If I was going out, I damn sure planned to look good. I also made sure to get myself ready in case I got lucky. A good bottom should always be prepared. It wasn't that I thought there would be a whole lot of options in Havenwood, but then, I hadn't expected to meet a group of friends like Knox's my first night in town either.

Not that I should consider it his group, since I didn't know him and he was straight.

Ugh. Life was really unfair sometimes. It had been close to two weeks since I'd seen him and his son at dinner. I'd wondered more than once how they were doing. How Logan had settled into school. The kid had a sadness in his eyes I recognized, one I'd had even when I was young but hid well so no one saw it.

I pulled a tight tee over my head, brushing my thumb against the small scar over the left side of my chest. I didn't know why I did that sometimes.

I ran my hands through my wet hair a few times, decided it looked properly mussed, told my mom goodbye, and then I was on my way.

To Griff's. Tiny-ass bar in a small town where I knew no one. I still couldn't believe I was there.

The drive to the bar only took a few minutes. I could hear rock music as I approached the building. I didn't get as many looks when I walked in this time. My eyes were immediately drawn to the bar, not because of my lumberjack, or you know, that was a lie. Knox was pretty to look at.

He was there, sitting on the end. Lawson and Remington fucking Monroe weren't there—I still couldn't get over that shit—but the blond, his twink boyfriend, and the dude with the brown hair were. I couldn't remember their names.

Griffin was behind the bar, and there was another bartender there with him, a woman with red hair.

Knox took a swig out of the bottle of beer in front of him and looked up, his eyes landing on me over his drink. He set the bottle down and glanced away.

"Oh, hey. Callum, right?" the twink said. "I'm Kellan, remember? This is Chase, Josh, and Knox."

"Oh yeah. Sorry. I was a little frazzled that night. It's not every day you drop everything and leave LA for a town in Virginia you've never even been to."

"We seem to have that effect on people. We've been drawing the gays like crazy lately," Kellan teased. "Wanna join us?"

"Sure."

"I'll scoot down," Knox said. There was an open barstool on the end. I sat in the one he'd left, which put Josh on the other side of me, then Kellan, followed by Chase.

It took one glance at Josh to see he had Grindr up on his phone—a man after my own heart.

"How are you liking Havenwood so far?" Kellan asked.

"It's good...different."

"Can I get you a drink?" Griff asked.

"Just water for now," I replied.

"What brought you here?" Chase asked.

I could feel Knox's eyes on me. He was probably just

waiting for me to speak, but it still made me shift. He really was gorgeous.

"Well, my mom, but outside of that, a bad breakup. You know how it goes." That wasn't completely the truth, though. "Just needed a change."

"This is why I stay single—so I don't have to ever worry about the breakup thing," Josh said with a grin.

"Well, that," Kellan said, "and you like sex too much and with many different people, not that there's anything wrong with that."

Griffin made a huffing noise behind the bar, as if he disapproved, before handing me my ice water.

"Why are you always bustin' my balls?" Josh asked Griffin.

"I didn't say anything."

"You made a noise," Josh countered.

"So? Maybe the noise had nothing to do with you."

"Simmer down, gentlemen," Kellan soothed. "You two are different from each other, and that's okay. Go back to joking and flipping each other off, please."

From there, the four of them started rambling about other stuff. Knox cleared his throat beside me, and I turned to look at him just as he rubbed a hand over his beard. I could already tell that was his thing.

"How's it going, Daddy?" I asked, right as he took a

drink. Knox spurted and started coughing, having sucked the beer down his throat wrong. "Oh God. Not daddy like that. Daddy because you have a son." Though he did look a bit daddy. I patted his back as if that really helped.

"I didn't… I wasn't…"

"Yeah, okay. You thought I was calling you daddy, but that's okay. It's obviously not the first time."

"Not sexually," he countered. "Just, these assholes tease me sometimes."

"And it would have been sexual from me, you're assuming? You know what they say about that…"

"What? No." He rubbed a hand over his beard again. "Let's stop talking about that. I'm doing fine. It's good to have my son here. I missed being a full-time dad."

Ugh. He was the sweetest. Gruff, sexy, bearded guys with a heart of gold were my thing. Who knew? "How's Logan adjusting?"

"He's…he's doing okay, I think. He started school. He says it's going well. It's late in the year, so it'll be hard to meet friends. I'm trying to do a lot with him, keep him busy, ya know?"

"Yeah, I do. Being a kid is hard. He's lucky to have you, though." I reached over and patted his hand. It was a simple touch. I'd always been an affectionate person like that.

Kellan said, "I feel like I'm left out of something. When did you two get so close?" He smiled. I didn't even know him, but I could hear the innuendo in his voice.

"What? Him? He's totally not my type," I teased.

Kellan was the first to burst out laughing, followed by Chase and Josh.

"Fuck you, guys. You don't know me like that!" I said it playfully, and thankfully they seemed to get it.

"No, but we do have eyes in our heads," Josh said. "We saw you the first night you came in here. You looked right past me to him. That's never happened before. I might have gotten my feelings hurt." He winked.

"Fine, well, whatever. You've all seen him," I replied.

"This conversation is weird. Can you guys stop talking about me like I'm not here?" Knox added, "And we're not close."

"He helped me with some wood." The second I said it, I realized how it sounded. "Not *that* kind of wood. I was making flower boxes with my mom, you perverts. Who knew I would find my people so quickly in Havenwood?"

Josh held his hand up, and I gave him a high five.

"I was out to dinner with Logan and saw him and

Mary Beth." Knox was apparently trying to pull us back to the topic at hand. He was no fun.

"Ooh! We should have a Welcome to Havenwood party for Logan!" Kellan said. "I mean, I know he visits, but this is different."

I frowned because even though I didn't know Logan at all, he didn't seem the type of kid who'd want all the attention of a group of adults on him. "That might make him feel…I don't know, some kind of pressure or something? Maybe I'm wrong. I don't know anything about him."

I looked at Knox, who had his brows pinched together. I felt the urge to reach out and straighten them. "No, you're right. I appreciate it, Kell, but I'm not sure how he'd feel about that. I think he'd take it like we pity him."

"Yeah, that makes sense," Kellan said. "He can take art classes with me if he wants. That might help him get more one-on-one time with kids his age."

"Maybe. I'll talk to him."

We got off the topic of Logan after that. I kept feeling Knox's eyes on me. When I'd turn, he would look away.

A while later, Josh said, "I'm gonna head out. Meeting up with a friend."

By friend, I was pretty sure he meant fuck buddy. "Are there...many options around here?" If I was going to live here and all, it wasn't like I was going to be celibate. I liked sex. I missed sex.

"Neighboring towns mostly. I go to the bars in Richmond sometimes. You're welcome to go with me if you want."

"Yeah, sure."

We exchanged phone numbers, and then Josh turned to Griff. "Wanna go fishing with me tomorrow?"

"I don't know. I might—"

"Shut up and take your ass fishing with me, Griff. I'll come over and drag you out of the house if I have to."

"Are you sure you'll be back?"

"I'll make time for you." Josh winked, and Griffin rolled his eyes. Josh kissed Kellan's forehead with a, "See ya later, babe," then said goodbye to the rest of us and left.

"I should probably head out too," Knox said. "I don't want to be out too late with Logan alone at home."

"Yeah, us too," Chase said, he and Kellan standing.

It didn't look like I'd have many options for hanging out tonight, so I stood as well. Everyone paid, and we said goodbye to Griffin and walked out. Kellan and Chase went one way, Knox and I the other.

"You're good with kids," Knox said, stopping in front of a big-ass truck. Totally didn't surprise me that this was what he drove.

"Nice Dodge. She's pretty. And yeah, I like kids."

He pushed his hands into his pockets and leaned against the grille. "How'd you know? About Logan? That he wouldn't be into the party?"

I shrugged. "I didn't really, I guess. Just a feeling I got. He reminds me of myself when I was his age, only I was a little better at playing pretend."

Knox closed his eyes and dropped his head back.

"Shit. I'm sorry. I didn't mean to say the wrong thing."

"No, you didn't. It's true. I can't get him to talk to me. Makes me feel like a fucking failure." He rubbed a hand over his beard again. "*Argh.* I'll figure it out. Maybe get him someone to talk to or something. I'm sure you don't want to hear this. Have a good night." He turned and went for the door of his truck.

"Hey…I'm always around to talk. I don't know how much help I'd be, but I'm here."

Knox nodded, mumbled a thanks, then got into his truck and drove away.

Foolishly, I'd been hoping he would ask for my phone number.

CHAPTER SIX

Knox

W^{AS I SUPPOSED} to have asked for Callum's phone number? The stupid question had been in my head all damn night. He'd offered to talk, which had been cool of him. He didn't have to do that. And when he and Josh spoke about going to Richmond, they swapped phone numbers... "What the fuck is wrong with me?" I grumbled quietly to myself. I was acting like a fool, dissecting our discussion over and over as if it had been something more than a person trying to be nice and make some friends.

Which went back to the phone-number thing. Callum probably thought I was an asshole the way I'd grumbled at him and walked away. I was good at grumbling, though I was a lot better than I used to be at *not* grumbling too. It was something I'd tried to work on over the years—talking about important shit. I'd been raised not to, and Carol and I had struggled with it in our marriage. I'd done well at being open with my kids because I'd always wanted them to be able to talk to me in ways I hadn't with my own dad, but the rest of it hadn't come as easily.

I set down the knife I'd been holding and doing nothing with for a good ten minutes. I was working on a bear carving. It was Saturday. I'd changed my schedule at the hardware store so I worked Monday through Friday when Logan was at school. I took him in, then he rode the bus home, and I was there a few hours later. Today I'd asked him if he wanted to come out to the barn with me, but he'd refused and continued lying on the couch with his book.

On the one hand, it was great that he enjoyed reading. It was important to me that my kids did whatever it was they loved. I didn't have any expectations, but part of me had been disappointed. He'd said he wanted to carve with me, but anytime I asked him to do that or go fishing or anything else, he said no.

It wasn't as if we weren't spending any time together. We ate dinner together every night and watched movies and played video games I sucked at—all things he enjoyed, so did I have the right to be disappointed that he didn't want to do any of my activities with me? Even though it was him who had mentioned it? I wasn't sure.

There was no manual on how to do this.

"*Dad!*"

The second I heard Logan's panicked, breathless voice, I shot off my stool, knocking it to the ground, and started running toward the house. Blood rushed through my ears, my heart thudding against my chest. Logan was standing on the porch, one hand holding the other against his body. Red ran down his arm. He was gasping some, and wheezing, like he couldn't get enough air and was trying to steady his breathing.

"Hey, it's okay. Slow your breathing down. Where's your inhaler?" He nodded toward his pocket, and I fished it out and held it to his mouth. "One, two, three." On the last number I squeezed the inhaler and Logan took a breath, filling his lungs, trying to open his airway. He held his breath as I counted aloud to ten, waited a minute, before we repeated the same process.

The albuterol began to work and I could already hear the difference in his breathing. I gently pried his non-bleeding hand away from the other to see a cut in the meaty part of his palm that was about an inch long and definitely would need stiches.

I pulled my T-shirt off and wrapped it around his hand. "You're good. We're good, okay? Keep your hand elevated to slow the bleeding, and wait right here. I'm gonna grab my keys and another shirt. We'll get you to the urgent care and all stitched up."

"S…s…sor—"

"Don't apologize. It's fine. We'll get it all sorted out later." Christ, I was already fucking up this single-dad thing. Never had stitches in his life, and a couple of weeks with me and he needed them.

I grabbed my stuff, plus a clean towel to wrap his hand in. When I got back to the porch, he was leaning against the railing, his breathing becoming easier. I tugged the shirt off and got the towel wrapped around his hand. "Let's go."

Tears streaked down his face. He was quiet, looking at his hand as we drove.

"What happened?" I asked, but he shook his head.

Luckily, the waiting room at the clinic was empty. There was a nurse standing at the front desk with the clerk. She looked up, saw Logan, and said, "Come on. We can take him straight back."

I gave my ID and insurance card to the clerk, who said, "I need to get some information from you first."

"Can you get it back there? I'd like to be with my son."

She nodded, and I followed along after the nurse. I was about to give Logan's information, when familiar blue eyes landed on me. It was Callum, and he was wearing a pair of scrubs. Well, shit. I didn't know why, but I hadn't expected that. His black hair was calmer than usual, flat on his head instead of styled like fingers had been running through it. He wasn't wearing the black stuff on his eyes either, though I'd already noticed he only did that sometimes.

"Hey, what happened?" He went straight to Logan and led him to a room.

I went to follow, and the clerk asked, "What's his name?"

"Logan Wheeler."

I told her his birthday next. I was standing outside the room, Logan looking over at me, when Callum asked, "Is that enough for now? Are you still able to get him registered? I'll make sure they stop by and finish up when we're done. They're friends of mine."

She asked if the address on my ID was correct, and when I said yes, she walked away. I went into the room with them, closing the door behind me.

"What happened here?" Callum asked him. He'd already put on gloves and was looking at Logan's hand.

Logan's eyes darted to me, then away. "I was, um…trying to lift some of my dad's weights. I don't really know how it happened, but my hand like, slipped or whatever. There was something on the weight bench that cut me? I don't know what it was."

"Well, there was your first mistake. Never work out," Callum said with a wink. "I'm kidding. Exercise is good for you, but maybe do it with Dad?"

"Buddy, you know I would have lifted with you." I squeezed his shoulder.

"Yeah, but I shouldn't need you. I want…wanted…" He closed his mouth, tightened his jaw and he looked away, obviously not wanting to continue speaking.

"Okay," Callum said. "This is what we're going to do. We'll get the area numb, and I'll get you stitched up. Then I'm going to tell you a story." Callum looked at me. "Dad, any allergies to medicines?"

"No."

"Medical history I should know about other than the asthma?"

"None."

"Tetanus shot?"

"I don't know if he's ever had one."

"We'll do it to be safe, then. I'll be right back." He tossed the gloves and left the room.

"Logan—"

"We'll talk about it later, Dad," he replied, and I nodded.

Then Callum was back with a nurse, who had two shots on a plastic tray. Logan's wide, panicked eyes turned toward me, so I went over, stood beside him, and held his good hand. "I hate needles too. I've always wanted a tattoo, but I'm too afraid."

"Really? You don't seem like you're afraid of anything."

I frowned. Did he really see me that way? "I'm afraid of a lot of things. Everyone is."

I held him while the nurse gave him the tetanus and numbing shots. I could feel Callum's stare on us, but I couldn't make myself look at him. I wasn't quite sure why.

A few minutes later there was an extra light in the room, a tray with supplies, and Callum leaning over Logan's hand, stitching him up, while I held my son's other hand.

"You're a doctor?" Logan asked.

"No, I'm a nurse practitioner. We see patients like a doctor does, though."

"Do you like it?" he asked next.

"I do. I like helping people." Callum looked up at Logan before getting to work on his hand again. "What about you? Tell me some things you like?"

Logan began to speak about books and games and

model airplanes. Callum asked questions and interacted, seeming truly interested. When he made Logan laugh, I strangely felt something shift around inside me, this swell of gratitude, because watching him, I could see Logan engage with him in a way he used to do with me.

"All finished!" Callum said not long after. "You killed it. Didn't flinch at all. I have grown men in here bigger than your dad who get all woozy and freak out."

Callum cleaned up Logan's hand, wrapped it, then tossed his gloves, washed his hands again, and leaned against the counter. "You have asthma," he said, and Logan looked away and nodded.

"Dad, he has a physician here for that already?"

It was throwing me every time Callum called me Dad, made me shift and feel something in my gut I couldn't explain. "Yeah, that's all taken care of. He's had it under control for a while. He had an attack before he moved here. Today I think it was more the panic and all from getting hurt."

"I hate it," Logan said softly.

"I'm sure it's not easy," Callum replied. "I'm gonna show you and tell you something I wouldn't say to just anyone, but I like you, and I think I get what you're feeling."

Both my and Logan's gazes were riveted on Callum

as though it was impossible for us to look away. He pulled the neck area of his scrubs down a bit. There was a small, puffy scar on his chest, where his heart was.

"When I was young, they realized I had something called a heart block. They had to go in and give me a pacemaker. It's something in my chest that shoots off little signals to my heart, reminding it to beat the way it needs to, otherwise it will slow down too much."

My own chest tightened as I listened to him.

"You've had it since you were a kid?" Logan asked.

"Yep. I see a cardiologist who checks it to make sure it's functioning properly. I'm okay, so I don't want you to think that I'm not, but I hated it when I was young. It made my mom fuss over me more, and my dad…well, we probably would have never gotten along anyway, but I think to him, it made him feel like I was broken. Even if that's not the case, that's how it felt to me. I hated being different growing up. And even though I could have—and honestly, I doubt I would have wanted to regardless—my mom was always very worried about me, so I didn't play sports or anything like it. Which again, made me feel different. It was silly since I really didn't want to play them anyway. I just wanted to look at the boys." He winked, and Logan chuckled.

"Yeah, I don't play sports either. I don't really like

them, but part of me wanted to play because all the other guys do…and Dad did when he was young."

"Hey, I don't care about that." I put a hand on his shoulder. "You know that, right? I couldn't care less if you played sports. I want you to be happy and do what you enjoy."

"I know." He looked down. "I just…want to be more like you, I guess. I'm smaller than all the other guys, and I don't like the things they do, and I can't breathe sometimes. I had an asthma attack at school once, and they were all staring at me like I was some kind of freak. They call me twig, and four eyes, and girly boy, and stuff like that. Well, they did in Colorado."

Christ, I thought my heart was going to break. And I wanted to pummel some middle schoolers. I wanted to hug him and tell him I loved him, but I didn't know if that would make him feel the way Callum had said his mom's attention did. There were a million things going through my head, but I knew this was the answer we'd been missing, the one Logan hadn't wanted to share with us, but he had today…because of Callum.

"Did they call you names too?" he asked Callum, who nodded.

"Sometimes, yeah, they did, but you know what? I wasn't nearly as brave as you. I never told my parents. I just dealt with it and always had a laugh or a smile or a joke so they didn't see that I was really sad inside. It's good that you're telling your dad. It's not healthy to hold it in. I did, and it got worse when I got older. I was really sad at one point. I had to take medication for it and see a therapist and everything."

Christ, that was incredible of Callum, sharing that with us. It made that strange draw to him I'd felt from the beginning pull me closer.

And he was good at this—at talking with kids. I should have told Logan how brave he was, how proud of him I was. "Hey." I knelt in front of him.

"I'll give you guys a minute," I heard Callum say in the background, but I didn't look up. I kept my gaze on Logan.

"I love you no matter what. I always will. If you never want to play ball, I won't care. If you don't want to work out with me or learn to carve or anything like that, I won't care. None of that stuff matters. I love you, and I'm proud of who you are, okay? And those other kids, that's their problem and their loss because they're missing out on the best person I know. You're smart and funny and have such a big heart. If they don't see that— well, it's probably not appropriate for me to say what I want to about them." I pushed his hair back and cupped his face. Wiped the tears leaking from his eyes. "It doesn't matter how big you are or any of those other things. They don't hold your worth. I'm the luckiest dad in the world to have you for my son, and I want you to know you can always, always come and talk to me about anything. You don't ever need to feel like you can't come to me. There is nothing I wouldn't do for you."

"I feel like there's something wrong with me sometimes. Charlie likes doing that stuff with you."

"Everyone is different, buddy. I wish I was as smart as you. You and Charlie are different people, and I love you both for different reasons."

He nodded, and I pulled him into a hug. Logan cried into my shoulder, took his glasses off and set them beside him. No one came in, no one bothered us, and I knew that was because of Callum.

I held my son and told him I loved him over and over.

I didn't know how much time had passed when he pulled away. I got him tissues to wipe his face. He cleaned his glasses and put them back on. "We good?" I asked.

"Yeah, Dad."

I couldn't believe he'd been dealing with all that and had never told his mom or me. I'd make sure to pay extra attention now—and talk to the school to make sure none of that happened again.

I opened the door and stuck my head out. Callum was standing at the counter, looking at a piece of paper. His eyes darted up as if he felt my stare. He smiled and came over.

"It's not your fault," he said softly.

"Doesn't feel that way."

"It's still not." He smiled again and walked into the room.

He gave us instructions for Logan's hand, then asked, "You guys have any fun plans for the weekend?"

"Dad's taking me to get a dog tomorrow. It's like a two-hour drive away. We have to make sure I'm not allergic. She's hypoallergenic, but I read that it can still cause some people with asthma problems because of the dander. I'm hoping not because I really want her."

"It sounds like you guys are taking all the right precautions. And there are other things you can do at home more often, like sweeping, dusting, vacuuming. Maybe get an air purifier. You're pretty lucky. I love dogs. I want one."

These were all things we did or had, but I appreciated him mentioning them.

"Do you want to go with us to get her?" Logan asked excitedly. "Oh my God, can he, Dad?"

My eyes made their way over to Callum. I could somehow read his expression, that he was telling me it wasn't a big deal, that I didn't have to say yes, but…I wanted to. I enjoyed his company. He intrigued me, and I wanted to know more about him. "Yeah, sure. We'd love the company if you're available. You can come over afterward, and we can grill or something." I told myself there was nothing different about this, that the flips in my stomach were nerves. This was the same as asking Law or Griff over, but it felt that way. I couldn't put my finger on why.

"I'd love to go, if you're sure. I don't want to intrude."

Was it me, or were Callum's cheeks slightly pink?

"You won't be intruding at all," I replied, then because this felt big, felt serious, I ruffled Logan's hair. "This brat seems to like you."

Logan rolled his eyes.

"I like him too," Callum replied.

"Should I, um…get your phone number? You know, so we can plan for tomorrow. We can pick you up, or whatever works."

Yep, his cheeks were definitely pink. I didn't want to let myself think about what that meant.

"I'd like that," Callum replied. I pulled out my cell phone and got his phone number.

CHAPTER SEVEN

Callum

W E'D DECIDED I should drive to their house and leave my car there since I was going over for dinner afterward. My stomach had been on a roller coaster all morning—swooping, ascending, then evening out for what seemed to be no reason at all. I was spending the day with a straight guy and his son. What was the big deal? Knox probably only invited me because Logan seemed to feel comfortable with me, and he was the kind of dad who would move heaven and earth to make his son happy. It was one of my favorite things about him so far.

I'd gone back and forth deciding what to wear, which was absolutely ridiculous. I settled on a simple pair of jeans, with a denim button-up shirt left open and a white tee underneath.

"Where are you off to today?" Mom asked when I left my room. It was only eight, and she sat at the table, drinking her coffee.

"I'm, um…going to Knox's house? His son has taken a liking to me, and they invited me—well, I don't know what town we're going to, actually. Somewhere that's a couple of hours away, for Logan to see about getting a dog. Then they asked me to dinner afterward."

"Oh." She paused for a moment. "That's nice. I'm glad to see you making friends here."

"Me too. I like them." I didn't know them well, obviously, but I really did like them. I wanted to get to know them better. It felt good, important, that Logan seemed to have connected with me. And Knox…well, my lumberjack was easy on the eyes and fun to be around, so that was a win-win.

I popped a bagel into the toaster, then made a protein shake—not for bulking, just for the protein. When the bagel was done, I added a light dusting of butter. I had a fast metabolism and had never struggled with my weight, but I'd always eaten light and was careful about what I ate.

I put the bagel on a napkin and grabbed my stuff. "I don't know what time I'll be home. I'll call you." Without thinking, I bent over and kissed her forehead. We both froze for a moment, like neither of us expected it. There was a pang in my chest at that thought.

"Okay. Have fun. I love you, Callum."

I smiled. "Love you too, Mom." Then I was out the door. I typed the address Knox had given me into my GPS. They lived outside the main town of Havenwood, off one of the old highways. I turned down a gravel road to see a large, two-story cabin, which immediately made a smile tug at my lips. It was such a lumberjack kind of home, tucked between way too many trees. Off to the right was a large barn. Knox's truck was out front. I parked beside it, and the second I was out of the car, Logan came outside.

"You're here!" he said enthusiastically.

"Wouldn't miss it. How's your hand?" I stepped onto the porch. There was a swing on the end of it. So quaint and homey.

Logan rolled his eyes. "Fine. Now you sound like Dad."

There was this little swell in my chest at that. Not that I was truly anything to Logan, but, hell, I couldn't really explain it. That I worried about him like his dad did? That I didn't sound like a fraud or his healthcare provider, but a parent? It wasn't something I'd ever thought about before—becoming a parent—but now I wondered if maybe it would be in my future. Not to Logan, obviously; I wasn't delusional. But maybe I would want a kid of my own one day.

"Well, I'm your care provider, so can I at least ask if it's giving you much pain?" He shook his head. "You guys cleaned it?" He nodded. "No redness or—"

"*Callum.*" The way he said it was with such familiarity, it nearly stole my breath. Why I was suddenly being so sappy, I didn't know.

"Fine, fine. I'll stop. Sorry I'm a few minutes early."

"It's okay. Come in."

I followed Logan into the house. It was incredibly Knox on the inside too. All earth tones, with lots of browns, greens, and black. He had a large dark-brown sectional in the middle of the room, and in front of it, a coffee table made from a really dark, solid wood. It had some kind of coating on it, I could tell, with blue running through the middle. The edges were rough, knobby, but in a way you could tell was on purpose. "Wow…this is gorgeous."

"It's called, like, epoxy resin river table or something. Dad made it. He can make anything. He's good at all that stuff. I'm…not." The dejection in his voice obvious. Logan felt bad about himself because he couldn't do things like this.

"Well, I bet if you practiced enough, you could. I'm sure your dad couldn't do all this at twelve either. And if you can't, who cares? I can't build tables, but I'm good at other things, and you are too. That's what makes us all unique and special. We all do and like different stuff."

"That's what Dad says, but he kinda has to say things like that," Logan replied.

"Maybe, but I don't. And really, your dad doesn't. My father wouldn't have reassured me that way. I have a feeling when your dad speaks, it's because he means what he says," I answered honestly.

There was a noise behind us, and I turned to see Knox standing in the doorway to another room in a pair of jeans and no shirt. *Holy mother of sexy, beautiful lumberjack gods.* My knees went weak, and I wouldn't be surprised if I was drooling. His black hair was wet and messy, and that damn beard had little droplets of water in it too. God, I wanted to feel it scratch against my face, my entire body, really…my ass…my…

Knox cleared his throat, jerking me back to reality. "Sorry. Running a few minutes behind. I didn't realize you were here."

But he'd listened to us talk. I could tell by the way he was looking at me, all intense and appreciative and…confused. That part threw me some. "It's okay. I was actually early. Is this a shirtless event?" I teased. Not that I was complaining. If there was a series of shirtless events featuring Knox, I would be at all of them.

"Ha-ha. Very funny," he replied, before looking at Logan. "Take your meds? Got your inhaler and everything?"

"Yes, Dad. God, when don't I have it, and when don't I take my medication?"

"Hey." Knox gave him a hard look that shouldn't have been hot but totally was. It wasn't angry, just warning. "I was only asking. There's no reason to have an attitude. I'll finish getting dressed, and we can head out."

He turned and went back into what I assumed was his bedroom. I could see the edge of a rustic, also dark wood, four-poster bed inside.

"Wanna go outside with me?" Logan asked.

I figured it wouldn't be appropriate to say I wanted to be locked in that bedroom with Knox, so I said, "Sure."

We went outside and sat on the swing. "Dad treats me like I'm a baby."

"I'm sure it feels that way to you, but I think he treats you like a son he loves."

"Did your heart thing make you feel weak when you were little?"

"It did. If people make a big deal out of it, sometimes

it still does, but I try to remind myself that it comes from a place of concern. And that I'm lucky people care about me so much."

"I wish I was more like my dad..." Logan looked down into his lap. "I bet he does too."

"No." I shook my head. My heart was thumping and breaking in my chest. It was so damn hard to feel like you weren't enough, like there was something wrong with you, that the people who were the most important in your life would love you more if you were different. I didn't believe Knox did anything to make Logan feel that, at least not intentionally, but I understood the emotions behind Logan's view. "He doesn't. I promise you that. He loves you, and he's proud of you. You should have seen how excited he was to have you come and live with him. He likes you just the way you are, and it might not mean much, but I do too. The world can only have so many lumberjacks."

I nudged his arm, and he chuckled.

"I'm serious, okay?"

He nodded and pushed his glasses up his nose just as Knox came out. "Why do I always feel like I'm missing something when I see the two of you? I'm feeling left out."

"Guy talk," I told Knox.

"Oh, and I'm not a guy?" Knox asked, locking the door.

"Not a cool enough one," I joked, earning a laugh from Logan.

"Fine. I see how you are. Don't invite me into your cool-kids club."

"It's actually a badass-cool-kids club," I corrected.

"Yeah," Logan added, then, "We'll consider your membership."

Knox smiled at his son. "Deal. Now let's get out of here. I swear you two took forever to get ready."

We laughed and headed for the truck. I couldn't remember the last time I felt so at ease, so comfortable. Like I fit, when really I didn't. Not with them. This wasn't my family, and I didn't even know if I could consider Knox a friend or if I was just the dude his kid liked.

"Should we play road-trip games?" I asked when Knox pulled onto the highway.

"No," Knox said in unison with Logan's, "Yes."

"Two against one. You lose. Also, that's a point in the no column for the badass-cool-kids club. You're not convincing us very well." I cocked a brow. Knox looked over at me through his thick lashes, those eyes of his holding me in some kind of trance.

"I have to play road-trip games to be cool?"

"Well, it's a start. I'm still not sure you'll be badass enough yet," I replied. Knox smiled through his dark beard and chuckled. It was a bright smile, one that lit up the space, the deep baritone of his laugh contagious. Oh, I was in trouble. He was too sexy and too kind. This wasn't going to end well for me.

"Okay, fine. Logan picks first. What do you want to play, buddy?" Knox eyed Logan through the rearview mirror. He sat in the back cab.

We spent the next two hours playing silly games with different colors of cars and license plates and funny facts about ourselves. They made me laugh like I couldn't believe, and both Knox and Logan seemed to enjoy themselves just as much.

Before I knew it, we were pulling up to an old farmhouse, where an older woman stood out front, watering flowers. She waved at us as Knox turned the truck off, and we got out.

"Hope you guys found it okay?" she asked, approaching us.

"Yes, ma'am," Knox replied. "This is Logan and Callum."

"Nice to meet you. I'm Margaret." She shook our hands. "Pups are around back."

She led us to the rear of the house, where there was a large walk-in kennel and a bunch of brown, curly, fluff balls running around. I didn't know why, but it struck me then how far we'd driven for a pet, but then I remembered they'd done research on dogs that shed less and didn't cause as many allergies. Knox hadn't made this decision lightly. He'd put thought into what was best for his son.

"You're welcome to go in and play with them, see how you do," the woman said.

"Thank you," Knox answered.

"I hope I'm okay with them," Logan added. Oh, this poor boy was going to be brokenhearted if he couldn't get a dog. I wished there was a way I could fix it, make it so that wasn't a concern of his.

"I bet you will. I have asthma too, and I do okay," Margaret told him.

"Really?" Logan asked.

"Yep. I'll leave you guys to it." Margaret stepped away and began pulling weeds from a flowerbed.

Knox opened the kennel, and the two of them went inside. I hung toward the back, not wanting to interrupt. It was special—picking your dog—a family moment. They didn't need me for that.

The mama dog wasn't in the enclosure with them.

All the pups began jumping all over Knox's and Logan's legs. There were chairs they sat in, and Logan was picking them up and petting them.

"I thought you liked dogs?" Knox asked.

"I do, but this is your thing. I didn't want to intrude."

He frowned. "You're not. You're a founding member of the badass-cool-kids club, remember? If anyone belongs in here, it's you."

Oh, stop melting my heart. Knox Wheeler would be the death of me. "If you're sure," I replied softly, joining them. "What kind are they?"

"Lagotto Romagnolo," Knox answered. I'd never heard of that before. They looked like a bigger poodle to me.

The three of us played with puppies for a good hour, and so far, Logan seemed to be okay. Knox studied him, likely looking for signs he was struggling, when Logan wasn't paying attention, and to be honest, I did too.

"I have a friend with asthma back in LA. He's great with dogs, but he can't have cats. You never know."

"Yeah, I think it really depends on the breed too. We've tried others and it didn't work, but Carol, my ex-wife, had a friend with a Lagotto, and he was okay around her. I just wanted to be sure."

"So can we get one, Dad?"

"I think so," Knox answered. Logan hugged him, and my heart squeezed again. "Which one do you want?"

"Her." Logan pointed to the little one. "I want the runt." She was chocolate brown with a white spot on her chest and some on her paws, and had the biggest, bluest eyes I'd ever seen.

"It's always the little ones that have the most heart and spunk," I told Logan as we petted his new puppy. "She's my favorite too."

I felt Knox's gaze on me the whole time.

CHAPTER EIGHT

Knox

W E HIT UP a drive-through before leaving town. "What do you want?" I asked Callum.

"I'll take the garden salad."

I frowned. "*Eww*, vegetables. What about your daily intake of grease, fat, dairy—oh well, there's cheese on the salad, I guess."

He chuckled. "I like to eat right. It's not like I don't ever treat myself or enjoy a meal of heart disease, but—"

"Oh shit. I wasn't thinking." Open mouth, insert foot. I hadn't even considered his heart condition. Hell, for all I knew it was more serious than he'd made it sound to Logan. I was sure he had to be careful with that kind of thing. Worry made the hairs on the back of my neck stand on end.

"No, no. Don't do that. I'm fine. That's why I don't like to tell people." I must not have looked convinced because Callum reached over and placed a hand on my thigh. "Seriously, don't stress yourself out. Not that you would. I mean, you don't really know me, but…" He pulled his hand back, and where he'd touched almost tingled. It was the strangest sensation, and one I couldn't ever remember feeling from the simple touch of another person. "I live a normal life. I don't have restrictions. I've had no problems since the pacemaker was put in. It's not a big deal. And I'll take a small fry with the salad. French fries are my weakness."

I cleared my throat, trying to figure out why my blood still felt like it was warming where he'd touched. "Who doesn't love French fries?" I was fairly certain my voice came out a little strained. Callum's forehead wrinkled as if he noticed it.

"Are you ready to order?" the worker asked through the speaker, making me jump. Damn it. I was losing my shit.

"Yeah, we'll take two number threes, with a Coke, a garden salad, small fry, and…" I turned to look at Callum again.

"Water," he replied.

Well, shit. Now I felt insecure about my food choices. What in the hell was wrong with me?

"Let me give you some money for mine." Callum began to pull his wallet out of his back pocket.

"No, no. My treat. You came all the way out here with us. It's the least I can do."

"Well, you're also making me dinner," Callum countered.

I was, but I was starting to wonder about that. Hopefully I had the stuff to make a salad or another kind of veggie. At least I knew I could make him fries. "Still my treat."

"Fine. You guys will have to let me take you for pizza or something sometime."

"Okay!" Logan said from the cab as the puppy jumped all over him.

"It's settled, then." Callum smiled.

"Sir?" the woman at the window said, and I ripped my gaze from him. I was losing it.

We got back on the road after that. Logan didn't pay much attention to us for the rest of the drive. He was too busy with his new puppy, who kept trying to steal his fries.

"See? Even she knows fries are the best," Callum teased.

"Are you a vegetarian?" I asked.

"No. I don't do a lot of red meat, but I eat it sometimes. I try and eat a balanced diet."

I nodded, and we kept going. We stopped once at a

rest area to let the dog out to pee. We'd brought a collar and leash with us, which she didn't know how to walk on yet. She pulled and tried to run, but she did go to the bathroom.

We were almost back home when she finally fell asleep on Logan's lap.

"Do you know what you want to name her?" Callum asked.

"I don't know… I was thinking either Frankie or Blue because of her eyes."

"What about Frankie Blue?" Callum asked just as I said, "Or both names."

Our eyes met, and I swear my skin got all tingly again. Jesus Christ, I really was losing it. So we'd said the same thing. Big deal.

"I like it!" Logan replied. "Frankie Blue."

"I like it too." I looked at him through the rearview mirror. He smiled at the puppy as if she was his whole world, and my damn heart swelled. It felt good making your kids happy. We were definitely going to have to figure out something special to do for Charlie too when she came to visit. "We should probably make a stop at the pet store. I didn't want to buy a bunch of stuff if it didn't work out. Sorry." I glanced over at Callum.

"What? Are you kidding? I don't mind. This has

been the best day I've had since I moved to Haven-wood."

I was sure he said it for Logan's benefit, but it still made me grin. He was a nice guy. I didn't know what had gone down to make him move here, if anything at all, but I had a feeling there was a story there. Usually, when someone came to Havenwood, there was. Now that I thought about it, I did think he mentioned something about a breakup.

We went shopping and got a dog bed, kennel, the kind of food Margaret had mentioned, toys, puppy pads, and any and everything else you could think of for a new pup. Frankie Blue was a little wild in the store and peed on the floor.

We got back to the house. Logan and Frankie Blue immediately stumbled out of the truck.

"Oh, don't mind me. I'll carry all this stuff in my-self," I teased, but really, I didn't mind. It was good to see him smiling and laughing.

"I'll come help," he replied, but I waved him off.

"What? I don't count? I'm crushed, Knox Wheeler," Callum said in this light, playful voice that sounded a whole lot like flirting. Was he flirting with me? My stomach flipped in response, though I wasn't sure what kind of feeling it was. I'd never been interested in a guy before, never even thought about it. There was no way I was now, I didn't think. How could you go your whole life only being interested in women, then suddenly consider liking the idea of a man flirting with you?

"Hey, I didn't mean to make you uncomfortable. I was just teasing. I get a little flirty, and I know—well, obviously, I was interested in you that first night at Griff's, but I didn't know you were straight. I respect that."

My eyes snapped to his, and that tumbling feeling was back, like my gut was doing somersaults down a hill. "Wait, you were?"

"You couldn't tell?" Callum replied, then added, "Oops. I figured you knew."

I knew he'd been staring at me weirdly and, well, now that I thought about it, that made sense. Kellan had said something about Callum noticing me, but it had come as a surprise. A man wanting me.

We were standing there, looking at each other over the bed of my truck. Callum crossed his arms on the edge and bent forward, head facing down and forehead on his arm. "Shit. Now I made it worse."

"No, you didn't," I rushed out. "It's fine. I wasn't uncomfortable. It wasn't something I'd considered, which makes me feel dumb now, but then, it would make me a cocky asshole if that had been my first assumption. I... Thanks." Jesus Christ. Had I really just thanked the guy for having found me attractive the first time I saw him? "Now I made it weird," I added.

Callum lifted his head, looked over at me, and laughed. The second he did, I was doing the same. I couldn't say exactly what it was that was so funny, but I couldn't have stopped if I wanted to. He wiped his eyes as if he laughed so hard, he was crying, before we finally settled down.

I shook my head as I went for the tailgate and opened it. "It's not very nice to laugh at me."

"But you were laughing at you...and me. I think we were both laughing at me too. Doesn't that make it okay?"

"Yeah, I guess. We're quite the pair. I mean, not *pair*, pair, but..." And then we were at it again, and I tried to remember the last time I had this much fun. The last time I laughed until my stomach hurt. I couldn't remember when that would have been.

As if reading my mind, Callum said, "I think you need to have more fun, Knox Wheeler. I'm going to take it upon myself to make that happen. I'm going to open up your whole world. I can feel it."

I wouldn't say it, but somehow I could feel it too.

"How about you take it upon yourself to help me get this shit inside," I teased.

"Yes, sir!" He saluted me.

"Smart-ass."

We grabbed the stuff and brought it inside. "I think Logan's out back," I said and nodded in the direction of the kitchen toward the rear of the house, where the door was. Callum followed behind me.

"Wow. Your home really is beautiful."

"Thanks. I've always wanted a place like this. Carol—my ex—she's a suburbs girl, and I get it. That worked for us when we were married, but I've always wanted some kind of cabin in the woods. Is that crazy?"

"No. I get the appeal. I mean, not that anyone would ever believe me when I say something like that. I grew up in Richmond and left for college as soon as I could. I've been a city boy ever since—apartments or condos, night life and all that, but...I don't know. I don't think I realized it at the time, but it felt like something was missing. Like I wasn't settled or...fulfilled? That probably sounds stupid, but—"

"No," I cut him off. "I get it. I've felt like that a lot." Though it wasn't something I ever shared with anyone, and I wasn't sure why I was doing it now. "It was hard for me when I moved to Havenwood. I'd been with

Carol since I was eighteen, and my kids weren't with me, yet a part of me felt more at home than I ever had. Which made me feel guilt. How could I be at home and settled without my kids?"

We were standing there, staring at each other as we stood by the back door, but neither of us moved.

"I think some parts of us can feel like things are right, while still missing someone. Or maybe you felt settled in new ways, but knew you were still missing something in others? That's possible too."

And that felt…right. Like he voiced something I felt but didn't have the words for. As happy as I was and as much as I knew Havenwood was my home, as much as being there was a dream come true for me, there were other things I'd been missing—maybe more than just my kids.

"Thank you," I found myself saying.

"For what?"

"This…the conversation and going with us today. How you were with Logan at the clinic and what you told him. He's taken a liking to you. There's some disconnect between us right now. He doesn't talk to me the way he used to, and I think he sees me as, I don't know, something other. Like maybe I'm part of the problem? And I don't want to be…or know what I did wrong. *Argh.*" I dropped my head back and looked at the ceiling.

"Hey." Callum reached out and put a hand on my bicep. I looked down at him. "You're not part of the problem. You love that kid like crazy. Anyone can see it. He knows it. He loves you too. He looks up to you. I think it's him who feels *other* right now, and he doesn't know how to deal with that. I've felt it before."

"Do you think he's gay?"

"Because he's small and doesn't like to build stuff and connected with me?"

Guilt slammed into my chest. Hearing it repeated that way made me feel all kinds of wrong. "No, I didn't mean that. Did it sound like I meant it that way?"

Callum shrugged. "I'm probably oversensitive to it. Would it be okay if he was?"

"Yes," immediately fell from my lips. He was my son. I would always love him.

"Then if he is, he's already a step ahead of a lot of queer kids. That's a good thing. Time will tell. Maybe he knows, and maybe he doesn't. Maybe he is, and maybe he isn't. Love him and support him and let him know you're here for him."

I nodded, and Callum dropped his hand away. Damned if I didn't feel again like I missed the contact.

"Thanks," I said for the second time. "I'm glad you're here. That we met you."

"I'll help with Logan in any way I can. He's a great kid."

"I didn't mean just for him." The words came out with no direction, no thought from me. "I mean…you know what I mean."

"I do. Because we're friends and I'm determined to make you laugh and open up your world, remember? I can be like…your gay best friend. Though you have Lawson, but I can be your other one."

"Or you can just be my friend. No gay in front of it, the same way Law's just my friend."

He looked up at me and smiled, this huge happy smile that told me I'd said the right thing. I liked the feeling, felt it radiate through my chest before settling into my bones.

"You're good at this friendship thing." Callum opened the door, then hooked his arm through mine. "Come on, Lumberjack. Let's go play with Logan and Frankie Blue."

In that moment, there was nothing I wanted more.

CHAPTER NINE

Callum

LAST NIGHT WITH Knox, Logan, and Frankie Blue had been...well, I didn't truly have the words for exactly what it had been. Surprising was one. Fun was another. Also comfortable, silly, happy, perfect. I was in deep already, and honestly, a little worried about myself. I'd done well in my thirty-three years not to be that guy who falls for a straight man. I'd had plenty of hetero friends, and the guys had always been strictly in the friendship zone, but I knew myself well enough to know how easily I could fall for Knox.

There was something about him—sexy lumberjack look aside. He was kind. He loved his son fiercely and had told me about Charlotte too. You could tell he couldn't wait for his daughter to visit over the summer. Knox said she was a spitfire—sassy, confident, and smart. He was sure she'd be president one day, which was a dream of hers. He was also funny, sometimes a little quiet. You could tell that the emotional stuff was harder for him to share, but he did it. There was no doubt in my mind that was for a reason, and he made an effort toward being more open.

So yeah, I was fucked, and if we kept hanging out, I would likely end up with my first straight-guy heart-break.

After a good stretch, I climbed out of bed and went into the kitchen. It wasn't until I noticed Mom wasn't home that I realized I'd forgotten to call her last night. Not that I had to; I was a grown-up, after all. But I'd told her I would. Guilt grew slowly, starting deep in my gut. I hadn't come in until late last night. She'd already been asleep.

Turning around, I went into my room, grabbed clothes, took a quick shower, added a little eyeliner, and then was on my way.

When I walked into Sunrise Café, it was even busier than it had been my first time there. Mom was seating someone—oh, it was Remington, Lawson's boyfriend. He was at the last empty table in the restaurant. Mom turned and saw me. Her eyes lit up, and again, it made me feel guilty. I was there, in Havenwood, and we were living together, but we didn't spend much time together.

Remington glanced up and noticed me, waved me

over, then said something to Mom. She nodded, and I headed toward them as she met me halfway. "Remy says you can sit with him."

Holy shit. It wasn't every day a musician invited you to have breakfast with him at the small-town café your mom worked in and his boyfriend happened to own. Damn, Havenwood was a strange place.

"Great, thanks. Listen, about last night. I'm sorry I didn't call. We were playing with Frankie Blue—the puppy Logan got—and then I helped Knox with dinner. Logan asked if I could play board games and watch a movie with them, and I just…I'm not used to living with my mom."

"I'm glad you had a good time. Knox is a nice man, and you're an adult. You don't have to check in with me."

"I know. But it's still respectful, so I'll try to do better, okay?"

Appreciation sparked in her eyes. It was so simple really, to make my mom happy. I wished my father had tried to do it more.

"Go join Remy. I'll get you both some coffee."

"Yes, ma'am," I replied before heading to the table where the musician sat. His red hair was messy. I was fairly certain he hadn't combed it today. He had on a wrinkled T-shirt, and a notebook sat beside him. "Are you sure you don't mind if I join you?" It wasn't as if we knew each other.

"Of course. Your mom is…well, she's great. She made me feel welcome when I first came to Havenwood, so I'm following her example."

I smiled, contentment settling in my chest. The people of Havenwood loved my mom, and I was so happy she had that. "Thanks." I sat across from him in the booth.

"I don't know that I'll be the best company," he said.

"Do you know you?" I teased. "You're Remington Monroe. I can't believe I'm even sitting here with you right now." His eyes darted down, and a sting of regret hit me. "Shit, sorry. I didn't mean to make things awkward. I'm sure you want to feel comfortable while you're at home and not have people fanboying all over you."

He gave a soft chuckle. "It's okay. Not your fault. I'm getting better at it. Anxiety stuff. And please, call me Remy."

"Remy." I nodded. Not gonna lie, I was freaking out a little inside.

Mom came over then with coffee and water for both of us. She and Remy teased each other for a moment. He ordered this skillet thing with meat, potatoes, and who the hell knew what else, while I got a veggie omelet and wheat toast.

"Mary Beth says you're a nurse practitioner?" he asked when Mom left.

"Yeah, I'm working at the clinic. I have a small patient load right now, and I'm doing a lot of urgent-care stuff, but I like it. How's…" The music business? Being famous? I had no idea what to even say. "Life."

Remy snickered, obviously seeing my discomfort. "It's good. I'm not performing right now. I'm mostly writing lots of new music." He held up his notebook. "Just trying to keep myself steady, ya know? And enjoying being with Law." He smiled, and it was clear as day, the love Remy had for Lawson. I could feel it in his stare, hear it in his voice and…shit, I wanted that. I wasn't sure I'd ever really wanted it before. I was positive I never had that much emotion in my voice about my ex—hell, any of them. I'd cared about Stan a lot, but I knew we weren't Lawson and Remy.

"That's great," I replied. "I came to Havenwood to get away from my ex. He apparently had a different understanding of *we're monogamous* than me."

"Oh. That's hard. Sorry about that."

I shrugged. "It is what it is. Maybe it was a good

thing. I'm liking Havenwood." Especially Knox and Logan. They were the highlight so far.

"It has a way with folks, that's for sure."

We chatted more about everyday things. Quirks of the town, their group of friends, where I moved from and stuff like that. The food came, and we ate together. Before long, I didn't feel like I was eating breakfast with Remington Monroe. He was just Remy, and there was something endearing about him.

We had just finished eating when Remy said, "Mary Beth…she talks about you all the time. She's real proud of you. Law says she told him I remind her of you. I don't see it." You could tell he hadn't meant it in an offensive way. If anything, it was self-deprecating.

His words didn't make sense at first, but then I looked at him, at his eyes and the secrets there, and thought about myself. There was an insecurity in him that I knew well, maybe sadness too. Not that I thought Remy was sad or even that I felt that way now, but I had, and I was sure he had too. I'd worked through my depression a long time ago, but I thought it was a battle Remy was still fighting.

"I see it," I said softly, just as Lawson approached.

"Mmm, I missed this face." He leaned over and pressed a quick kiss to Remy's lips. It was like Lawson lit up Remy's soul, the light so bright, I felt it.

"It's only been a few hours since you've seen me," Remy replied.

"So? I always miss you."

Remy rolled his eyes, but I could tell he liked it. That Lawson was maybe the only person Remy would believe when they said that. Lawson was Remy's reason for…well, everything, I was pretty sure. And the way Lawson looked at him, talked to him, I could see he felt the same.

A deep, penetrating ache landed in my chest. I cleared my throat. "Thank you both for your friendship with my mom. It, um…it means a lot to me."

Lawson nodded at me as if I'd somehow passed some test. "You're welcome, man. And hey, next time we have a get-together at our house or something, you should come."

"I'd like that." I really would.

Lawson smiled, kissed Remy again, and returned to work.

Mom brought my check over a few minutes later, and Remy said, "You're welcome to join me anytime. I'm usually here a few mornings a week. If I'm writing, I might be a little lost in it and either won't notice you or will forget you're sitting with me, but you're welcome."

"Thanks. I appreciate that." Somehow, I didn't think he was exaggerating either.

Remy stayed at Sunrise. I paid, told Mom I'd see her later, and was on my way. I didn't go straight to my car, though. I walked around, explored the town a little. There was a hilly, shady park not far from Sunrise.

I ended up a few streets away and saw Safe Haven, the art studio. I remembered Kellan saying he owned it and talking about Logan taking classes, so I jogged across the street and went inside.

Kellan was leaning against the counter, talking to a woman and a little girl, who looked about five. He glanced up at me and smiled, then held up his hand as if to say he'd be a minute. I browsed around the studio, admiring the paintings, pottery pieces, and other forms of art decorating the space.

When the woman and her kid left, Kellan approached. "Well, if it isn't the other Havenwood twink," he said playfully.

"There are only two of us, huh?"

"The only two who are fabulous." He winked.

Kellan reminded me of people I would have known in the city. I wondered if he'd ever left Havenwood or if he'd been here his whole life.

"Looking to take a class?"

"Me? No, I'm not very artistic."

"Lots of people think that, but they are. You should give it a try."

"Maybe… I just left Sunrise Café and was exploring. I saw the studio and remembered you owned it, so I thought I'd stop by."

"Check out the schedule. You might see something you like." Kellan pointed to a corkboard, and we went over.

A flyer caught my eye: **Adult-Child Paint Night!**

I immediately thought of Logan and Knox. Logan liked art. He drew and painted some. He'd shown me some of his work the night before. The thing was, I didn't know if Knox realized he was an artist too. That table he'd made was art. I thought maybe the two of them had more in common than they saw on the surface. Maybe they needed to look at things in a different way.

"Do you do gift certificates? Or gift classes or anything like that?"

"Yeah, of course. Which one are you interested in?"

"I'd like to pay for one of the adult-child paint nights, only I'm not sure what date." There were a few days and times listed.

"That's fine. You just pay for the class, and I'll write on the certificate what it's for. They can call and schedule for themselves."

"Great," I replied, feeling more giddy than I probably should.

"How many adults and children?" Kellan went back to the desk, and I followed him over.

I opened my mouth, almost said two adults and one child, but this wasn't for me. This was about Knox and Logan. I was a random guy who hung out with them once. "Just one of each."

Kellan got everything taken care of for me. I was grateful he didn't ask who it was for, though in all honesty, he probably knew. He'd mentioned Logan taking a class that night at Griff's.

I couldn't help being nervous, though. It would be just my luck that I was overstepping. For all I knew, Knox and Logan had no interest in something like this, but if Logan did, Knox would too.

I paid, thanked him, and stepped out of the studio. I was halfway back to my car when my phone buzzed in my back pocket.

Tugging it out, I saw a text on the screen. **Hey...thanks again for yesterday. It was fun.**

The giddiness was back, wreaking havoc on my insides. It was only a text. People did it every day. Yet here I was, acting like he'd invited me on a date or something.

Logan had fun, Knox added, and I deflated a bit. Not that I didn't want Logan to have a good time. Obviously, I did, but I wanted Knox to have had fun as well.

No problem. I'm a fun guy. Makes sense. Stupidly, I wondered if that made him laugh.

Me too, though. I had fun too.

A tingling sensation formed at the base of my spine.

Again, makes sense. I'm a fun guy. ☺

Funny? Funny-looking?

I rolled my eyes. **Oh God. Dad jokes! I thought you were a sexy**—I backspaced that word, damn it—**tough-guy lumberjack? Not an old guy with dad jokes.**

Okay, that one was maybe pretty bad.

You're forgiven, Dad.

Knox's reply came back quickly. **No...not the dad stuff. I thought we were friends?**

We were. Or at least, I really wanted to be friends with Knox Wheeler. **We are.**

I frowned when a response didn't come back right away. I thought about saying something else or telling him about the class, but I also didn't want to be *that guy*. I didn't want to seem like I was sitting around looking for a reason to talk to him, while at the same time I was driving myself crazy, thinking maybe I said something wrong in those two simple words. He was screwing with my head, that was for sure.

I got all the way back to my car before my phone buzzed again. I fumbled it with too much enthusiasm…over a text.

Sorry. I had to help a customer. Logan asked this morning if maybe you'd want to come over and hang out again tonight? I told him you might be busy. I'll understand if you have other things to do, but I thought I'd ask. I know he's twelve, so it's probably weird that he's wondering, but I just…I want him to have friends.

I finished reading that message as the next one came through.

And since we're friends and all too…maybe it's less weird if we both wanted to see if you could hang out. That's what I meant to say.

I leaned against the car, closed my eyes, and held my phone to my chest.

Knox Wheeler was going to wreck me, break me in ways no one else had. I knew it right then and there. The stupid, sweet man already had my pulse thumping, and even though I knew I'd likely fall for him and that he was straight, I wouldn't say no. I would spend time with him, whenever he asked, and deal with the consequences later.

CHAPTER TEN

Knox

I T WAS RIDICULOUS that I'd felt silly inviting Callum over earlier. There was this strange restlessness going on beneath my skin, running through my veins. It was unfamiliar and confusing, so I tried to tell myself it wasn't there.

I finished my workday, climbed into the truck, and headed home. I'd been back and forth between the store and my house a few times, trying to take care of Frankie Blue while Logan was at school. It would be hectic for a while, and maybe getting a dog so soon hadn't been the best idea, but Logan's happiness made it worth whatever sacrifices I had to make.

"Logan?" I called out, stepping into the house.

"Up here, Dad!"

I went upstairs to see him sitting on the floor with the puppy, who immediately came running over to attack my feet.

"Hey, silly girl." I bent and petted her. "Did you take her out?"

"Yep. I took her out and cleaned her kennel. She had one accident on the floor, and I cleaned that up too."

"Wow, I'm impressed." This definitely wasn't typical behavior. Like most kids, chores usually took some prodding.

"I wanna make sure I prove to you that I can handle a puppy."

"Good man." I pushed to my feet. "Homework?"

"A little bit."

"You should maybe start it now. Callum will be here in about an hour, and that way you won't have to do it while he's here."

"Awesome! I'm glad he's coming over."

Logan and Frankie Blue followed me downstairs, the latter stumbling over her feet slightly. Logan grabbed his backpack from the hook by the door, then went to the table and got started on his homework.

"How's your hand?"

Logan rolled his eyes. "It's fine, Dad."

I already had boneless, skinless chicken breasts marinating in the fridge, so I plucked out the vegetables I'd gotten at the store on one of my trips home today, washed my hands, and started cutting.

Logan frowned. "What are you making?"

"Um…salad? I know you've had one before."

"Yes, but you don't usually make them."

"Yes I do." I threw a chunk of cucumber at him before remembering we had a puppy now. Luckily Frankie Blue didn't notice, and Logan threw it back.

"When you do, you get the bagged stuff, but you have like, real lettuce and all sorts of options. I don't remember you ever putting bell peppers in a salad before."

Leave it to kids to unknowingly call you on your shit. Not that it was really shit, but yeah, I was trying to make a pretty fucking special *salad*. "First, the bagged stuff is real lettuce. Second, maybe I just think we need to start eating more balanced meals."

His frown deepened. "*O-kay.*"

"Do your homework, twerp."

He nodded and did as told. I finished up with my salad, covered the bowl, and put it in the fridge.

"How's school going?" I'd spoken to them about watching out for anyone teasing Logan, and they readily agreed.

"I thought you wanted me to do my homework?" Logan countered.

"I do, but I also want to check in with you. Is that

okay?"

He sighed. I sat across from him at the table, and he said, "It's fine, Dad. No one has been mean to me or anything. They don't really know me well enough to think I'm a dork."

"Hey, you're not a dork."

"You have to think that."

This was so foreign to me. While I hadn't been the popular kid everyone wanted to be friends with, I always had my group of peers. I always fit in, and if I didn't, I didn't give a shit. I didn't know what it felt like to be littler than everyone else or picked on. The thought of Logan dealing with it made my chest ache and anger rage.

"No, I don't have to think that, but even if I did, other people who aren't your parents don't think you're a dork. Callum likes you. You guys have a badass-cool-kids club I'm not even allowed to be a member of."

He gave a small grin. "I know, and I'm *fine*. I just don't like to talk about it. I feel like even more of a loser when we do. But no one has been mean to me. No one has picked on me. No one has said much of anything to me unless they have to."

It wasn't hard to read between the lines. Maybe he hadn't been picked on, but he hadn't met any friends yet either. Fuck, I hated this. I wanted to go down to that school and force the other kids to see how great Logan was. How kind and funny and smart.

"Want to work on our model airplane tonight?" It wasn't the same as kids at school, but I wanted him to know I enjoyed spending time with him.

Logan didn't reply right away, and then there was a knock at the door and he shoved out of the chair. "I'll get it!"

"Hey," I said. He stopped and looked at me. "I love you, buddy."

"I know." And then he was gone. I heard him talking to Callum, the two of them chatting about Frankie Blue and how her first night had gone.

"Dad's in the kitchen. I'm finishing up some homework. The math here is different, so I'm having a little trouble with it," Logan told him as they walked in.

"Math is my specialty. I can help if you want."

"Really? That's the best!"

Callum looked over at me and smiled widely. He had perfect teeth, straight and white and, shit, I'd never noticed someone's teeth before. But then I was smiling too—he had this contagious grin you couldn't help returning when he aimed it your way.

"Oh, I see how it is," I teased. "You don't ask *me* to

help with math."

"Dad, I love you, but you suck at math. We both know that."

I laughed because he was right. "You have a point there. I'd likely be asking you to explain it to me."

"Exactly." Logan pushed his glasses up his nose. Callum pulled one of the chairs over and sat beside him, and they immediately started talking numbers and process and I was already lost. It only took Callum a few minutes to explain something before Logan was hooting. "Oh my God! You're right. How did I not see that?"

"See? It's actually kind of cool how it works." Callum jotted something down.

I didn't see how math could ever be cool, but to each their own. They were blabbing again, talking about multiplying this by that and all sorts of other shit.

I opened the fridge and poured them each a glass of lemonade, hoping Callum liked it, then set them on the table.

"Thanks, Dad."

"Yeah, thanks, Dad. Now go away somewhere and leave us alone." Callum winked, and goose bumps ran the length of my arms.

My skin felt a little too tight, which was weird, so I said, "Fine, just try and get rid of me. I'll go out to my shop for a few minutes while you two smart guys take care of this."

"You're smart," Logan said. "Just in different ways."

"Thanks, buddy."

Callum waved me away playfully. I left them to it. There wasn't much I could help with. Plus, if there was anything school related Logan didn't want to talk to me about, maybe he would share it with Callum. As soon as I had the thought, I wondered if that was fair. He couldn't want to spend his time befriending a kid, but then, that didn't feel right. There was an honesty to how Callum laughed and spoke with Logan, like he enjoyed it and not only did it because it was polite.

I unlocked the old barn and went straight for my workbench. I sent off a quick text to Charlotte, saying hi and that I loved her. It was earlier there, so she was likely just getting out of school or at gymnastics practice or something.

I picked up the carving of a lion's head I'd been working on, losing myself in it for who knew how long. Eventually, there was a sound by the door, and I looked up to see Callum standing there.

"Hi." He looked almost bashful as he said it, his eyes darting away.

"Hey."

"Can I come in?"

"Of course."

"Homework is finished. Logan's out back with Frankie Blue." He bit his lip, and I wondered what it meant. Was he nervous? Why would he be? But then I'd had no reason to feel jittery when I'd asked him to come over tonight either.

"Thank you for helping. I appreciate it. I should have asked. Shit, I didn't even think. I'm not trying to push my kid off on you. I feel like I'm always apologizing or thanking you for something where my son is concerned." I rubbed a hand over my face, which I did when I was nervous or frustrated. All I wanted was to do right by Logan, and I really hoped I was.

"Then maybe you should stop, hmm? If I didn't want to do it, I wouldn't. I love kids. Logan is even more awesome than most. Also, I've seen you with him, and the last thing I would ever think is that you're trying to pawn your son off on someone else." I watched as he walked over to the wall on the right side of the barn. There was a long table there where I had my finished pieces—a boat, an old tree that reminded me of when I was a kid, and a few others. "You did these?" Callum reached out and ran his fingers over the tree, almost in reverence. His nails were painted black, which was a first.

Well, for me. I'd never seen him with painted nails before. It struck me suddenly how strong he was, how confident. I hadn't noticed any other adult men in Havenwood painting their nails or wearing the eye stuff, yet Callum was who he was and didn't care. It was one of my favorite things about him.

Finally, I replied, "Yeah, I did. Keeps me busy." I walked over and joined him. "When I was a kid, we had a tree like this behind our property. My dad built a tree house in it. He wasn't good with words. It was always just the two of us—my mom passed away when I was little—and I knew he loved me, but he was very much the real-men-don't-talk-about-their-feelings type. Never in a hateful way. If I'd ever tried to talk to him, I knew he would have tried to listen, but he wouldn't have gotten the why of it, ya know? It didn't make sense to him."

"People are nuanced. They're rarely one thing or another—hateful or good, talkative or not. Your dad probably learned that from his parents, or maybe it's simply how he was built."

"Exactly." Somehow, I knew he'd get it. "Anyway, this tree house. I built it with him. I think I felt closer to my dad than I ever had, when we made it. I felt like I was his equal, if that makes sense. I was one of the guys, and we were building our tree house. Sounds stupid, I'm sure."

He nudged me with his hip. "No, it doesn't. Go on."

"I don't really know the point of my story. Maybe that I loved building that tree house with my dad." I paused, thought. "And I guess maybe, when I found out I was having a son, I saw me and Logan doing stuff like that together? And maybe we will. When he first came here, he told me he wanted to work with me in the barn, but now I'm seeing it was more that he felt like he *should* want to, or maybe to try and prove wrong the kids who teased him. He might want to, or maybe he won't, and that's okay too. Again, it's not like that. I want him to be happy and healthy and comfortable in his skin, but...I want him to always feel as comfortable with me as I did when I built that tree house with my dad. I want to bond with him over something that's just ours, more than it being a certain kind of activity. We have the model planes, but that's it. I don't want him to look back and only have one memory like that, the way I do."

Holy shit. I couldn't believe I'd said all that. I didn't even know where it had come from. It was true, and I knew I felt it, but the thought of sharing that with someone had never been there.

"You will," Callum replied softly.

"You think so?" I found myself asking. Christ, I was embarrassed I'd said that, but I didn't want to take it back either. I needed to hear that, and for whatever reason, I trusted it coming from him.

"I know so." He did the hip-nudge thing again. "You're doing well by him. You're working hard to change patterns you learned from your dad. You're making sure your son knows his worth doesn't depend on doing typically masculine things. My dad would have never done that."

"I'm sorry," I replied, not knowing what else to say. "I mean, about your dad. That had to be hard."

"It's over now. I don't have anything to do with him, and I think that's fine by both of us. You with your dad?"

"He passed away."

"I'm sorry."

"We keep saying that to each other."

"Well, I have one more thing to say: you're pretty good at this talking thing, Knox. You said you weren't, and I don't think you see it, but you are."

With him. I didn't know why, but it was easier with Callum. It was as if he'd cast some spell over both me and Logan. "Eh, you're a good listener, I guess." I crossed my arms and leaned against the table.

"Now you're just trying to prove me wrong." He playfully rolled his eyes. He had the black stuff on those again too. Eyeliner, I thought it was called. "It's beautiful—the tree. All your work is, but this one especially. You can see the love that went into it. This one is my favorite. I was drawn to it immediately."

I didn't know what made me do it, but I picked up the tree and set it in front of him. "Then it's yours."

His eyes widened. "What? You can't do that."

"I just did."

"Knox, you can't—"

"Take it. Please. I insist."

He looked at me almost as if I were a stranger. Our eyes met. He was only about two or three inches shorter than me, but much leaner. "Thank you, Knox."

"You're welcome."

"As fate would have it, I also have a gift for you. Well, you and Logan, actually. I was feeling a little silly about it, but now I'm not." He reached into his pocket and pulled out a folded envelope. I took it from him, opened it, as he added, "So maybe it is a little silly, but...I don't know. You're an artist. I thought so after I saw the table, but I see it even more now, and Logan is an artist too. I thought this could be something you guys tried together. Please don't feel obligated if you're not interested—*oh*." He said the last word when I pressed my finger to his lips.

"Shh. It's not silly. It's perfect and not something I would have done on my own. Thank you." My hand dropped. I had no fucking clue where that shit had come from. I was pretty sure I wouldn't touch any other friend's mouth that way.

"You're welcome." He blinked a few times, licked his lip, then bit the damn thing. He was staring at me with this intense heaviness to his gaze, and I was looking back at him and couldn't turn away. It was probably weird, us standing there gawking at each other. My brain kept telling me to back up, to look away, that I was being creepy, but I still didn't move.

"Dad! Callum!" Logan said excitedly.

Callum and I both leaped away from each other like we'd been doing something we shouldn't have. "What's up?" I cleared my throat.

"Frankie Blue will bring the ball back if you throw it to her. Come see!"

"Sounds like we have an extra-smart girl," I said.

We followed Logan out of the barn and around to the back of the house. Callum kept the tree clutched to his chest the whole time.

CHAPTER ELEVEN

Callum

"WAIT. WHY DID I want to help with this again?" It was midmorning, and I was in the backyard at Knox's with him and Logan. It was the weekend after our dinner, when Knox had given me his tree carving, which I still couldn't believe. It was special to him, that much was obvious, and while he could make another one, it meant something that he'd chosen to give it to me. I tried not to let it mean more than it actually did—friendship, appreciation. I'd never felt more than that from him, except that moment in the barn. When he'd touched my lips and the way he'd looked at me. There had been something in his gaze that was unfamiliar coming from him, something that maybe confused him too, but then I figured I was projecting what I wanted to happen rather than what was happening, and yep, I was totally going to be stupid, falling for a straight guy and getting my heart broken.

"Callum?" Logan said questioningly.

"Hmm?"

"You were spacing off."

"Sorry. I was trying to figure out why I thought helping your dad build a fence would be a good idea," I lied.

"It'll be fun. Plus, Frankie Blue needs an area where she can run around by herself without us risking losing her," Logan replied.

"Well, I guess it's a good thing I like her."

"What are we? Chopped liver?" Knox asked.

I rolled my eyes playfully. "Oh my God. You're such a *dad*. That sounded so old."

Both Logan and I laughed. Knox flipped me off, before his eyes darted to his son.

"Oooh! I saw that!" Logan said.

"Saw what? I have no idea what you're talking about." Knox winked at him, they both chuckled, and my heart went a little flip-floppy. Ugh.

"Okay, guys," Knox said, "we're gonna do this, and just think, every time we come outside, we'll see it and be proud of something we accomplished. It'll feel good, I promise. No obligation from either of you, though."

He was so sweet, and so cautious when it came to Logan, it made me melt every time. He didn't want his son to think he doubted his abilities, and he wanted to teach him things like this, but he also didn't want him to feel like it was something he had to enjoy.

"What do we do first?" Logan asked.

"How's your hand?" The second I said the last word, it clicked that Knox and I asked the same question simultaneously. "Jinx?" I looked at him, hoping I hadn't overstepped. Yes, I'd been the one to stitch him up, but I wasn't there as Logan's healthcare provider. I was there as a friend.

"See? Someone's on my side," Knox replied. "He gets mad at me every time I want to see it."

"You guys treat me like I'm a baby." As if realizing what he said, Logan looked at me. "I mean, Dad does, but you kinda are right now too."

Nope, nope, nope. Don't like what he said. Don't like the fact that he'd spoken like you and Knox are a unit. You absolutely are not.

"Well, I'm the one who stitched that up so perfectly, so I don't want you to mess up my work. Let me look real quick." I examined his hand, and it was, in fact, healing beautifully.

"Can we start now?" Logan asked. I could see the outline of his rescue inhaler in his pocket. He was good about keeping it on him.

"Yep. Let's do it," Knox replied.

It was a chain-link fence. He was enclosing a small area off one of the doors so they could let Frankie Blue out by herself when need be. He'd already dug the holes and added the concrete and poles so we only had to do the rest of it.

Knox lifted some of the supplies and started walking toward the edge of the house where the fencing would begin, and I wasn't admiring how his body moved or his tight muscles, I swore.

Logan and I listened while Knox explained what needed to be done. He was thorough but never condescending, and as we began the process, he gave us pointers and occasionally asked for help.

I loved watching him when he explained something to Logan. He had this way about him where he went into detail about how everything worked, even if it didn't have anything to do with the fence. I'd noticed it before, but it was even more noticeable today, when he was talking about drainage and rain gutters and how the slope of the roof helped, or about a bird nest we saw and he explained how they built them.

God, he was such a good dad. A good man. I couldn't help being in awe of him.

We'd just finished a section, and he lifted his shirt to

wipe the sweat off his face. Holy fuck, his abs. It took everything in me not to whimper. He ended up pulling the dark tee off and tucking it in the back pocket of his jeans.

Knox's green gaze caught mine, and I was pretty sure my cheeks reddened. They felt hot in a way that had nothing to do with the heat of the day.

He smiled. "What?"

Oh, bless his heart. He was so oblivious. It didn't even compute with him that he attracted me.

"Nothing."

He kept staring at me, and I didn't look away either. I felt gross and sweaty and probably looked a mess.

"I'm gonna go inside and pee, then bring Frankie Blue out for a minute," Logan said, snapping us out of whatever moment that had been. We both turned to look at him.

"Okay. Drink some water while you're in there," Knox told him. "And maybe you can bring another bottle out for me and Callum?"

"Sure thing," Logan replied, and then he was gone.

"Thanks for helping today. Don't think I told you that already. I'm sure it's not your favorite way to spend a Saturday."

Actually, I was fairly certain there was nowhere else

I'd rather be. "Eh, I like Logan and Frankie Blue, so…"

"I see what you're doing here. I'm not calling myself chopped liver again so you can tell me I'm old."

"If the shoe fits…" I teased. "Not really, though. You're what? Forty?"

"Forty-four. Christ, that's weird to even say out loud."

I rolled my eyes. "That's not old. You're only eleven years older than me." Not that our age difference mattered. "And I mean, look at you." I waved my hand up and down.

"What's wrong with me?"

"Um…nothing. Come on, you've seen you." I wasn't going to lie to the guy.

Knox frowned. I couldn't tell if he was uncomfortable I'd said it, surprised I had, or if he didn't see it.

"Knox. Oh my God. You don't know you're fucking gorgeous, do you?" I asked in shock. Maybe not my finest moment, but still.

The surprise on his face deepened, before he put a mask over it. "'Course I do."

I couldn't tell if he was being serious or not. Did he really not see it, or was it that he wasn't used to a man thinking that about him? Knox didn't strike me as the insecure type, but hell, maybe he hid it well.

"Knox…"

"You got something." He took a step closer, then another one. "Right here." He reached out, and his thumb brushed under my eye. My stomach got light and my pulse sped up while I was thinking, *Great, I just told him he's hot, and I had stuff all over my face? Typical.* "Piece of a leaf." He pulled back, and I missed his calloused touch instantly.

He cleared his throat and moved away. A second later Frankie Blue was jumping all over us. I knelt and petted her as Logan walked over and gave us each a bottle of water.

We drank them down before getting back to work on the fence again. Stupid me still felt his touch against my face.

We were almost done, Knox and I working on one of the corners, adding the fencing. I held it while Knox did his part. Our arms were touching, shoulder to shoulder. He didn't seem to notice, but I definitely did.

There was a deep bark, and we both turned around to look just as a big-ass horse dog rounded the corner. "Oh shit." I backed into Knox quickly, and he held on to my arms to keep me steady, my back against his chest.

"It's okay. He's the sweetest boy you'll ever meet," Knox said as Lawson and Remington fucking Monroe walked around the corner. Their eyes landed right on us. I felt Knox tense up, and I pulled away.

"He won't eat me, right?" I asked, trying to ignore the way Lawson's gaze shot between me and Knox.

When he didn't reply, Remington said, "No. He's a lover, not a fighter. We were, um…close and thought we'd introduce Bear to Frankie Blue."

I took another step away from Knox. Logan and Frankie Blue had gone back in the house a few minutes before and now came barreling back out. The two dogs went right over to each other, and Logan said, "Bear!" before the three of them started playing.

"Hey, Callum," Remington said. He had on an old T-shirt, inside out.

Jesus Christ. What in the hell world had I stepped into? "Hi." I glanced at Blond Curls. "Hi again, Lawson."

"You can just call him Law if you want."

"Just, huh?" Lawson said, apparently snapping out of whatever daze he'd been in. He wrapped an arm around Remy, pulled him close, and kissed the top of his head.

Remy looked at him like he hung the moon, making something squeeze in my chest. Law grinned at him, giving him the same intense stare. Just like that time at Sunrise, it was clear as day how much they loved each other, and I suddenly felt very, very alone. I'd had boyfriends, lots of them, but no one had ever looked at me with the adoration they did each other. "We're, um…building a fence," I said stupidly.

"I see that," Lawson replied.

Knox rubbed a hand over his beard. "You guys want a drink or anything?"

"Nah, we can't stay long. We have a family thing. Believe me, I'd rather be here," Lawson said, and Remy chuckled.

"They're getting better," Remy said.

"Yeah, because they like you more than me," Lawson countered.

"Who wouldn't?" Knox asked.

"Aw, you better be nice to me, Knoxy."

My eyes widened at the nickname Lawson used for him. "Knoxy? That's so cute! I think I'm gonna call you that from now on."

"So…it was nice being friends with you and all," Knox teased me, then playfully tried to push me away.

"Aw, Knoxy doesn't like it? I'm *so* sorry, Knoxy," I joked back.

"If you're not nice to me, I'm not cooking you dinner for helping."

Knox was basically a grill master. I loved his food, so

I said, "You win!"

We smiled at each other. I felt eyes on me, so I looked at Lawson and Remy to see them watching us.

Knox cleared his throat. "You guys wanna stay for dinner later? Shit. Family thing. I forgot."

Yeah, because this wasn't awkward at all. It shouldn't be. There was no reason for it to be, but it most definitely was.

Frankie Blue, Logan, and Bear all came running for us then. We laughed and talked about random stuff. Mostly they laughed and talked and I watched, feeling a little out of place.

Law and Remy were nice, though, and the awkwardness seemed to fade away. It was only about twenty minutes later when they said they had to head out.

"We need to hang out soon, brother," Law said, clapping Knox on the arm. "We've both been busy."

"Yeah, we will. Thanks for bringing Bear over."

They said their goodbyes, and the three of them left. Knox acted completely normal, turning to look at Logan and me. "You guys ready to get this knocked out or what?"

"Let's do it!" Logan replied. "It's kinda fun, huh, Callum?"

I grinned at him. "It's lots of fun," I said, meaning it.

CHAPTER TWELVE

Knox

"**A**RE YOU EXCITED for the class?" I asked Logan as we drove to Safe Haven, Kellan's art studio. I'd called a few days before to register for one of the classes, using the gift certificate Callum had given us. Logan had gotten his stitches out today, though it hadn't been Callum to do it, and now we were having a night out.

"I'm excited to beat you at something," Logan teased, looking over at me. His dark, floppy hair needed a cut.

"Oh, I see how you are. It's all about beating your old man, huh? You're better than me at lots of things."

"Yeah, sure. Whatever."

"Okay, I'm making a list. First—"

"Oh my God, Dad. Please don't. I shouldn't have said anything. Yeah, I'm stoked for the class. I like to paint."

I nodded, but I really didn't want to let it go. Logan

didn't seem to do well with compliments from me. When Callum and I spoke about it, he hammered home the fact that it was because I was his dad. It was easier to believe from someone like Callum, and Logan did believe him more, because like he'd said, he thought I *had* to say those things.

Not for the first time, it struck me how good Callum was at this kind of thing. Did he want kids of his own one day? He would be a great dad. He was making this whole transition a hell of a lot smoother for both Logan *and* me. It was strange. I couldn't quite figure out how it happened, what made us fall into this easy friendship and what made Logan connect with him, but I was thankful. I liked spending time with him. It was…different.

I pulled into one of the parking spots across the street from Kellan's studio. Logan and I got out, crossed, and went inside. A couple of people were already there, one of them a boy about Logan's age. He had red hair, was a little taller than Logan, and looked over at him and waved. Logan returned it.

"Do you know him from school?"

"No. I don't recognize him."

"Hey! You guys made it! I'm so excited to have you in my class today." Kellan nodded for us to go through the short, swinging counter door so we could join them in the studio area. "What's up, Logan? We're all so happy you're living here now."

"Thanks," Logan replied, then, "Whoa. Did you make that?" He pointed to a piece of pottery.

"I did."

"That looks cool."

"I'll teach you sometime if you want." Kellan winked at me, and I was so thankful. I was lucky to have such great friends.

"That'd be awesome. Can I, Dad?" Logan looked up at me.

"Yeah, buddy. Of course."

"Ooh, that's cool! I want to learn it too," the red-headed boy said.

Kellan called him over. "How about I introduce you guys? Logan, this is Dale. Dale, meet Logan."

They said hi to each other, Logan's a little softer and more insecure. Dale didn't seem to have that problem. He said, "That's cool that we both like art. Do you like video games too?"

Then they were chatting about games and levels, and I thought maybe for the first time since Logan came to live with me, I breathed a little easier. Christ, I wanted this for him. Wanted him to have a friend.

Logan and I went over and sat on the stools beside

Dale and a pretty woman with strawberry-blonde hair and these big blue eyes, who I assumed was his mom.

"Hi, I'm Amanda."

I shook her hand. "Knox, nice to meet you." I didn't recognize her, but I figured I couldn't know everyone in town.

Dale and Logan were still chatting, Dale pointing at his easel.

"We just moved here a couple of months ago," she said.

"I've lived here since not long after my divorce, but Logan moved out with me not too long ago."

"My parents moved here a couple of years ago. My husband and I separated about a year back. It hasn't been easy. We wanted to be closer to family, which is how we ended up in Havenwood." Amanda smiled.

"It's a great place to live," I replied, and she smiled again.

The class filled up, and Kellan started. He was a great teacher, walking us through each step as we painted an ocean-and-sunset scene. I wasn't gonna lie, mine wasn't great, but that was more my ability than Kellan's instruction.

Logan basically ignored me the whole time. He and Dale seemed to really hit it off. It felt so damn good to see him laugh with someone his age.

We were almost finished with the painting when Amanda leaned my way. "I have to admit, I'm really glad you guys are here tonight. Dale hasn't befriended anyone yet. I was getting a little worried."

"Logan hasn't either. Dale goes to Havenwood Middle School?"

She nodded. They might not have had any classes together, or they just hadn't noticed each other, but it was good to know they would be at the same school.

"I haven't met many people yet either," Amanda added, "so I get it. Sometimes those things are hard in a small town."

I went to reply, but then Kellan was announcing class was over.

As we cleaned our supplies, Logan asked, "Dad, can I hang out with Dale sometime after school? Or on a weekend or something?"

"Yeah, please, Mom?" Dale asked Amanda.

This was all so new for me, I just sort of looked at Amanda, who chuckled. "It's okay with me if it's okay with Mr.…."

"Just Knox is fine."

"Knox. We can switch phone numbers."

"I can give Dale my phone number too!" Logan said

excitedly.

Amanda and I swapped phone numbers, and the boys did the same. They left first. Logan and I spoke with Kellan for a few minutes, and then we went to the truck and headed home.

"Dale's super cool, Dad. We have a class together. I didn't even realize it."

"That's good. I'm glad. Maybe he can meet Frankie Blue sometime."

"That would be awesome. He has three game systems. He said I could go over. Sorry I didn't hang out with you much. I know Callum got it so we could spend time together. He said you were really excited to take the class with me."

I wasn't surprised that Callum had said something like that to Logan in confidence. It was so *him*, trying to make Logan feel good that way. "I was, but it's okay. I still had fun, and it was nice to see you meet someone."

"Dale is awesome! Can I text Callum from your phone and tell him?" They didn't have each other's numbers.

"Yep." I unlocked it, pulled up the texts to Callum, and handed it over. Logan frantically moved his fingers over the screen, then laughed at something I assumed Callum said back to him. "He's a good guy, isn't he?" I found myself saying.

"Callum?" When I nodded, Logan said, "Yeah, the best. I'm glad we met him. He…he's easy to talk to. Not that you're not, but he just, gets it…gets me. That doesn't hurt your feelings, right? I don't want to."

"It doesn't." The truth was, it did slightly. I could both wish Logan wanted to talk to me that way and be grateful he had Callum at the same time. I knew they had in common the fact that they'd both had childhood health problems, but again, I wondered if there was more to it. I didn't know how to do this or if I should bring it up at all, but I wanted Logan to know he could come to me with anything. That I would love him no matter what. This was maybe the perfect opportunity to say it. "He's a good person for you to talk to. It's okay if you choose to talk to him, if you guys have stuff in common, ya know? But I also want you to know you can always come to me with anything too. That nothing will ever change how much I love you or anything like that."

"Okay…" Logan replied, confusion making him draw the word out. "I mean, I know that. Why would you not love me 'cuz I'm littler or a dork?"

"You're not a dork, and I wouldn't. I was just saying, if there was ever anything else."

Logan was a smart kid, so I wasn't really surprised

when he said, "Oh my God, Dad. Do you think I'm gay?"

Well, shit. The way he said it, I figured I'd gone about this all wrong. "I don't think anything, buddy. But if you were, that would be okay."

"I'm not. I don't notice boys that way, and I notice girls that way all the time. They're really, really pretty. Did you think I'm gay because I'm friends with Callum?"

"I didn't say I think you're gay. I was just saying—"

"But why? You're friends with Callum, Law, Remy, Chase, and Kellan, and you're not gay."

My pulse sped up, blood rushing through my veins.

He added, "That's kinda like stereotyping."

Which was what Callum had basically said too. My face heated, and I rubbed a hand over my beard. "I can see how it looks that way. I don't mean it, but I guess it doesn't matter how I mean it if it comes out wrong. You're right. I'm friends with all of them, and no, I'm not gay. I didn't mean to sound like I was assuming anything about you. It's my job as your dad to make sure you always know you're loved. That's all I was trying to do." Though from the sound of it, I'd fucked it up royally. "Can we pretend this conversation never happened?"

Logan chuckled. "It's okay, Dad. You're old. You don't get it."

"I'm not old, and you're grounded," I joked back.

"Whatever you say." Logan typed out another message for Callum before giving me my phone back. Then he was on his, I assumed messaging with Dale, so we were quiet the rest of the drive. When we got home, we took Frankie Blue out, had a snack, having eaten dinner before the class, and Logan showered and took care of what he needed to do to get ready for school the next day.

We watched a show, and then it was bedtime. When he got to the stairs, he stopped. "Hey, Dad?"

"Yeah?" I turned to look at him.

"Thanks…for everything, but also for what you said in the truck. You're, um…you're an awesome dad. I know Callum didn't have the same thing, so it's cool you wanted to make sure I know you'd always love me."

"I…"

"Don't get all *emotional dad* on me. It's weird." He laughed, then ran up the stairs, Frankie Blue on his heels. I sat there dumbstruck for a moment, feeling…hell, pretty proud.

I didn't know what made me do it, but I grabbed my phone from the coffee table and called Callum.

"Is everything okay?" he asked. "Logan?"

"What? Yeah, he's fine. Why?"

"Oh. You scared the crap out of me. You've never called before. We've texted but not talked."

He was right. I hadn't even thought of that. I hated talking on the phone and did it as seldom as I could, unless I was talking to my kids or Carol. "Is it an okay time?" I asked, this unfamiliar insecurity in my chest.

"Of course. You can call me anytime you want. I heard the class went well and Logan met a friend."

"He did. Because of you."

"I didn't do anything. It was just—"

"You did," I cut him off. "And thank you."

There was a short pause before Callum replied. "You're welcome."

We were quiet again as if we didn't know what to say. I still didn't know why I called, so I said the first thing that came to mind. "Wanna hear how much of a dumbass I was on the drive home?"

"*Duh.* Is that even a question?"

I told him about the conversation with Logan, and he told me I was only a bit of a jackass. He asked what we painted, and I told him more about Dale and Amanda, and he was a little quiet when I did. "How was your day at work?" I asked, and Callum rambled about things he could tell me that didn't break patient confidentiality, and about making dinner with his mom and how much he enjoyed it.

Then he told me about a movie he found on TV, and I turned it to the same channel so I could see what he was talking about. We laughed and watched it, poking fun here and there.

It was…*nice*. When the movie was over, I kept talking to him as I turned off the lights and went to my room. I didn't know how we could have so much to say to each other—it hadn't been long since we last spent time together—but we did.

"I should go," Callum said a little while later. I was lying on my bed, trying to figure out why I felt a stab of disappointment at that.

"Yeah, me too. It's getting late."

"Good night, Knox," he said softly.

"'Night."

Callum disconnected the call, and ridiculously, I found myself looking at my phone for a moment. Shaking my head, I put it on the charger, then went into the bathroom for a shower.

When I was in bed, I wrapped my hand around my cock and jerked off, blue eyes in my thoughts. I tried to tell myself they belonged to Amanda, but I wasn't sure they did.

CHAPTER THIRTEEN

Callum

"IT'S GOING TO look good out here when we're all done," I said to Mom as we worked on tearing out some of the old brush in the backyard. It was her day off, and she'd told me last night she'd planned on being out there. She had a garage full of supplies and had been taking on one project at a time. I was making a point of trying to spend more time with her. It was one of the reasons I was there, after all, and I hadn't been doing the best job of it.

"It will. I like that I can do whatever I want, ya know? And everything I'm physically able to do by myself, or with your help if you want, I'm going to do. There will be some projects I have to hire out for, but I just…"

"Want to stand on your own," I finished.

"Yeah." Mom looked at me and smiled.

"I get that. I felt the same in college. After I went

through that depressive stage, I just…"

"Wanted to stand on your own," she supplied the same as I'd done for her.

"Exactly."

"I…" Mom paused, closed her eyes, and shook her head. "I'll never forgive myself for how I reacted when I found out."

It was something I would never forget, something that still hurt, if I was being honest, but I also knew I couldn't dwell on it forever. "I know, and it's over. You're here now, and you've been for a long time. That's what matters."

"No, it's not. Not fully, at least. You're my son. I…"

"Hey, don't. We've dealt with this already." Mostly. I reached out and wiped the tear rolling down her face. "Oops. I have dirt on my hand, and now all I did was make you messy." I was hoping to lighten the mood, that she would chuckle and we could stop talking about things we couldn't change.

"I should have known earlier."

"How could you have?" I asked. "I faked it well. I knew most of my life, Mom, and I hid it with jokes and smiles and fake girl crushes. You didn't know because I didn't want anyone to know."

"I still *should have known*."

I frowned, something in her tone setting off some kind of alarm inside me. "Why?"

Mom opened her mouth, closed it, then said, "Because you're my son, of course."

"Well, moms aren't perfect, because if they were, that would mean sons have to be perfect, and I'm definitely not that."

Mom grinned. "I think you're pretty perfect."

"You have to say that. You're my mom." As soon as I finished speaking, I chuckled.

"What?"

"It's just funny. Logan says that to Knox all the time—that Knox has to think whatever it is he said because he's Logan's dad." I turned, tugged my gloves back on, and began pulling brush and putting it into the wheelbarrow. "First, building a fence, and now this. Havenwood is going to work me to the bone."

Mom came over and got busy as well. "You and Knox spend a lot of time together."

We did, and I liked it, was liking it more and more. "He's a good guy, and Logan is great. I think Knox mostly hangs out with me because Logan took to me so quickly." Though that didn't really feel true. I told myself that to try and help keep the emotional distance I needed to build between us, but I didn't believe it for a second.

It had been two weeks since the art class when he called me out of the blue, when we'd talked for hours and watched a fucking movie on the phone together, for Christ's sake. That was shit you did in high school.

Since then, I was at his place about four times a week, and we texted often throughout the day and night. We'd also ended up chatting on the phone a few more evenings too. Those were all things that didn't include Logan, though we had yet to hang out without him.

"No," Mom said, "that's not true. Knox wouldn't do that. Both Knox and Logan just realize how great you are."

"You have to say that; you're my mom," I teased again, rubbing a hand over the scar on my chest, then bent down to lift some of the broken twigs, plants, and weeds from the ground. It was easier to talk about this stuff if I wasn't looking at her. "I like being with them. It's kind of weird. I feel like…I don't know, like I slipped into place, if that makes sense. Like I fit. Which is dumb." Especially now with Logan having met Dale, who apparently had a single mom. She and Knox had spoken a few times, and I had this vision in my head of them dating, which he had every right to do, and me not fitting in with them anymore.

"No, no. Why is it dumb?"

We hadn't done this—ever—talking about guys or anything like that. I was in the closet, and then she told me to deny myself. I did, and by the time I came out of it, I was too angry with her to open myself up this way. But I wanted to do it now, I thought. "Because I'm scared I'm going to like him in a way he won't like me. And that I'm going to get closer to Logan too, and somehow I'm going to lose it all because I'll mess it up, or he'll realize I tried to insert myself into his life in a way I was never meant to. Like they're a round hole and I'm this square peg, telling myself it works when it doesn't." I wanted to be suited for them so bad, and while I felt like I did, I doubted Knox would feel the same. Not in the way I was starting to want.

"Oh, sweetie." Mom knelt beside me. "You don't know for sure if that will happen. Knox likes you. I hear you guys talking on the phone, and he's always inviting you over. Maybe you'll fall for Knox, and maybe you won't. Maybe he'll feel the same, and maybe he won't. That's always a risk when you put your heart out there, but isn't it worth it? There's no chance at all if you walk away. I'm not saying to take needless risks. You have to protect your heart, but...I don't want you to be alone. I've spent my life feeling alone, even when I was with your dad. I want better for you."

"You deserved better than him. Have you dated since then? You should get out there, find yourself a good man."

She shook her head. "Oh, I couldn't. I'm old and have too many issues of my own."

"That's not true."

"We're talking about you, not me," she said with a smile.

Why had I never thought of that before? Of Mom being alone. "Well, I think you should date. I'm going to see if I can figure out the eligible bachelors in this town."

"Don't," Mom rushed out, panic in her voice.

"I was kidding. I won't overstep. I'm sorry."

She waved off my concern, but I couldn't tell if it was honest or not. "I'm an old lady. I have my house and my projects, my job and my son. That's all I need."

Reaching over, I gave her a hug. "I'm glad I'm here."

"I'm glad you're here too."

Talk of men dropped from there. We finished clearing out the brush, and Mom told me more about her plans—another garden she wanted, a gazebo, and a swing. She wanted her own little oasis, and I wanted it for her. I liked working with her, talking to her, getting close to her again.

Still, Knox was on my mind the whole time. I kept telling myself I would fall for him, but the truth was, I already had. I wasn't in love with him, but I liked him beyond his sexy lumberjack look. I wanted…more with him, but that was something I needed to force down. His friendship was the most important thing, and I was desperate not to lose that.

So I'd pretend I didn't want to be the hole to his peg, ones that fit together really fucking well. We were friends, and that was all, and one thing that would help with that was to find someone who did like sticking their pegs in sexy little holes like mine.

Which meant a hookup app. Josh had offered to go to Richmond with me sometime, but I wasn't sure if he meant it, and now that I thought about getting laid, I realized I was really fucking horny and wanted it now instead of waiting to plan a weekend away.

It took less time than I would have thought out here to find a top looking for a hookup. The guy was visiting in the area and wanted a night out, but since we were both with family, we didn't have a place to go.

I booked a room at the hotel I stayed at when I first got to Havenwood. We were meeting at six, and since I was a good little bottom, I showered, douched, and took care of everything I needed to do. I'd even skipped dinner for extra precaution.

"I'm heading out," I told Mom a little while later.

"Going to Knox's?"

"Um…no?"

She held up her hand. "I don't need to hear any more."

We both laughed, and a knot loosened in my chest, maybe one I'd had there since that day Mom asked if I was gay and then told me I could pretend I wasn't.

"I love you, Mama."

Her eyes filled with tears. "You haven't called me that in a long time."

"I know." But I thought I would more now.

We said our goodbyes, and I drove to the hotel, pretending it was a coincidence that the guy I was meeting had black hair and a beard, like Knox.

CHAPTER FOURTEEN

Knox

THE HOUSE WAS too quiet.

Logan hadn't been living with me for long, but I was used to always having him there, and sometimes both Logan and Callum. Even Frankie Blue looked lonely as she glanced at me from the dog bed, like I was a disappointment and not nearly as fun as Logan. "I know, girl. It's not my fault. He has a friend now, and it's his first sleepover. We have to let him go." She ran over to where I sat on the couch and put her front legs on the cushion. "You're a good puppy, aren't you?" I scratched behind her ears. "Maybe we should invite Callum over? What do you say?"

As soon as I had the thought, I struck it out. For some reason, I felt...silly inviting him over, though I couldn't figure out why that might be. He was my friend. I enjoyed spending time with him. He was at the house all the time. In fact, I hadn't done much with any of my friends outside of Callum in a while. Even after Law had come over when we worked on the fence, I still hadn't made it to his place or to Griff's to hang out. Though it was different now, having Logan at home. We were taking a biweekly art class and had homework at night and spent evenings working on our model planes. It wasn't as easy to sit at the bar, shooting the shit.

Which meant I should take advantage of tonight and hit up Griff's, maybe call Law or Josh to see if they would be there.

Just as I leaned forward to grab my phone from the coffee table, it rang. Callum's name popped up on the screen, and I felt a strange jolt in my pulse.

I grabbed my cell and stood up, answering the call. "Hey, man. What's up?" Was it me, or did my voice sound weird? Why in the hell my voice would sound unsure was beyond me.

"Have you guys eaten?" he rushed out with what sounded like a bit of annoyance in his voice.

"Um...no? Are you okay?"

"I'm coming over. I mean, can I come over? And I'm bringing dinner. If you say I can come over, at least. I'm bringing all the food and maybe some snacks too, so is there anything you like? Well, first, do you guys have plans?"

I couldn't help but chuckle at how he'd rambled. "No, I haven't eaten. I think I said that already. Yes, you can come over. You're always welcome here. Or we can..." My words trailed off. I was going to say we could go to Griff's, but I didn't. I suddenly realized I didn't feel like going out. I wanted to relax at home with Callum.

"We can what?"

"Nothing. Hurry up and get your ass over here. It's just me, though, so if you're looking for Logan, you might be disappointed. I'll have to be enough."

"Oh."

My chest tightened. "Is that a problem?"

"No, no. Of course not. It's...it's nothing. Ignore me. I'll be there soon with all the food."

"As long as you don't forget the food," I teased.

"Not a chance." Callum hung up, and I found myself staring at my phone for a moment. I had no fucking clue what that was about. He'd never been so obsessive about dinner, and obviously something was wrong. I just didn't know how those two things fit together.

I was wearing a pair of jeans already, but I tugged on a white T-shirt, then brushed my teeth. My insides felt jittery, which was a bit fucked. I had no reason to be nervous, so I told myself it was because Logan was at his first sleepover. I *was* stressing about that already. I'd made him crazy checking in about his medication, and his inhaler, and bringing his phone charger, and calling me anytime, it didn't matter how late. I'd also made sure to tell Amanda about his asthma. He'd wanted to kill me, and I could understand why. But thinking about that didn't change the jumpy feeling inside me, just added to it.

"Come on, Frankie Blue. Let's go outside." She came running, and we went out the back, into the fenced-in area I'd built with Logan and Callum. I tinkered around back there for a while, then threw the ball for Frankie Blue over and over and over again. She never got tired, and before I knew it, I heard a car pull up out front. Frankie's ears perked, and she began yapping. "It's just Callum," I told her.

I went through the house, puppy feet tapping along the hardwood floors behind me. I opened the door just as Callum got there. He swept inside, a pizza box and other stuff in his hands. "Well, hello to you too," I joked, closing the door and following him into the kitchen.

"I got pizza, and it's veggie because that's my favorite and I deserve it tonight. You can eat it. Green stuff isn't bad for you. You need more colors in your diet. Bar foods and appetizers aren't a food group. But I was nice and got you chicken wings because I know you like them. We also have brownies because I love brownies. Do you like them?" He set everything on the table and turned to me.

"Yeah," I replied, still trying to wrap my brain around everything he said. "And I eat colors and vegetables. I've been eating them even more lately."

"Yes, but you act like it's torture."

"Do not."

"Do so," he countered. "You're like a big kid with your food. I don't know how you have a body like that without eating better."

My pulse did this strange, stumbling thing.

Callum's eyes went wide. "Not that I'm checking out your body or anything, but, you know, it's hard to miss a lumberjack." He turned away, began opening boxes, and then went straight to the cabinet where I kept the plates and grabbed two. He moved around the space as if it were his, familiar with it, which I guessed he was. Callum had eaten with us and hung out with us how many times by now?

"I'm not a lumberjack," I finally managed to say, my voice slightly more raspy than usual.

"Yeah, okay. Whatever you say." He faced me again and playfully rolled his eyes.

There was my sarcastic Callum. Shit. Not mine. He

wasn't mine. Why had I thought that?

He frowned. "What's wrong?"

"Nothing."

"Good. Let's eat. I'm very angry about men right now, so it's not the time to test me."

I laughed. "I'll try to keep that in mind." He handed me a plate, and I got two pieces of pizza and some chicken wings.

He was already taking a bite of his as he sat down. "You don't even get what I went through today."

Concern ate at me. "What happened? Is there something I can do?" I took the chair across from him.

"Pig out with me and let me vent." He didn't give me a chance to respond before he continued. "So…I decided I needed to hook up. It's been a while, and it's slim pickings in these parts." It felt like something heavy sat on my chest, but Callum kept going, obviously unaware I felt weighed down for no reason. "I got on an app and met this guy. I paid for a room. Do you know how hard it sucks to have to get a hotel room to have sex? Well, it does, but I did it, and I skipped dinner, just to be safe, and got all ready for him—a lot of work goes into this, thank you very much. I mean, I eat well and take my fiber daily and know my body really well, so it likely would have been okay, but yeah, I went through all that, and he didn't show! He stood me up."

"Wait. Why did you have to skip dinner to have sex?"

Callum froze mid-bite, holding a piece of pizza at his lips, then lowered it slowly. "Oops. I guess I forgot who I was speaking to for a moment. This conversation is now over. How's the...weather."

"You were just in it. Why are you changing the subject? That's not like you." A low voice deep inside me reminded me how much I liked that I knew him.

He looked unsure, but said, "If you think about it, you'll figure it out. And I don't *have* to skip my meal. I was being proactive, and this is not the conversation we should be having over dinner. My fault, but I'd like to fix that now."

The truth slammed into me like a battering ram, at first making me feel stupid for not putting two and two together, and then I was fidgeting in my seat because...well, because that's not something I've ever had to think about.

"Oh my God! You shifted!"

"I didn't shift," I replied even though I obviously did.

"Don't worry. Your butt is safe around me. It feels pretty fucking good, I'll have you know. Please don't get all bottom-shamey or weird."

He stood and walked away, looking out the window with his back to me. I could tell I'd struck a nerve without meaning to.

"I shouldn't have said anything. I don't know why I did. I was just frustrated, and we're friends, and I don't know anyone else here the way I do you."

My heart was beating like crazy then, like I was running a marathon while all these random thoughts collided in my head. That I was talking sex with Callum. That I felt…weird at the thought of him having sex with someone, and not because it was with a man; just that he was having it with someone, anyone. That he trusted me and felt comfortable with me. It was all making my brain spin, and I didn't know what to focus on, so I chose him. "I would never shame you, bottom or otherwise. And I know my butt is safe with you." That was something I'd never imagined myself saying. He chuckled softly but didn't turn to look at me.

I walked over, stood behind him. He smelled like rain and wildflowers on a spring day—something uniquely him. It was a scent I recognized, a scent I knew, and I had never realized it was something I was familiar with until that moment. It was mixed with the soft musk of a cologne he didn't usually wear, but maybe now did because he'd been meeting someone to have sex with.

"Hey," I said. When he still didn't turn around, I said it again, softer, with an unexpected plea in my voice. "Hey."

Callum turned. He leaned against the counter, but he was still close, so fucking close. I hadn't noticed I'd moved so near to him. "I would *never* shame you, and I didn't mean to make you feel like I'm uncomfortable with your sex life. It's just not something I've ever thought about that way, and it threw me. But you're my friend, and you can talk to me about anything. Hell, you've listened to me enough."

His eyes glistened slightly.

"Did I say something wrong?"

"No." He shook his head, swiped at his eyes to dry them. "No, not at all. You're a good friend, Knox. And like I told you before, you're better at talking than you realize. It was just…a strange day. I had a much needed conversation with my mom, and then the whole preparing to meet up with someone only to be stood up. I'm being stupid. We're fine. Let's finish eating."

He tried to walk around me, but I reached out, put a hand on his waist. Callum's breath hitched, and I thought maybe I held mine. "You're not being stupid, but yes, I want to feed you. I can't believe you missed dinner for that asshole." He looked up at me, and I winked.

"Fucking tops. They just don't get it." His voice was lighter then, more playful, but it didn't sound real.

"Sit. Eat. And tell me what happened with your mom."

So that's what we did. We went back to the table, and he told me about their past—about when she found out he was gay. "And today was nice. We worked in the yard together. I swear this town is trying to kill me. But for the first time we talked about guys, and it just…it felt good. It made me realize how much I'd missed her. How much we missed out on because I couldn't fully let go of my anger from the past."

"Which you had every right to feel. Plus, you're letting go now. That's what matters."

"Yeah…yeah, I guess so." He smiled, glanced away. "Thanks, Knox."

"You, um…have something." I motioned toward his face. Callum went to wipe what looked like pizza sauce but missed it. "Here, let me." I reached over. It was weird and almost in slow motion. I watched my hand ease close to him as if I wasn't the one controlling it. I touched his cheek, which was soft, so fucking soft and warm, and…different. I swiped at the pizza sauce with my thumb. His eyes fluttered, his thick, dark lashes against his skin. There was this jolt of…fuck, something. I jerked my hand back as if he burned me.

"Well, that was embarrassing. I'm a bit of a mess tonight. At least it happened with you. My friend. And not some guy I was…"

"Hooking up with," I finished for him, that tightness returning. "Wanna come out to the barn with me?" I asked, though I wasn't sure why. "I can show you what I'm working on."

"Yeah." Callum smiled. "I'd love to." Then he stood and gave me his back, and somehow I felt cheated out of something, like the movement had put a barrier between us and that he'd done it on purpose.

CHAPTER FIFTEEN

Callum

I WAS SO fucked, it wasn't even funny.

I wanted Knox. There was no pretending. It wasn't even just wanting him in bed, though I wanted that too. It was *him*. I wanted to date him, to be with him, and there was only one way this could end for me. It wasn't good.

We went out to the barn. He turned on the lights and asked, "Do you want something to drink? I have beer and water in the fridge out here."

"Water is good. Thanks." I went over to the shelf where he had his work and studied the pieces. Knox came over and handed me a bottle. "You really are talented."

"Thanks. I like woodworking. Gives me something to do."

"Gives me something to do, he says, like he's not creating gorgeous pieces of art." I looked at him and winked. "I wish I could do something like this."

"You stitched my son's hand. You take care of people who are sick. That's a little more important than hardware-store owner who plays with wood in his barn." Oh, the things I wanted to say to that comment. Knox apparently realized how it sounded. "Shit. I didn't mean…"

And then we started laughing. God, I loved the deep, rich sound of Knox's laughter. It fit in all the crevices inside me and filled them up.

"Come here," he said suddenly before walking to his workbench.

I followed. He pulled out one of the stools.

"Sit."

"Yes, sir," I teased, but I sat.

Knox began rummaging around, finding a small piece of wood, a knife, gloves. "Here."

I looked at him, and then he was slipping goggles on my face. "What are we doing?"

"I'm going to teach you. Just something little."

My heart melted into a ridiculous puddle of goo. Knox Wheeler would be the death of me.

He sat down, and began instructing me, where to start, how to move my hand, pulling it away from me when it got too close to my body. "Never toward yourself," he said.

"Yeah, that's probably smart."

Once I got the hang of it, he said, "You keep going. I'll watch."

"Okay," I replied, hoping I didn't chop any fingers off and having no clue what I was actually doing or making.

"How did you end up out here?" he asked. "I mean, obviously your mom, but I remember that first night you said she didn't know you were coming."

"A man, of course. My boyfriend. We'd been dating about a year or so, and I walked in on him cheating on me. Such a typical fucking story. Makes me feel like a cliché. Anyway, found out he'd been fucking this guy—well, and others—the whole time, and some of my friends knew. No one thought it was important to tell me, apparently."

"Shit. I'm sorry."

"I'm not," I said truthfully. "Sure, at the time I was hurt and angry, but now that I have some space, I realized I didn't love him. And if he hadn't cheated, I wouldn't be here. I'm liking here more than I thought I would. Here feels...right."

I ventured a glance at him. Knox's forehead was wrinkled, like he was in thought. He was so cute when he concentrated, his mouth tense, surrounded by that sexy beard of his.

"Yeah, here feels right to me too," Knox replied.

My heart jumped.

"Havenwood, I mean. It has that effect on people."

Because of course that was what he was talking about.

"Be careful. Not that direction. Here." Knox's hand was suddenly on top of mine, guiding me. "You want to keep the strokes going in the same direction. I know it doesn't seem like it makes a difference, but it does."

He kept his hand there, and I tried not to tremble, tried not to breathe wrong, so he wouldn't see how much I loved the feel of his big, rough hand on mine. "I, um…think I got it."

"You're a natural." He smiled.

"You have to say that because you're my teacher," I teased, and Knox chuckled.

"Why does that sound familiar?" He pulled his hand back, and I missed the touch instantly.

"Have you, um…been serious about anyone since the divorce? Dated?" Why, why, why had I asked that?

Knox shook his head. "A few dates here and there. Hookups, that kind of thing, but I haven't been serious. It's hard with kids involved, ya know? Probably even more now with Logan here. I don't want something I do to hurt them. Plus, I don't know if I want to get married again or anything. Carol and I are close. It wasn't a messy divorce or anything. I just…don't know if marriage is for me."

"I get it. I don't have any plans to get married. You can be serious about someone and committed to them without that." I looked down at the tool in my hand. "Logan said Dale's mom was flirty with you. Who knows, maybe you'll change your mind." Those words hurt to say more than they should have.

"She's a nice woman, but I'm not interested in her."

I turned to him, and he was close, Jesus, he was fucking close. Had he been that near to me the whole time, or had one of us moved? Both of us moved? "Good," I replied, then wanted to snatch the word back. I had no business saying it, and I didn't know why I did. The lines between my brain and my mouth seemed to be misfiring. "I'm sorry. I shouldn't have… I don't know why I… I know we're friends and that's all…" I really needed to pick a sentence and go with it.

Knox closed his eyes, and I assumed this was when he was going to tell me I needed to go, or that he was straight and only wanted to be my friend. What he said was, "I felt weird…when you said you were supposed to meet with someone tonight."

Blood was rushing through my ears. My heart was going crazy, my chest tight. Holy fuck. I was going to stroke out. "Why?" I managed to ask.

"I don't know." Knox's voice sounded far off, full of questions and confusion.

This time when he reached out, when I felt his hand on my face, he wasn't wiping away pizza sauce or a stray leaf. He brushed his thumb beneath my eye, over my cheekbone, and I felt like my brain was buzzing. Yep, totally going to stroke out.

"Your skin is so soft," he said in this deep whisper I almost couldn't make out.

"Oh," I replied ridiculously. What was wrong with me? Why was that how I answered, and why in the fuck couldn't I make myself say anything else?

"Sorry. I—"

"No!" I rushed out when he went to pull away. I put my hand on his, danced my wood-dusty fingers along his skin.

"I don't know what I'm doing here."

"Do you want to stop?" I asked, my voice sounding needier than I wished it did.

"No." Knox leaned in, his lips gentle and unsure against mine.

I closed my eyes, savored the feel of his rough beard against my skin. I had no idea why that did it for me. I wasn't sure if it had before Knox, but yes, the contrast of his wiry hair and the gentleness of his questioning lips was making me crazy.

As much as I wanted to grab him, to hold him and deepen the kiss, I let it move at his pace. Knox pressed a few closemouthed kisses against mine before his tongue teased the seam of my lips. I opened them for him, wanted to taste him and let him taste me. It was tentative at first, but then his hand was in my hair and he was pulling me closer, kissing me deeper.

Our tongues moved together, dipped and retreated, danced. Knox pushed off his stool and stood between my legs. My hands went to his hips, my head tilted back as he kissed me like I'd never been kissed before. Like I was his favorite thing in the world and he was savoring me.

He growled into my mouth, all deep and raspy. My brain shut off, and I went on instinct, my legs wrapping around him, my hand journeying from his waist to the bulge beneath his jeans, and oh, fuck yes, he was big. But then his body went tense and he jerked away from me as if I'd electrocuted him.

"Shit. I'm sorry. I shouldn't have touched you like that. I got ahead of myself." Fuck, why had I pushed? I was pretty sure he'd just had his first kiss from a man, and I'd rushed him. "I'm sorry," I said again.

"It's not your fault." He shook his head, took another step back. "I'm… I've never done this before. I've never kissed a man or thought about it and…"

"And I pushed. I'm sorry."

"Don't do that. Don't blame yourself. I liked it; clearly, I liked it." He signaled toward the very obvious erection in his jeans. "I…I don't know. It's a lot." Knox stepped back more, then began to pace. He rubbed his beard before dropping his head back. "Fuck. You're my friend. I don't want to lose that. And Logan…he loves you, and this…I don't know how to process it, or what it means, or what it would do to him, because I don't know if…"

If he would want more than a release? Than a kiss? If he would want a relationship with me and what how he felt about it either way would do to his son? The part about Logan, how much his kids meant to him, was one of the things I liked so much about Knox. "It won't happen again." I stood, and Knox's eyes zeroed in on my bulge. I turned away.

"I don't want to screw this up." And then because he was Knox, he came over to me, put his hands on my shoulders. "I don't want to hurt you…or Logan…but I don't know. My brain is a bit of a mess right now."

"I'm fine," I lied, stepping away from him. "You won't hurt me, and we won't hurt Logan. We just go back to how things were and pretend it didn't happen." The words were bitter on my tongue. This hurt infinitely worse than being stood up tonight.

"Cal…" he said, and my heart jumped. It was the first time he called me that, the name I usually hated, but I liked the way it sounded coming from his lips— comfortable, familiar.

"It's fine, Knox. I get it. Logan comes first. Fucking around with me would make things awkward. Not to mention what's going on inside you personally." I didn't even know if he *wanted* to fuck around with me. "I need to go."

"Callum," he said again.

"It's fine. I'm just…I'm just gonna go." I turned and walked out.

Knox didn't come after me.

CHAPTER SIXTEEN

Knox

IT HAD BEEN almost a week since I'd seen Callum, and I couldn't stop thinking about him, about the way he'd tasted, and melted against me, and hearing the noises he'd made when I'd kissed him.

When I'd. Kissed. Him.

I was still trying to wrap my brain around that.

My closest group of friends were all gay or bi men, except Griff, so it wasn't that. I couldn't stop thinking…shouldn't I have known? Had I somehow been lying to myself my whole life? In denial? How could I not have known, and what did all this say about me? What did my attraction to Callum mean for me, because there was one thing I couldn't deny: I'd liked kissing him.

And I wanted to do it again.

When I told him being here felt right, then mentioned Havenwood, I hadn't meant the town; I meant being with him.

But then all the other stuff created this storm inside my head again: Never being with a guy before. What did I want from Callum? From us? What would it mean for Logan? Or for Charlotte when she came? And if we did keep this going and we crashed and burned, how much would that break my son's heart?

I didn't know what to make of any of it. Things were already different. Callum hadn't come over all week. We'd texted a couple of times, and I knew Logan had spoken to him, but when Logan asked if he could come hang out, Callum always had an excuse.

The thing was, no matter how good Callum said I was at talking, I didn't feel I was. The thought of sharing this with someone, honestly made me feel a little dizzy and faint. It didn't help that the person I talked to the most lately was the man I was all tied up over.

But I needed to talk to someone, and the only other person I felt comfortable with was Law.

So I called him up. It was late afternoon. Logan was home from school and had called to check in. The shop was slow, so I knew I could cut out early if Law was available.

Instead of hello, Law said, "Wait. Who is this? The phone said someone named Knox, but I rarely see him anymore, so I'm confused."

"Be nice, man. I'm dealing with some shit." I said it teasingly.

"What's wrong?"

I looked around the hardware store as if Callum or someone else were going to jump out of a hiding place where they were eavesdropping on me.

"You got a little time? If you and Remy are busy, I don't want to interrupt, but—"

"You wouldn't be interrupting. It so happens Remy is on a hike with Griff, so I'm sitting around the house with Bear. Want me to come to you?"

"Nah, I'm leaving work early. I'll come over on my way home."

"Sounds good," he replied, and we hung up.

It was ridiculous how nervous I felt on the drive to my friend's house. He'd come to me when he was struggling with some things with Remy before his boyfriend had come out, so as much as I wasn't a fan of spilling my guts, I knew Law was someone I could trust. Still, I couldn't get over the fact that Callum was a first for me. Even though things hadn't always been easy between Law and Remy, at least they'd both known they were into men.

And I must be into men too if I liked kissing Callum.

As soon as I pulled up in front of the house, Law opened the door and Bear came running out. He was all legs and clumsy, the biggest, goofiest teddy bear a dog could be. "How's it going, boy?" I rubbed behind his ears. "Frankie Blue is going to smell you on me and know I was with another dog." Bear almost knocked me down, and Law chuckled.

"What's up, brother?" I said as I stepped onto the porch.

He led me inside. "Not much, man. Just living life. Being happy. Don't think we're here to talk about me, though." He tucked his curls behind his ears.

"It would be much easier, so why don't we do that instead?" I teased.

"Doesn't work that way. You wanna beer?"

"Nah, I'm good."

We headed out the back door and to the chairs on his patio. It was quiet out, nothing but trees and nature in front of us. I rubbed a hand over my face and dropped my head against the chairback. Maybe I should have taken that beer.

"Is everything okay with Logan?" Law asked.

"Yeah, that's not it. Things are going really well where he's concerned. He met a friend and had his first sleepover last weekend. They play video games against each other even when they aren't together, and we're taking some classes with Kell and shit like that. I…" How did I even start this? *So…I was wondering how I know if I'm bisexual?* How fucking dumb did that sound? And again, wanting Callum was pretty much the answer to that question.

I sat there, unable to make the words come out. It was fucking ridiculous, and I was frustrated, but this was so damn new for me.

"I'm going to go out on a limb here, and it might be a crazy choice, but, well, I have eyes in my head, and I've had something on my mind for a while now, so I'm gonna go with it. Is this about Callum?"

I whipped around in his direction so quickly, I was surprised I didn't get whiplash. How had he known? "What? Why…? What makes you…?"

"Shit, I don't know. I could be way off, but by the look on your face, I'm thinking I'm not. I know the two of you have been hanging out a lot. Even Mary Beth has mentioned it here and there, little things like, she ordered dinner out because Callum was with Knox or something like that. Then when we showed up that day, you guys were working on the fence… Hell, I don't know, man. Something seemed different with you, with the two of you together. I mean, he wanted you the second he walked into Griff's that first night. Anyone could see that, but it was even more that day. Not just a physical thing, but more of a connection? Familiarity? Comfort? And you were the same with him. Remy noticed it too. We've never seen you like that with anyone."

I sighed and let go. "Yeah, you're right, and yeah, it's about him. We…we've been spending a lot of time together. Logan is fucking crazy about him, man. They just connect. It's amazing to sit back and watch them sometimes. But he and I…we, um…we get along well too. He's become a good friend and then…" I was being silly. I was a grown-ass man. It shouldn't be that hard to talk about this.

"Did something happen between you guys?"

"I kissed him." My whole body flushed with heat just thinking about it. "Fuck, did I like it. But I freaked out a bit, and he left. He hasn't been over since, and I'm worried I fucked things up. That I hurt Cal and made my son lose someone important to him, that *I* lost someone important to me, and *fuck*." I leaned forward, elbows on my knees, face in my hands. "I don't want to lose him."

"Okay," Law said softly. "It sounds like the two of you need to talk about it. But I also think you need to clear your head first and figure out what it is you want and whether you're willing to go for it or not. Is it just friendship you're missing from him? Do you want to try for more? And if you do, can you accept that? It comes with its own set of struggles, one being your kids."

"I know. Shit, I know." I shoved to my feet, walked over to the edge of the patio and looked out at the land. "Shouldn't I have known? Before now, I mean, shouldn't I have known if I was attracted to men?"

"I didn't acknowledge it before Remy."

"You were eighteen. I'm in my forties."

"Damn, you're old," he teased, and I chuckled, having needed it. "Seriously, though, that's not something I can answer for you. Maybe there have been little clues, noticing things about men your whole life, and you haven't let yourself see it or acknowledge it. Maybe it's something about Callum for you, and the two of you have connected on a different level. Sexuality isn't cut-and-paste. It's not the same for everyone. I think the most important question isn't why you didn't know, but are you okay with it now? Because that's what matters. That's what affects you going forward."

I pushed my hands into my pockets. He was right, of course he was right. "I really like him. I can't even one hundred percent put my finger on what makes him different." Maybe everything about Callum seemed to make him different. "I just…feel it. Feel him."

"That's how it was with Remy."

I nodded, but I didn't think we were similar. Lawson was crazy in love with Remy. He always had been. It was Remy for him from the start, while I hardly knew Callum and wasn't in love with him, but Christ, I cared about him. Wanted to feel his lips move against mine again and listen to him laugh and see his blue eyes light up when he did. But… "I'm scared." That wasn't easy for me to admit. I hadn't ever been scared of anything except when it came to my kids.

Law sighed, stood, walked over, and put a hand on my shoulder. "Welcome to the club, brother. We're all scared when it really matters. Has nothing to do with being gay, straight, bi, or something else."

Again, he was right. I knew he was. Turning, I looked at him. "Damn, you're good at this."

Law gave me a confident grin. "I'm good at most things."

"Cocky motherfucker."

"If the shoe fits." Law shrugged, then sobered. "I get that this is a lot, and with kids, I know things are different for you than they were for me. You have them to think about, and I get being worried since Logan and

Callum are so close, but there are two things that stand out to me. The first is, I know you. You're a good man. You wouldn't do anything to hurt Logan. If you moved forward with Callum and it didn't work out, you would make sure he was okay and you would still be close to him, like you are with your ex-wife. The second is, I've never seen you like this. Yeah, you have fun. I've seen you hook up and date around, casually, but this feels different. Don't you owe it to yourself to see why that is? Don't you deserve that?"

I wanted it to be that easy. Wanted to be able to answer him yes and tell him none of the other stuff mattered and mean it. But the truth was, I didn't know if I could, so I just said, "Thanks for the talk, man. I should get home to Logan."

Law nodded and squeezed my shoulder again.

I was no closer to having an answer than when I'd come.

CHAPTER SEVENTEEN

Callum

TWO. FUCKING. WEEKS.

It had been two fucking weeks since I'd seen Knox, and I wanted to strangle him…and maybe myself, which, yeah, was a little weird, but I couldn't put all this on him. I hadn't made any effort either, and the few times Logan had asked when I was coming over again, I'd made excuses, but still, I was doing it to make sure Knox was okay. To let him work through whatever was going on inside his head. And maybe because I was scared to see him too.

This was exactly what I'd been afraid would happen, and I'd let it anyway. Now everything was a mess.

I'd enjoyed my time with Knox and Logan so much, I hadn't even taken the time to make friends in Havenwood outside of them. Remington fucking Monroe had offered to have meals with me at Sunrise, and I hadn't done it. Josh had said we could go to Richmond sometime, and I hadn't done that either. Kellan was fun to talk to, and that was another thing I hadn't pursued. Not that they were actively pursuing it with me, but at least they had offered.

I was determined to make that change today. I would get out. I would make friends. I would get over Knox Wheeler and find a way to be friends with him again.

It was a Friday, and I happened to be off at the clinic. I put on some workout clothes and made my way to the gym. I remembered them saying Josh owned it, so that might be a way to chat with him again and make some plans. Plus, it was about time I got back into a decent exercise routine. It was something I'd always done in LA but hadn't found the time for since moving to Havenwood.

I saw Josh and his dark hair the second I walked in. And okay, I couldn't miss his body either. Josh looked like one of those guys you admired on Instagram, with the perfect physiques and muscles and, well, obviously he was gorgeous. Currently, he was leaning over the counter, talking to the employee on the other side of it, a woman who looked to be in her mid-thirties.

He glanced my way, then did a double take, and smiled. "Hey, man. How's it going?"

"Pretty good. Was thinking it's about time I joined

the gym before I started to lose my girlish figure," I teased, making him laugh.

"You've come to the right place. Well, the *only* place in Havenwood, but that's beside the point." He glanced at the other worker. "He's a friend. I'll help him, Jasmine."

Oh, I liked that, liked that he called me a friend.

"We'll get you taken care of in my office."

I followed Josh toward a door, which he unlocked and let me inside. He left it open, signaling for me to sit down.

"You liking Havenwood so far?"

"Yeah, getting my bearings. I have a bigger patient load, but still doing mostly urgent care. I probably should start looking for my own place, but I haven't quite made it that far yet."

"Yeah, I hear ya."

I handed over my ID and debit card. He took the rest of my info, asked me about different packages, and signed me up.

When we were finished, he said, "Still looking to head to Richmond sometime? Kell used to be my bar buddy, but now that he and Chase are together, he's left me on my own."

My stomach twisted uncomfortably. Not because I

didn't want to be friends with Josh, because I did. Not even because I didn't want to head into Richmond with him, because I did miss dancing, clubs, and gay bars. No, the discomfort was all Knox related because if I went out, I would have the chance to hook up—which I should want, damn it. I missed orgasming with other people, thank you very much. The annoying part was, I didn't want anyone but him.

"Yeah," I replied. "Yeah, I'd like that."

"Good. I would say we could go tonight, but Kellan and I already told Nat we'd go out with her. She and her boyfriend broke up."

"Nat?"

"Natalie. She's a good friend of mine and Kell's. And she's a nurse, so the two of you will have that in common."

"Oh, I think I've heard her mentioned before."

"Do you want to go with us? And if you're free next Friday or Saturday, we can go to Richmond."

"That'd be great," I replied, meaning it. The whole not-wanting-anyone-other-than-Knox thing was still there, but I needed to put myself out there, needed to find more friends. I liked the idea of hanging out with Josh, Kellan, and Natalie.

"Great. Sounds good. I still have your number, so I'll

text you. We're doing Mexican for dinner at seven, and then we'll head to Griff's."

Josh smiled, but it wasn't a flirty smile, more of a friendship smile, which I was glad of. As hot as he was, it wasn't him I hoped would want me.

Stop it! Stop thinking about Knox!

"I'm looking forward to it. Thanks for inviting me."

"No worries. I know what it's like to be the new guy. Plus, everyone is pairing up around me. First Kell, then Law. I need some single buddies." He laughed.

"There's Griff and Knox too."

"Yeah, they're great, but Knox is straight and I can't see him heading into Richmond with me to party."

There was a sharp pang in my chest, even though there shouldn't be. Knox *was* straight, and even though we'd kissed, which probably meant he was bi, he'd made it clear that was a one-time thing and he didn't want anything more.

"And Griffin is…Griff." He shrugged. "I mean, straight too, not that a straight guy can't go to a gay bar. I'm sure both of them would, but it's not the same. Going out like that isn't Griff's thing."

Hmm, well, that was interesting. He'd said two things about Griffin, the second one not really needed after the first. "You guys are close?" I asked.

"To tell you the truth, I don't even know how to

answer that. Kellan's my best friend, and Griff was always just his overprotective brother. We've been hanging out a bit, and we're friends, but…I don't know. It's hard to put into words. I've never known anyone like him."

Josh had spoken casually. There wasn't any obvious desire or anything to what he said, yet it still struck me for some reason. But then, what did I know? It wasn't as if I knew much about Griffin or Josh.

"Anyway, I need to get back to work, and I'm sure you came here for more reasons than to talk to me. I'll text you and see you tonight."

I stood, and we walked back into the main part of the gym together. Josh said goodbye, and I went over to start my workout. Kellan showed up not long after. He spoke to Josh for a few minutes, who pointed me out. Kellan came over, and we exercised together. He mentioned my going out with Josh the next weekend, so he must have said something. He told me about his favorite bars in Richmond, and we shot the shit about random things.

Afterward, we had a smoothie and sat to chat some more. I liked Kellan. I liked both him and Josh. See, I could do this. I could make other friends in Havenwood. I didn't need Knox Wheeler at all.

Damned if I still didn't miss him, though.

CHAPTER EIGHTEEN

Knox

L OGAN WAS STAYING at Dale's again, so when Law said he and Remy were going to Griff's, I decided I'd go have a beer too. I'd tossed around the thought of calling Callum, asking him if he wanted to go, or just inviting him over, but I was still confused. The truth was, the longer I stayed away from him, the more I told myself I wasn't really attracted to him. That it had been a fluke, and we were friends, and the next time he was standing in front of me, I'd realize I didn't want him.

Clearly, I wasn't brave enough to test that theory.

I was sitting on my stool at the end of the bar, Law was beside me, Remy on the other side of him, followed by Chase. Josh wasn't there, but that wasn't unusual. He often came later or went off to find a hookup or something.

"How's everything going?" Law asked softly as I nursed my beer. It didn't take a brain surgeon to know he was talking about Cal.

"Same."

"You still haven't talked to him?"

Shame curled my spine as I shook my head. Christ, what was wrong with me? I was acting like a child. I was going to stop seeing the guy because we kissed once? Someone who meant something to me? Someone I missed?

"Oh, I didn't know they were hanging out," Griff said suddenly. "Not that it matters."

I looked up to see Callum, Josh, Kellan, and Natalie walk through the bar toward us. Josh and Natalie were smiling. Callum had his head tilted back, laughing. When he put a hand on Josh's shoulder, something caught in my throat.

He was wearing a short-sleeved, blue button-up shirt, left open. He had a white tee beneath it, tight enough that I could see exactly how slender he was, maybe even make out the muscles of his abs. He had on a little bit of eyeliner and looked happy and confident, not knowing or caring that a few guys looked at him in disapproval as he moved.

I felt Law's eyes on me, but I couldn't look at him, couldn't turn away from Callum, and then suddenly his gaze caught mine and held. There was something there, something I couldn't fucking read, but I really wanted to know.

He gave me a small smile, then turned away.

"If it isn't the three musketeers, back together again. Is it four now?" Griff asked.

"Maybe," Josh replied.

Maybe? What did that mean? Was Callum going to start hanging out with them more? Not that he shouldn't. Why the fuck not, but there was a question in the back of my head that I wasn't proud of. *What about us?*

Josh leaned over the bar counter. "You miss me?" he teased Griff.

"No. Why would I miss you?"

"Aw, I'm crushed, Griffy. I thought we'd grown so close," Josh countered, and everyone but me and Law chuckled.

"How was dinner?" Chase asked Kellan.

"Good. We spent the whole time talking about how much some men suck." He blew a playful kiss at Chase. "Not you, of course."

My pulse shot up at that. Had they spoken about me?

"It was nice to be there for Natalie," Callum said, then risked a quick glance at me that didn't hold. Was that his way of making sure I knew it wasn't about me? Fuck, I'd never been the type to assume the world revolved around me, and I felt like shit that I was acting this way now.

"I can't believe I got dumped," Natalie said.

"His loss, sweets." Kellan wrapped an arm around her.

"This is why my life is easier than y'all's. Relationships make everything hard—not that kind of hard," Josh said to Kellan, who had opened his mouth. "It's why I just fuck my way through life."

There were more chuckles, then a scoffing sound from Griff, but I wasn't sure anyone noticed it.

Kellan said, "Callum and Josh are going to Richmond next weekend. We should go, Chase. I haven't been dancing in a while."

There was an unfamiliar buzzing in my ears, a rush of blood, a tightness in my chest. This unexpected feeling of possession made my fingers twitch to grab Callum and pull him to me, to tell him I wanted him to be mine.

Law's hand came down on my shoulder in support. Callum's blue gaze landed on me again as confusing thoughts and feelings twisted and turned in my head and chest. I had no right to feel this way. He should go wherever he wanted and sleep with whoever he wanted, but even the thought of it made me feel like I was cracking apart inside.

"I'm gonna head out. I'm not feeling so great." I tossed some money on the bar and stood.

"Remy and I will go with you, make sure you get home okay." They both went to stand as well, but I shook them off.

"Nah, I'm fine. I didn't drink. Just feeling like I'm coming down with something." It was weak of me, an easy way out, but I felt like my world was spinning and I couldn't figure out which way was up or down.

I was jealous, that much was clear, but the tightness in my chest and the need in my bones hammered home that it was more than that, more than a kiss. I wanted Callum to be *mine*, wanted to touch him and explore him and walk into the bar with him laughing by my side.

The second I stepped outside, I sucked in a lungful of fresh air, and wondered if he would come after me, if I wanted him to. But I needed to think, needed to figure shit out because this, this changed everything. And there was still Logan to worry about on top of it.

I didn't remember the drive home, but suddenly I was there, sitting on the couch with my hands in my hair, elbows on my knees, when there was a soft knock on the door.

My heart rate jumped and my hands shook because I knew it was him, knew that if I opened the door, nothing would be the same again.

Still, I pushed to my feet, took quick steps, grabbed the doorknob, tugged it open, and of course Callum was there, hands in his pockets, looking unsure. The tightness in my muscles began to loosen, the fog in my brain clearing.

"I'm sorry. I know I should have called first. I don't even know if Logan is here and, shit—this was a bad idea. I'll go."

Callum went to turn away, but before I knew it, my hands were reaching out, landing on his hips and tugging him to me, and I was crushing his mouth beneath mine. Callum didn't miss a beat, melting against me, opening his mouth for me, letting me dip my tongue inside. My whole body came alive, a lightning storm in my veins and fireworks behind my eyes.

He felt so damn good and tasted so damn good. Nothing else mattered except that he was Callum and I was Knox. That we wanted each other. That we cared about each other and liked each other.

Then his hand was against my chest, pushing slightly, so I immediately stepped back.

"Wait... I... Holy fuck, you kissed me again. I

didn't expect that, and I want that, *God*, do I want that, but I think we need to talk first. Is Logan here?"

Warmth spread through my chest that he confirmed where Logan was before going any further, that Logan was important to him and he wanted to be sure things were okay. "No. He's at Dale's. Come in."

He did, and Frankie Blue came running, apparently just realizing he was there. A guard dog, she was not.

Callum knelt and petted her, talked to her as I closed the door, and then I could do nothing but stand there and watch him.

When he stood again, he said, "Hi."

"Hey." I grinned.

"So, um…that, the kiss. Jesus, Knox. That was really fucking hot. And maybe this isn't fair, maybe I have no right to say this or expect anything from you because you've never been with a man before, and because of your kids, and holy shit, how did this happen? How did I fall for a straight guy with kids?" He shook his head and stepped back.

"I think it's pretty safe to say I'm not straight. If I were, I wouldn't want to kiss you again, right? I must be bi, and I'm still trying to make sense of it all myself."

"I *know*. That's what makes this harder and what makes me worry I don't have the right to say this, but I can't just be someone you're figuring out your sexuality with. I like you, Knox, a lot, probably too much, but—"

"I like you too," I cut him off. "Is that not obvious?"

"No... I... Well, that's a thing. Guys who get off with other guys but could never have anything more with them. I know that's not you, and I'm not asking for matching *His and His* robes or anything. And again, I know this is new for you and you have your kids to worry about, especially Logan right now, but I...I need us to either not kiss again, to decide that's a thing we're not going to allow to happen, but we stay friends and neither of us is immature about it...or I have to know it means something to you. That it's more than getting off, because..." Callum shrugged. "Because you have the power to hurt me. Because I care about you and I have to protect myself. I don't want this to be something that happens when you're jealous I might be with someone else."

Well, shit, when he said it like that, the guilt twisted me up again. I *had* been jealous tonight, but... "That's not what this is. Don't you know me better than that?"

He nodded, sucked his bottom lip into his mouth, and I wanted nothing more than to nibble it myself. "I do know you, probably better than I should for how long we've known each other. I had to say it, though."

Because he was strong, because he didn't take shit. I loved that about him. Still, it wasn't that easy. I walked over, sat on the couch. "I don't want to hurt you, and I want you, Christ, I want you so much, it feels like someone set my insides on fire."

He gasped. "That doesn't sound pleasant."

"In a good way." I smiled, maybe sadly. "And I'm not going to say I wasn't jealous tonight, because I was. And I want this…to see what this is between us, but I'm on shaky ground too. I need to figure shit out myself before I risk hurting Logan. Can you imagine how confused he would be if I told him we were together? Then what if it didn't work and he lost you?"

"He won't ever lose me. I wouldn't do that to him. I know I've had my head in my ass the last couple of weeks, but I wouldn't walk away from him. Not really."

"Okay." I didn't think it would happen on purpose, but there was always the chance. "What are you asking for, Cal? I want to explore this, want you to be mine, but I think we need to get our legs under us before we consider telling Logan. I need to sort through stuff in my head before I pull him into it."

Callum stood there for a moment, and damned if I wasn't holding my breath. Then slowly, he walked over to me. He knelt on the floor between my legs. "I would never risk hurting Logan that way. I would never rush you either. I just needed to know this is real."

"It's real," I told him, my voice scratchy and vulnerable. "There's no one else I want but you. I won't be with anyone else, but I have to take it slow and not be…public with it yet. I know that's not fair, but…"

"One step at a time," Callum said softly. He put a hand to my face then, stroked his fingers over my beard. "I love this. I love the way it feels against my skin." He leaned in, put his cheek to mine, and rubbed them together.

Desire shot straight to my groin. "I like the way you feel against me."

Callum nodded, making his face brush against mine again. He sat back on his heels, and I wanted to drag him closer again, pull him on top of me and learn his body, even though that scared me too.

So I waited, watched. He caressed my arms, danced his fingers from my wrist to the inside of my elbow and back again. My eyes were riveted on him, watching a man touch me this way.

Callum leaned forward, this time his mouth taking the same route, up and down my left arm, then my right. It was so simple, but the way my heart slammed against my chest and my cock throbbed was anything but easy.

It was maybe one of the most erotic moments of my life.

"Can we take your shirt off?" he asked. "I love your chest. Such a sexy lumberjack." Callum winked playfully before sobering. "I won't go too fast. I just want to…touch you. Savor you, find all my favorite spots."

A groan started deep in my chest. Christ, what did you even say to that?

I tugged my shirt over my head. Once it was free, Callum pushed me so I leaned back, resting against the couch. He kissed my stomach, right near the edge of my jeans, and I nearly fucking came right there.

"Someone likes that," he said against my skin. I could hear the smile in his voice, even though he wasn't looking at me.

He kissed me again and again, all around my lower stomach. My hand was in his hair, and my body arched toward him. "You feel so good," I whispered. "You might kill me."

"Don't do that. I just got you."

I couldn't help watching him, studying him as he pressed his lips to my skin over and over. The first time he lashed his tongue against me, I moaned and tightened my hold. My eyes almost drifted closed, but I didn't want to miss seeing him—Callum, this man who had come to mean so much to me, my own home felt empty when he wasn't in it.

His eyes met mine as he licked a trail up the center of my stomach, from my belly button to my chest. "Oh fuck," I groaned.

His body was pressed against my dick, and I couldn't help but thrust up against him. That time, my eyes did close. It felt so good, *he* felt so good, but then I heard him say, "No. Don't close them. Look at me, watch me. I want to make sure you know who you're with."

He wanted to make sure I acknowledged I was with him, with a man. "I know who you are, who I want."

Callum rasped his tongue over one nipple, then the other. Rubbed his cheek against the hair between my pecs. Nuzzled my armpit, which shocked me, but damned if that didn't feel good too.

He kissed my collarbones, my throat. My whole body felt like I'd been hooked up to jumper cables, like each time he touched me, power shot through me.

"I want your mouth," I admitted.

"Say my name, then."

"Callum...Cal." I cupped his face. "I know who you are," I said again, this time looking into his eyes.

I pressed my mouth to his, pushed my tongue inside. We were urgent then, grabbing for each other, arms wrapped around each other. I went off instinct, pushed his top shirt off his shoulders, separated enough to jerk the other over his head, then pulled Callum up to the couch. He was on his back, and when I leaned over him, I saw the puffy skin of his scar…and kissed it. "I can't believe something is in there, working with your heart." To make it beat correctly. Fear suddenly gripped me.

"Hey, I'm fine. Seriously. It causes me no problems. There's nothing to worry about."

"Okay." Why did I sound so needy?

I kissed it again, and then Callum had a hand on either side of my face and pulled my mouth to his again. I rutted against him, felt his erection through his jeans, and it didn't freak me out. It was just…him. Just us.

We kissed and thrust our groins together. Each move of his body against mine made the best sensations rush through me. My balls were full. I was achy and knew if we kept going, I'd blow my load.

Callum wrapped his legs around me, kissed me deeper, pumped his hips against me. My vision went blurry, and pleasure darted down my spine, my orgasm shooting through me. Callum's hands had moved to my hair, pulled it tightly as his body bowed beneath mine, and I knew he was coming too.

"Wow…that was…wow…" I lay down, my cheek to his chest. "Shit. I'm heavy."

I went to move, but he locked his arms and legs around me. "Don't you dare go anywhere."

So I didn't. We just lay there, breathing together. He ran his fingers through my hair, and my eyes started to get heavy.

"No regrets?" he asked, his voice breaking.

"None." I kissed his scar again. It had been a long time since I'd held someone like this, since I lay with a lover. I hadn't refrained from sex over the years, but this felt different. "Do you want to stay? Logan isn't supposed to be home until later tomorrow afternoon."

"Are you sure you don't need some space?"

I pushed up on my elbows and looked down at him. "I'm sure."

"Then you're gonna have to give me something to wear. This guy made me come in my jeans."

I laughed. "Oh, I see how it is. All my fault, right? Christ, that seduction. It took everything in me to hold off as long as I did."

"Oh, baby. You ain't seen nothin' yet."

My dick began to plump up again. Fuck, he got to me. "Be good." I stood, held my hand out, and pulled him to his feet. We took turns cleaning up. I gave Callum a pair of boxers to wear and threw his clothes in the washer. "I'm gonna take Frankie Blue out real quick."

He nodded, seeming a little unsure, but I got it. This had been an eventful night, to say the least. I was running on my postorgasmic high and wondered if I'd crash and freak out.

Once Frankie did her thing, I put her in her kennel, then went to my room. Callum was sitting in the chair in the corner. My heart clenched. "Did you change your mind?"

"No, I just… Are you sure?"

Maybe I shouldn't be. Maybe this should have been scarier than it was and I needed to take more time. It was all new for me, and I didn't have a guidebook on how I was supposed to respond.

Step one after your first experience with a man: take a few days to think about it. Now, expect that you might freak out, and that's normal…

Obviously, there was no how-to manual, so all I could do was follow how I felt.

And I couldn't remember the last time I felt so good, the last time things felt this right. "I'm sure. Now get your ass into bed."

"Damn, look at you, so bossy."

But he came. Callum curled into my side, and we went to sleep.

CHAPTER NINETEEN

Callum

I WOKE UP before Knox did. At some point during the night we'd separated. I was positive that was on me. I was a bit of a wild sleeper. I had my legs spread and a hand on his face, but he didn't seem to notice.

I pulled back, rolled to my side, and…well, watched him like a fucking creeper. He was so sexy, he nearly stole my breath.

Part of me was still trying to believe last night happened, but I guessed I wouldn't be there, in his bed, wearing his boxers, if it hadn't.

I didn't know what we were, if he was my boyfriend or what, but we were something, and the thought made my chest swell. I wasn't real fond of the fact that we had to keep it a secret for now, but I understood why. This was a coming-out for Knox, and I knew how messy those could be. And that they never stopped happening. We came out to different people our whole lives.

His eyes fluttered, then opened. I held my breath, waiting for him to say he'd changed his mind, but he didn't. He just smiled and asked, "Has anyone ever told you that you sleep like an octopus on drugs, who can't stay still?"

I laughed. "Maybe a time or two. Did I keep you awake?"

"Nah, it was fine."

As I leaned down to kiss him, I heard a noise from the other room. Frankie Blue started going crazy, the front door opened, and then Logan's, "Dad?"

"Oh fuck." I scrambled out of bed as Knox did the same. There was panic in his eyes, and I tried not to take it personally.

"Bathroom. Go into the bathroom."

I scurried to the en suite and closed the door as quietly as I could.

"I'll be right out!" Knox called. I figured he was tugging on jeans, and then his bedroom door opened.

I heard a woman's voice. "I'm so sorry. We tried to call, but it went straight to voice mail. I think your phone died. Something came up, and we have to run out of town for my uncle. Sorry to bring Logan back so early."

"No, no. It's fine. My fault. I must have forgotten to

charge my phone last night," Knox said.

"Where's Callum?" Logan asked. *Fuck.* "His car is out front. We haven't seen him in forever, and I have some stuff to tell him."

There was a pause, and I was silently telling Knox to hurry the fuck up and come up with a lie.

"He, um…he's upstairs. He came over last night, and then he wasn't feeling too good, so I told him he could crash here."

Yeah…in his bed. And now I had to sneak out of his room like I was a teenager. This was already getting messy.

"Who's Callum?" a young boy asked. Jesus, I could hear everything perfectly through the walls.

"He's my best friend," Logan replied. "Well, my other best friend. He's Dad's other best friend too, besides Law. He's awesome. You'll have to meet him sometime!"

My heart melted, and I closed my eyes. How could I risk this? Logan had quickly become the world to me. What if this thing between Knox and me ruined everything? It was me who would end up alone.

"Oh, cool," the other boy replied.

They spoke a little more before I heard goodbyes. The door closed, and Logan said, "I'm gonna go talk to

Callum."

"Wait!" Knox rushed out. "I don't know if he's up yet. We don't want to wake him. Why don't you take Frankie Blue out real quick, and we'll give him some more time."

"*Dad,*" Logan whined.

"Go on, she's your puppy."

Suddenly Frankie Blue's feet were padding around the floor. The bedroom door jerked open, and I scrambled out of the bathroom. Knox pulled a pair of shorts and a T-shirt out of his drawer and threw them at me. "Spare bedroom upstairs."

I nodded and ran out, not breathing until I was upstairs, safely behind the door. I had no idea how I was going to explain wearing Knox's clothes, and in some ways, it didn't matter. I was still flying high on what Logan had said about me. It was one thing to have him talk to me about his problems or for Knox to tell me Logan cared about me, but another to hear him tell his buddy that I was one of his best friends. I'd never thought I would have something like that. Hell, I'd never known I wanted it until he'd come into my life—until they both had.

Yeah, I was fucked.

I put on Knox's shirt and the shorts and sat on the

bed. I wasn't there long before I heard Frankie Blue in the house. Taking a deep breath, I stood up and opened the door.

"Can I go see if Callum is awake?" Logan asked.

"Let's give him a few minutes, buddy," Knox replied as I was walking out of the room. Frankie heard me and ran for the stairs, so I kept going.

Logan looked up and saw me on the landing. "You're up! I can't believe you had a sleepover and I missed it!"

I bit back a smile and wondered if Knox was losing his shit. "It wasn't planned." I headed downstairs. "I think I ate something that didn't agree with me." Lies, lies, lies. I had done something that very much agreed with me. "I feel better now."

Logan came over and gave me a hug. I ruffled his hair, while holding on to Knox's too big shorts with the other hand. "You look funny in Dad's clothes."

Yeah, well. I wasn't sure what to say about that, but Logan continued talking anyway. "I thought maybe you were mad at us or something. You haven't been around at all."

I tried to hold back my emotion at hearing him say that. Knox was right. If this went bad, we risked hurting Logan. And chances were that it would go bad. Did I really think Knox was suddenly going to want a serious relationship with a man? "No. I would never be mad at you. I just had—"

"It was my fault," Knox cut me off. "But everything is fine now." His eyes caught mine and held, with an intense look I couldn't read. "Do you have plans today?"

"No." I shook my head as though he didn't know what the word meant. I was in uncharted territory and feeling off-balance.

"We're getting a late start, but what if we took a drive to the beach today? Could be fun. We're expecting rain next week, so this is our chance to do something fun like that."

"Oh my God! Really? Can you go, Callum?" Logan's small body bounced with excitement.

My heart broke open, tugged them both inside, this intense want filling me up. I wanted this. I wanted to be a part of them. "Yeah…yeah, I can go."

"I'll go get my stuff!" Logan ran for the stairs.

"Did you take your—"

"Yes, Dad. *God*," Logan cut him off and then was gone.

Knox looked unsure for a moment, then nodded toward the kitchen. I followed him. When we were tucked out of sight, he brushed his hand down my cheek. "We'll figure it out. No regrets," he said again, and not gonna lie, I almost died. Then he reached over, grabbed a clip that went on chips, lifted my shirt, and clipped his shorts so they didn't fall off me. "And I don't think you look funny in my clothes. It's kind of hot."

"Only kind of?" I tried to act like I wasn't secretly swooning inside.

He smiled, almost shyly. It was such a juxtaposition on someone like Knox, who was so big and oozed confidence.

"More than kinda." He paused, leaned in, and pressed a kiss to my lips. "I, um, we should get ready. Your clothes are in the dryer, and I don't know if they'll be done in time."

I was struck stupid for a second, looking up at him, then wishing I could drop to my knees for him. *Bad Callum.* "We'll have to stop by my place anyway."

Which was what we did. They got ready, we had a quick breakfast of bagels and eggs, then drove to my house. Knox had a cooler for drinks, and beach chairs and other supplies in the back of the truck.

He and Logan waited in the car while I ran inside, changed into shorts and a T-shirt that fit me much better, and grabbed a few other things, before the three of us were taking the hour and a half drive to the shore.

The truck was rarely quiet the whole drive. Logan

rambled about his time at Dale's, and video games, and then launched into his ever-expanding list of random facts he knew. I could counter each one with something medical, and some he typed into his phone for future reference.

"I'm feeling a little insecure over here. I have the two smartest guys around," Knox joked. The second he did, I could see the panic in the set of his jaw and the wideness of his eyes, but Logan didn't catch what Knox had said.

"You're smart, Dad. And you're also good at other stuff. There are lots of ways to be smart."

Damn, the kid was wise beyond his years. I was still concentrating on being Knox's guy.

"You're right, buddy." Knox glanced at him in the rearview. "There's no one way to do or be anything."

"Hey, Callum told me that before too," Logan added.

"I did? I don't remember." I'd probably said a lot of things to him I couldn't recall.

"Yeah, when I was talking to you about fixing things and working on stuff, you said Dad was awesome, but I didn't have to be him. That I was awesome too, and there's more than one way to be a man."

"Oh," I replied softly. I tried to be nonchalant about it, but when I glanced over at Knox, I saw him looking at me. Again, I couldn't read his expression and didn't have the time to study it because he looked back at the road.

"Cal's right. I think you're a pretty great man," he told Logan. Without turning my way, he added, "Callum too."

The air around us turned thick, but not the uncomfortable kind. One that was full of want, at least from me, and connection, and this feeling that everything was finally right.

"Are we almost there?" Logan asked, oblivious to it all.

Knox chuckled. "I wondered when that would start."

"Hey, I'm better about asking than Charlotte," Logan countered.

A pang landed in my chest. I wanted to meet her, wanted to know the youngest Wheeler.

"That you are," Knox said, then to me, "Wait until you meet her. She's stubborn and sassy and one might say impatient, but don't you dare tell her I told you that."

"She's a brat," Logan added, but one look from Knox and he apologized. "And yeah, she's more like Dad than me. She fixes stuff at home for Mom all the time. But she also wants to be the Hulk when she grows up, so she's a little weird."

We all laughed. And even though the day wasn't close to being over, I already knew it was one of the best of my life. "What do you want to be?" I asked Logan.

"I don't know...I'm deciding between video-game designer and doctor."

Okay, well, those things couldn't be more different, but I said, "Both solid choices."

"I want to help kids with health stuff, I think. Like asthma or heart stuff, like you."

"That's why I went into the medical field."

We spent the last twenty minutes of the car ride talking about other things.

Once we arrived, we got everything unloaded, found a spot, and ate the lunch Knox had packed. "I put carrots and ranch dip for you. I know you like that rabbit food," he told me.

Jesus, he was going to ruin me. He always did kind things like that for people. "You should like that rabbit food. It's good for you."

"What's that? I can't hear you," Knox teased before animatedly biting into a chip.

"Oh, excuse me. You have heart disease in your beard," I joked back as I reached over and took the crumb out of his facial hair. His eyes turned fiery and hungry as I did. I more than liked that look aimed at me.

After we ate, the three of us played Frisbee, which was fun because Knox was shit at throwing it. Of course, Logan and I didn't let him live it down.

"All right. I quit. I don't like either of you members of the badass-cool-kids club right now," Knox said. "I'm going to the water."

"Me too!" Logan said.

"Last one there is a rotten egg," Knox replied.

I pulled my shirt off and chased them, but they beat me to the ocean.

We played around, splashing each other and laughing. Logan hung off Knox's neck with one arm and tried to help his dad spray me with water.

"I give up!" I covered my face. "You guys win, though it's not fair you're ganging up on me."

"Aw, poor Callum." Knox reached over and wiped at my face as though his wet hand could help. As if realizing what he was doing, he jerked it back quickly. "Okay, I'm older than you guys, and I need a rest." Knox began making his way toward the shore, Logan and me trailing behind him.

We got back to our spots, and Logan and I fell into chairs.

"I'll be right back. I need to take a leak," Knox said.

"You guys aren't very nice to me," I teased Logan,

but then noticed his skin looked a little off. "You good?"

Logan started coughing. He looked down, his breaths quick and sharp, with a familiar wheeze.

Jumping to my feet, I dug his inhaler out of the bag and knelt in front of him. He was sucking in more whistling, rapid breaths.

"Here, take this, we're good. We got this." His hands were shaking, so I put the inhaler to his lips. "On three—one, two, three." I squeezed medicine into him as he took a deep breath. I counted to ten. He was still wheezing. I waited a minute like I was supposed to before I said, "One more time." Hard press on the inhaler, deep breath, count to ten. It wasn't until I looked at my hand that I realized it was shaking too. I'd seen a lot in my time as an NP, but this was different; it was someone I cared about. Someone I loved, and I wasn't used to this in that situation. "There we go. Concentrate on me. You got this," I said again as I rubbed his back.

Suddenly Knox was there. He was kneeling beside me and talking to Logan until he began to catch his breath.

"Come here." Knox pulled him into a hug.

"I'm fine, Dad," Logan replied, but I noticed he held on too.

I moved out of their way. When Knox stood, he turned to me. "Hey, thank you. I—"

"It's fine. I didn't do anything." Which I hadn't, not really, but I was still shaken up.

"Yes, you did." Then…then he hugged me too. Knox cleared his throat. "How about we relax a little and then get on the road to head home."

Logan and I nodded. We only lasted another half hour. Knox wouldn't let Logan help pack up or carry anything back to the truck. Not long after we were on the road, Logan fell asleep, and Knox reached over and placed his hand on my thigh.

I looked his way. We smiled at each other, and I realized I'd been right. Outside of Logan's asthma attack, this had been one of my favorite days.

CHAPTER TWENTY

Knox

IT DIDN'T MATTER how many asthma attacks I'd witnessed in Logan's life, they always shook me up. There was nothing like the feeling of helplessness when your child couldn't breathe and you couldn't do anything to fix it. There was his inhaler, but that didn't always do the trick. Luckily, he'd been better when we got home and we hadn't had to do a nebulizer treatment.

Even though it was days later, I couldn't stop remembering what it had been like—flying high, realizing how much fun I had with Callum, thinking of how good he was with Logan and how great our day turned out, only to walk back to them and see Logan struggling.

And Callum was there. It made the inside of my chest feel tight and funny. The whole day had, for different reasons. It had been one of the best I could remember having in years. The only thing missing was Charlotte. I'd called her that evening, and it had been so good to hear her voice. I couldn't wait for her to meet Callum. I hoped she loved him as much as Logan did.

Summer was fast approaching, and we'd find out. Logan would be going to Colorado for two weeks, and then he and Charlotte would fly here to stay for a few weeks. I'd be lying if I didn't admit I was nervous as shit too. I still didn't know what in the hell Callum and I were doing, how far I could let it go and what it meant for me, for my family. All I knew was he made me happy. He made Logan happy. The thought of not having Cal in our lives left an emptiness inside me I wasn't sure I'd ever experienced.

Even though he was at our house nearly every day, we hadn't done anything else except steal a few kisses when Logan wasn't around, but each one just made me crave more from him. Made me crave all sorts of things that were unfamiliar with a man.

But I sure as shit wanted them to become familiar.

"Knox! New shipment arrived!" Hank, one of my employees, called out, and I became aware I'd been standing there staring into space while daydreaming about Callum. I was suddenly like a lovesick teenager, and the kicker was, I didn't care. I liked it.

I pulled my head out of my ass and got back to work. It was Friday, the night Callum was going with Josh to

Richmond. We hadn't spoken about it all week. He didn't bring it up, and I didn't feel like it was my place. Cal had every right to go out and have a good time. He deserved it. The guy was working like crazy and spending time with us and his mom. I'd want a night out too, but damn, it twisted up my insides.

I wanted him to have fun but to know he was only mine. Wanted everyone to know it.

Logically, I knew he was just going out for a night of dancing and wouldn't go home with anyone. But my thoughts were all mixed up on whether I had the right to expect that when I couldn't give him more.

Realizing I was again obsessing about Callum, I forced myself to cut that shit out and took care of what I needed to do.

Sometime later Logan called to say he got home from school, the way he was supposed to do every day, and the rest of the afternoon flew by.

It was almost six when I pulled up in front of the house and was surprised to see Callum's car out front. Ignoring the excited jump in my pulse, I got out of the truck and went inside.

"I know it sounds confusing, but it's really not. XY is…"

I smiled at the sound of Callum's voice as he explained math to Logan. It felt good hearing them together, coming home to them as if we were a unit.

I walked around the corner and into the dining room.

Callum looked up, a spark in his eyes but an unsure smile on his face. "Hey. I hope it's okay that I came over. Logan called and said he was having trouble with his math. End-of-the-year tests are soon, and he wants to do well."

My son pushed his glasses up his nose. "And no offense, Dad, but you still suck at it."

"Gee, thanks." I walked over and ruffled Logan's hair. "And of course it's okay. You're always welcome here, especially if it means I don't have to try and do math," I teased.

"So are you saying you only like me for my mathematical abilities?"

It was obvious he was being playful too, only I answered seriously. "No."

"Of course not. He's your best friend," Logan added. "That'd be like me only liking Dale 'cuz he's good at video games."

Well, not exactly like that, but it wasn't as if I could tell Logan that.

"How about I make us dinner while you guys finish

up? I saw this ad for a seasoning to make for grilled vegetables and chicken, so I got the stuff to fix it. I figured it would be a hit with Rabbit Food over there."

Callum's eyes darted to mine. "You saved a grilled-veggie recipe for me?"

I frowned. He sounded as if no one had ever done something so simple for him. "Of course. I gotta make this special dressing, then baste the veggies as they grill; the chicken too. Hopefully you'll like it." He was giving me this strange, twisted-up look I couldn't read. "It's fine if tonight isn't a good time. We can do it another day. I know you have plans with Josh."

"You have plans with Josh tonight?" Logan asked. "Is he your boyfriend?"

My chest tightened at the thought.

"He's not my boyfriend," Callum said. "We're just friends. Sheesh, are you trying to marry me off or something?"

"No, but if he was, I was thinking maybe you wouldn't spend as much time with us, is all. Like you'd be busy with your own stuff," Logan replied, and fuck, did I agonize about the same thing while also being concerned for my son, who was obviously worried about losing Callum.

"That will never happen. If I find a boyfriend one

day, he'll have to know that you guys are my friends and I spend lots of time with you."

"Okay." Logan nodded. "And if Dad gets a girl-friend, he'll do the same. We heard Dale's mom talking on the phone with a friend from out of town about how cute he is. It was gross and weird. I mean, he's my dad."

And…this conversation was getting uncomfortable quickly. I turned away a little, ran a hand through my hair and scratched my scalp even though there was no itch there. Logan, having no idea what was going on, continued, "But then we thought that meant we'd be brothers, and I've always wanted a brother instead of an annoying sister, so that would be cool."

I risked a glance at Callum, who wouldn't meet my gaze.

I took a deep breath and said, "I'm not going to date Dale's mom. Ever. She's a nice lady, but I'm not looking for…" Shit, I couldn't even say I wasn't looking for a relationship, which would have been my answer before Callum. This time, he did raise his eyes to mine. "I'm not interested in her. Be nice about your sister, and Callum will be a part of our lives for as long as he wants to be, so no worries there. You should probably get back to your math now." Which really, he didn't need to as it was Friday, but I was hoping he wouldn't think of that. I turned to Callum. "What time do you need to head out? So I can make sure dinner's done."

"I don't. I canceled with Josh earlier in the week."

"Oh." My body immediately relaxed, the tenseness that had been in my chest, maybe since he'd come to Griff's with Josh last week, finally easing out of me. "You, um, didn't do that for us, did you? Because you don't have to." I was trying to make sure he knew I understood. He couldn't wrap his whole life up in us. If he wanted to go out and dance, he should be able to. His lips turned downward in a frown, and I wasn't sure I'd said the right thing.

"I didn't do it for you guys, I did it for me, but I'll keep that in mind for the future." Callum turned to Logan. "Okay, let's get going on this. You're so close to getting it."

I watched them for a moment, their heads together as Callum explained complicated steps to Logan. I was pretty sure I'd fucked up somehow, and wanted nothing more than to fix it.

CHAPTER TWENTY-ONE

Callum

I TRIED NOT to have my feelings hurt that Knox said I
didn't have to not go out with Josh for him. I wasn't
stupid. Logically, I understood what he was saying. Josh
was a friend, and whatever I had going on with Knox
didn't mean I couldn't go out with friends, but then,
part of me started questioning what we were to each
other.

I knew he couldn't go public yet, and I knew he
cared about me, but was he saying that it didn't matter if
I was with other guys? That had been one of the main
reasons Josh and I were heading into Richmond. Were
we that casual that we would be with other people? It
probably didn't help that it all went down around a
conversation about Dale's mom finding Knox attractive—obviously, who wouldn't, but it was a reminder
that Knox had always been with women, and if they were
dating, it would be happening much differently than it

was with Knox and me.

But then, he'd also said he wasn't interested in her—again, something I knew—but my emotions and my logic were currently at war with each other.

Logan and I finished math while he made dinner. When we were done, Logan shoved to his feet. "I'm gonna meet Dale online to play our zombie game!" Then ran out of the room with Frankie Blue on his heels.

"Hey! Dinner in thirty minutes!" Knox called after him, getting a mumbled reply as Logan took the stairs.

"It's all on the grill," Knox said, and then we just hung out there awkwardly. "Did I do something wrong?"

I shook my head. He was near the back door and I was at the table, which meant if Logan came downstairs, he would have a partial view of me, so I went over and leaned against the counter in front of him.

"If this is about Amanda, I'm not interested in her," he confirmed softly.

"I know. I was just thinking it would be easier if you were. And that these kind of innocent comments will become a thing because no one knows about us or that you're maybe interested in someone who isn't a woman. That's the default, and it just hit me, is all. I hate that to most people, I'd never even be an option as someone who is good for you."

Knox reached out and cupped my face. "First, there's no maybe about it. I'm interested in you. I *want* you. Hell, all week I've been driving myself crazy thinking about you going out with Josh and how much easier it would be for *you* not to want *me*. You could find someone you didn't have to hide with, who didn't have kids and who wasn't coming to terms with their sexuality, so I get it. And while I want you to have fun and know you deserve a night out, I wanted to ask you not to be with someone else, but I didn't know if I had the right."

"You have the right," I rushed out. "It killed me thinking about you with Amanda or anyone else. You have the right, if you want it." My ex cheating on me had hurt. I wouldn't do that to someone else.

He brushed his thumbs over my cheeks, his pinky and ring fingers teasing the skin of my neck. "Thank God." Knox lowered his mouth to mine and pressed a gentle kiss there. His beard rubbed against me in the most delicious way. "You have the right too. I'm sorry I can't make this easier on us yet. I'm trying, but I know it's not fair to expect you to deal with this, so again, I'll understand if it's too much."

"It's not." The chance to have Knox was worth anything. I circled my arms around his neck, pulled him down to me, and we kissed again. Our bodies aligned, and he dipped his tongue into my mouth as I tugged at his hair.

It was killing me not to drop to my knees for him. I wanted Knox in my mouth, wanted to hear the sounds he made and feel his hand in my hair as he thrust between my lips.

"*Fuck,*" he said, pressing his forehead to mine. He ran his hands up and down my back as if he had to keep touching me. "The way kissing you makes me feel."

"And how is that?" I asked playfully, just as we heard Logan on the stairs, and we jerked away from each other. It was like someone threw cold water on me, ruining the moment.

"Dale had to eat, so—" Logan skidded into the kitchen. "Why do you guys look weird?"

Wait. We did? I rushed a hand down my shirt as if that would change something.

"We're not weird. You are," Knox teased Logan, and just like that, it was back to normal.

The three of us went outside. We played with Frankie Blue, and I helped Knox finish dinner, which smelled delicious.

It was a nice evening, so when dinner was ready, we ate outside. Knox talked about plans to build a screened-in porch, and I pointed out where a nice garden could go. He had so much space. "When I get a house, I really want to have my own garden. Mom and I used to garden together when I was a kid, and I love the idea of growing my own vegetables—these are great, by the way. You did good. I like the seasoning."

"Yeah, I like it too. Guess eating healthy isn't so bad. I wouldn't mind putting a garden here sometime. You'd have to help me, though. I don't have much of a green thumb."

"Really? I'd love to. When I lived in LA, I had a condo and no space. I've always wanted a garden of my own." Then it hit me, what I'd said. This wasn't my house. The garden would be Knox's, and I'd be helping. "Not that this one would be mine; you know what I mean." Ugh, I was so stupid. I wanted to have my very own garden with Knox.

"It can be all of ours." Knox winked.

"Not mine. I don't want it to be mine." Logan looked at me. "No offense, Callum."

"Oh, fine, whatever. I see how you are. Some founding member of the badass-cool-kids club you are."

We laughed and finished eating dinner. Knox told Logan to do the dishes, and he showed me the progress on his carving.

Afterward, Logan asked if we wanted to watch a movie, and Knox teased, "You're not gonna play games with Dale tonight? We're cool enough that you want to hang out with us?"

"Well, I don't know about cool, but you guys are all right," Logan countered, and I loved it, loved being involved in this thing with them. Wished it was permanent.

"I have an idea," Knox said. "What if we video-call Charlotte and have her watch with us? That way it will be like a whole family thing."

My hands started to tremble, and my heart swelled that I was included. There was nothing in the world I wanted more than to be part of their family.

"And Mom too!"

I didn't know why but that made my stomach twist. "Are you sure you want me involved?"

"Wouldn't be right without you," Knox replied.

We went into the living room, and Logan used the tablet to get his mom and sister on. He turned it toward me. "Mom, Charlotte, this is Callum, our friend I told you about. He worked on math with me and had dinner and stuff. Now we're gonna watch a family movie."

Carol was a pretty woman with honey-colored hair and freckles. For a moment her eyes flashed with confusion, likely over family and me.

"Um…hey. Nice to meet you both." I waved and tried to ignore the nerves in my gut.

"Hi, Callum. Nice to finally meet you," Carol said. "The boys don't stop raving about you."

"Thanks. Logan's great, and Knox is a good friend. I'm lucky they let me hang out with them."

I noticed Knox wasn't looking at me and was fiddling a lot with the remote.

I said, "I'm really excited to meet you, Charlotte. That's a pretty name. My mom said if I was a girl, that's what she was going to name me."

"Thanks," she replied but didn't seem overly interested. "I like Charlie better. Dad always calls me Charlie-girl. I'm trying to get Mom to do the same."

"I'm doing my best," Carol replied. "I forget, but I'll make more of an effort."

"I know, Mom."

"I'll call you Charlie, then. That's a great name too," I told her.

She nodded. "Logan says you're gay."

"Charlie!" Knox and Carol said at the same time. "I'm so sorry," Carol added.

"No. It's fine. It's true. I am." It wasn't something I was ever willing to hide again.

"All Daddy's friends in Havenwood like boys."

Aaaaand, we needed to get off this conversation. Charlie seemed very blunt, and I could imagine her asking Knox if he did too.

"Oh my God, Charlotte, you're so dumb," Logan said. The two of them started arguing from there, before Knox and Carol got them under control.

We watched a superhero movie. I had to fight not to look at Knox through the whole thing. Instead of admiring the sexy men on TV, I wondered if he was thinking about what Charlie said.

When it was over, Carol said, "It really was nice to meet you, Callum. Thanks for taking that in stride. I'm glad the boys met you. They both obviously adore you."

Goose bumps spread over my skin. Did she know? Was that what she was trying to say?

"Charlie, come say good night to your father," Carol told her.

"I'll call him tomorrow. I'm sleepy."

We said our goodbyes, and I was hoping Logan was ready for bed, which of course he wasn't. He asked for another movie. I stood and stretched. "I should head home."

"Do you work tomorrow?" Knox asked.

"No."

"Can you stay? It's okay if you're tired, but if you want to watch another with us…"

"Okay." How could I say no to him?

We watched a second movie, and my eyes found themselves on Knox more than on the screen. Each time I glanced his way, he was looking at me.

It was the longest two hours of my life before it was over and Logan was yawning. "I'm gonna go to bed."

"Brush your teeth first," Knox said. "I'll take care of Frankie Blue."

Logan rolled his eyes. "'Night, Dad. 'Night, Callum."

We sat there quiet as Logan went upstairs. My brain was spinning about the whole night—speaking with Carol and Charlie and how Knox felt about her comment regarding all his friends liking boys.

Before I had the chance to bring it up, he asked, "Take Frankie Blue out with me?"

"Yeah, of course." As soon as we stood and headed for the back door, Frankie was right behind us. Knox turned on the light, and she darted outside. He closed the door behind us, but we didn't go farther into the yard.

The wind blew, and I trembled. Even though it was nearly summer, a cool front had come in this evening and was supposed to linger through the weekend.

"You cold?" he asked.

"Kind of...or maybe a little nervous too." It had been a long time since I'd been nervous with a man, but this thing with Knox often had me feeling that way, like I didn't have my footing, because this was so new to him and so important to me.

"Come here." He tugged me close, right against his body, and wrapped his arms around me. "You feel good." He rubbed his hand up and down my back. "It was...it was nice tonight. You meeting Charlie and Carol."

I leaned back slightly and tilted my head up. "Yeah? I was scared it would stress you out."

"Oh, it did that too." He chuckled, and so did I. "But it was nice. I really want you to meet Charlie in person. She's a little spitfire. You'll like her."

"I already do."

Knox got small wrinkles around his eyes and along his forehead as if he was deep in thought, before he lowered his mouth to mine. That was basically all it took for my dick to start plumping up. Knox Wheeler went straight to my head, like this high that was good for me and I never wanted to come down from.

His hand slid down my back, stopped above my ass

as if he wasn't sure, then kept going. He palmed me, pulled me closer, and I grinded against him, feeling the hard ridge of his erection.

"Do you wanna go hang out in my room with me?" he asked teasingly, making me laugh.

"What if we get caught?" I played along, though it really was something we had to worry about.

"We'll be quiet. I just…wanna touch you…"

Um, yes, please. "Beat you there!" I tugged the door open and ran into the house. Knox chuckled, then called Frankie Blue back in.

I went straight to his room, pushing the door so it was only cracked behind me. I heard Knox with the dog, and a moment later the door pushed open and he closed and locked it behind him.

As if there was a sudden magnetic pull between us, one second we were standing ten feet apart and the next our mouths smashed together, teeth clanked, tongues searched, his hand finding its way to my ass again. I groaned into the kiss, wrapped my arms around him, hands tangled in his hair, as I savored the taste of him and the feel of his beard against my skin.

"Fuck, I don't know if I've ever been this hard."

I smiled against his mouth, slid a hand down his body, and cupped his bulge. "Let's see what we can do about that." I placed a kiss to his neck. Knox dropped his head back to give me better access, but instead I said, "Take your shirt off," before I began working the button on his jeans.

He did as I said, nearly ripping the damn tee off, showing me all that golden skin, the patch of hair between his pecs.

"Tell me if it's too much," I added. "I know this is new to you and—"

"It's not too much. I want you, Cal." Then Knox was tugging at my shirt until it was free. He dropped it, kissing me roughly, urgently, pulling me to him, and then we were stumbling toward the bed until we fell on it.

Once there, we kissed some more. I shoved my hand down his pants, rubbed his cock through his underwear. Knox hissed, arched toward me, ran his teeth over my throat and sucked the skin there into his mouth.

"Fuck." My eyes rolled back, and he sucked harder, nipped at me and then sucked again. My balls were full, and as embarrassing as it was, I was seconds away from shooting my load just from being against him and feeling his mouth on me. "I wanna blow you."

That got his attention. Knox's mouth left my tender flesh. "Yeah?"

"Fuck yeah."

I playfully pushed at him, and Knox rolled over to lie on his back. I tugged his jeans and briefs down his thighs. He lifted for me, and I watched as his cock stood proud, long and thick, with dark pubes and full balls. I wanted to rub my face all over him, let him mark me with his scent. "Jesus, I'm going to have fun with this." I wrapped my hand around him and stroked.

Knox nearly jolted off the bed. My eyes darted to his, nervous it was too much, but there was only wild desire in his gaze.

I went to lean over, but his hand on my chest stopped me. "Wait. I want to see you too."

His fingers trembled as he reached for the button on my jeans, then tugged the zipper down. I knelt beside him, letting Knox control this as he pulled down my jeans and trunks. My cock popped free of the material, and I silently said a thank-you to the sex gods. I'd been dying confined like that.

"I…wow…"

I laughed. "Well, shit. I can't complain about that reaction."

"Never been this close to someone else's dick before."

"Can I get up close with yours now?"

Knox laughed. "Yeah."

"Good. And just so you know, I expect a wow every time you see me naked." I stood, got my clothes off, then climbed back onto the bed with him. I settled between Knox's spread thighs, pressing kisses there before swiping at his sac with my tongue. His skin tasted salty, his scent musk and soap, and I fucking loved it.

Knox moaned when I sucked his balls, then let my tongue make a journey from the root to the tip of his shaft. Precome leaked on his belly. I pushed his cock out of the way, met his eyes as I licked it.

"Oh fuck, that was sexy." His cock jerked. "This is gonna go quick."

"We can take it slow next time," I told him. "Come in my mouth." Then, then I took him deep. Knox moaned again. His thighs flexed. His hand went into my hair, knotted there.

Each time he got to the back of my throat, I swallowed around him, went faster, sucked harder, used my hand, then just my mouth as I buried my face into the hair of his groin.

Knox was groaning and saying my name over and over. "Cal…Callum…"

He thrust gently, and I pulled off. "Don't stop. You can give it to me." I went down on him again, and he pumped his hips into my mouth. It wasn't the hardest

I'd taken it. I could tell he was testing the waters.

My dick was aching, needing a little friction, but I wanted Knox to come first. His hand tightened in my hair, his muscles constricting, his breathing faster as he thrust and still kept saying my name like it was a prayer.

"You sure? You…"

My answer was to keep going, take him deep. His body tensed, his cock spasming as he shot, filling my mouth with his release. I swallowed, he shot again, and I took that one as well.

Shoving up so I knelt again, I wrapped a hand around my cock, jacking myself. Knox's eyes were riveted on me, on my hand moving along my shaft, and then he was sitting up, reaching for me. "Can we do it together?"

"Fuck." I didn't think I'd ever heard anything hotter.

He covered my hand with his, and it only took a few more strokes before my balls tightened and the whole damn world exploded behind my eyelids. My load splattered against his leg, running all over our hands.

And then…we were quiet. I watched him, waiting for his reaction, only to see a slow smile spread across his face. "Come here." Knox tugged me to him and kissed me. He didn't seem to care that his come had just been on my tongue.

We lay together, kissing lazily for what felt like

hours. Eventually, I said, "I should clean up and go home."

"I wish you could stay…maybe in the spare room, so you can have breakfast with us? Or in here with me and you can sneak out early."

"No." I shook my head. "But it means a lot that you want me to."

Knox nodded and kissed me. "I'll get dressed and walk you out."

Again, I turned him down. "I'm a big boy. I can get to my car on my own. I promise."

"I didn't mean—"

"I know."

He watched as I went into his bathroom and cleaned up. As I got dressed. After pressing one more kiss to his lips, I said, "I'll lock up behind myself."

"Call us tomorrow?"

"Of course," I replied, and left before I changed my mind.

CHAPTER TWENTY-TWO

Knox

THE NEXT FEW weeks seemed to fly by. Callum worked extra shifts, trying to build his patient list. Still, we spent most of our spare time together. Most evenings he ended up at our place, having dinner with us. He'd hang out until Logan went to sleep, and then we'd sneak into my bedroom like a couple of horny teenagers and mess around before Callum went home. I often asked him to stay, but he never did. I tried not to let myself wonder why.

I'd lost count of how many blowjobs he'd given me, and while I hadn't ventured there yet, I was a pro at jacking him off now. Not that I'd never had any practice, since I'd been doing it to myself my whole life, but it was still a little different doing it to someone else. I had to learn his body, how he liked to be touched and how much pressure he wanted and how fast I had to move my hand to get him there.

And, of course, the adjusting to the whole someone-else's-dick-in-my-hand thing, but I'd discovered quickly that I liked it, and that was all that mattered. Who cared if I'd never been with a man before? I was with Callum now, and it was exactly where I wanted to be.

The school year had ended a few days before, and Logan would be going to Colorado the next day. Callum was taking him to the airport with me, and he was working today to make up for the missed shift.

Dale was staying with us tonight so he and Logan could spend some time together before he left. I was in my shop, working on a table I was making for Cal. I knew he wanted to start looking for his own place soon, and I liked the idea of something of mine there.

When I heard a vehicle, I got up and went to the door to see Law getting out of his truck.

"Hey, brother. What's up?"

"Not much. Thought I'd come by and see how you're doing. Remy's been doing this meditating thing in the woods with Griff. I don't know what the fuck that's about." He laughed.

"Not your thing, huh?"

He came into the shop with me. "Eh. I'd do it if he wanted me to, but gotta admit I'm thankful he doesn't."

I was pretty fucking sure there wasn't a damn thing

Law wouldn't do for Remy.

He continued, "It's good he's getting out, and I like that he and Griff enjoy spending time together. Good for Griff too, though he's been doing that more. He and Josh seem to be spending more time together, even if they're always nitpicking at each other at the bar. Guess it makes sense, considering the two of them are the only single ones left out of all of us."

My eyes shot to his. I hadn't told Law that Cal and I were officially anything. I thought maybe part of me wanted to protect it.

"Don't look at me like that. I'm not an idiot. I saw how you nearly lost your shit when you thought he was going to get laid with Josh. Plus, the two of you are always together, and he came into Sunrise with a hickey on his neck a few weeks back. Tried to hide it, but I saw that shit."

I laughed. Yeah, I'd gotten a little carried away the first night he blew me.

"Want a drink?" I asked.

"Water is good."

I grabbed two bottles from the fridge, and we went around back and sat in the chairs there.

"Don't gotta talk about it, obviously. It's your thing, but I wanted to let you know I'm here if you want to."

I opened the bottle and took a drink. The thing was, I thought I wanted to share some with Law. "He's got me all tied up, man. I've never felt this way, and I sure as shit haven't felt this way about a guy. There's something special about him…like he just fits with us, fits with me."

"Scary?" Law asked.

"As fuck," I replied, and we chuckled. "But I want it, want him. There's just so much at stake with the kids and everything."

"Nah, that's excuses. They'll be okay. If you and Callum don't work, he doesn't seem the type to bail on Logan. The rest of it, if you're worried about how they'll react or how others will, it'll work itself out. The people who can't accept it aren't people you'll want in your life anyway. If you're good, the kids'll be good, even if it takes a little adjusting."

I nodded, hoping he was right. "I think Carol knows. She hasn't come out and asked me, but she's hinted."

"And she'll be okay with it? She won't cause problems?"

How sad was our world that he had to even ask that?

I shook my head. There was no doubt in my mind that Carol would always have my back. I was lucky to have been married to her and would be her friend forever.

"Then the rest will fall into place. I think the most important thing is you and Callum. Do you want the same things? Are you okay with more than secretly sucking on a guy's neck? With being public?"

I rolled my eyes, knowing he was trying to be playful, but he was right. Regardless of how right it felt when it was only me and Callum, it'd be naive to think it would all be easy. Callum and I needed to make sure we were on the same page, which meant I needed to figure out exactly what I wanted from this. All I knew was, I wanted him. "Yeah, I hear you. Now I'm done with the mushy shit for today."

Law laughed, but even though we didn't talk about it anymore, it was never far from my mind.

"YOU HAVE YOUR medication?" I asked Logan as we stood in the busy airport.

"Yeah. This is the third time you've asked, and you put it in my carry-on."

"What about your phone charger?" Callum confirmed. "That cash your dad gave you, and oh, your school ID and list of emergency numbers?"

"Oh my God. You guys are treating me like a baby. *Both* of you." His eyes darted between Callum and me. "Sheesh, who knew I'd know what it was like to have *two* dads."

My whole body stiffened. Did that mean he knew? If so, he sounded like he was okay with it, but what if he had questions and—

"Why are you making a face like a dead fish?" Logan added, which snapped me out of it.

"I'm not, you little brat. And I like that I have someone to gang up on you with." I said it teasingly, but it was a way of testing the waters, maybe for both of us.

Logan rolled his eyes. He didn't have the chance to say much in reply because it was time for him to board. Since he was flying unaccompanied, we were able to come to the gate with him. We'd already spoken with an employee who would get him into his seat and all that.

"Come here," Callum said, and Logan went. "I'm going to miss you."

"It's only two weeks," Logan countered.

"Well, apparently you won't miss me," Callum joked.

"I will. Take care of Dad while I'm gone. Make sure he eats all his vegetables." Logan hugged him again while the three of us laughed. It made my heart hitch, seeing them together. It always did.

Logan came over to me next. We hugged, and I pressed a kiss to the top of his head. "I love you, buddy. I'll take good care of Frankie Blue for you while you're gone."

"Thanks, Dad. Love you too."

Logan walked toward the flight attendant waiting for him, then stopped and looked over his shoulder. "Don't have too much fun without me while I'm gone!"

It was said innocently, and I would miss my son, but I was definitely hoping to have lots of fun with Callum while he was gone.

"We'll try," Cal said.

"He's in good hand, Dads." The flight attendant smiled and turned around. I froze, my gaze darting to Logan, who just smiled and walked away. He didn't correct her or question me. It could have been because he didn't think it was true but didn't bother to tell her, or maybe he knew we were together.

"Breathe, Knox. It's fine."

"I'm not breathing?" I asked, and he chuckled.

"So like...we're not listening to him, right? Please tell me we're planning on having lots and lots of fun while he's gone."

I smiled, felt like my damn body was glowing. It was

a ridiculous way to feel, but that's what he did to me. "Oh yeah."

"Can we start today?"

My dick stirred at the question. Christ, he did it for me, in every way possible. "As if there's another option?" He laughed again. I loved the sound of his joy— excitement and happiness with this masculine sort of melody.

We hung around until Logan's plane took off, before I said, "Come on." And then I didn't let myself stress, didn't let myself worry. I put my arm around him, and sure, it was in Richmond, where we weren't likely to see anyone we knew, but it meant something to me. It was the first time I'd been able to do something like this with him in public, and while I hadn't known I needed it, the pressure that eased from my body said I did.

Callum didn't bring it up, and I appreciated that. He leaned into me as we went, walking through the airport together, with him on my arm.

We grabbed a quick drink and then headed back to Havenwood, talking and laughing the whole way there. Everything was always so relaxed, so easy with Callum.

The second we got home and into the house, I pushed him against the closed door and took his mouth. His hands shoved under my T-shirt, his fingers pressing into my back, then around to my abs and up to my chest. "God, I love your body," Callum said as I kissed his neck. "All solid muscle."

"I love yours too." I pressed the palm of my hand over his erection, massaged it through his jeans, an ember of want igniting and growing as I teased him and ate all his sounds.

"I can blow you all over the house for two whole weeks." Callum went to lower to his knees, but I stopped him.

"Wait. I want to try sucking you."

His pupils flared in what I hoped was desire. "Yeah?"

"Yeah."

Callum's teeth teased his bottom lip before he entwined his fingers with mine. "Let's go!" And began dragging me toward my bedroom.

Another laugh started deep in my chest as we raced toward the bed, stripped each other out of our clothes, and again, I pressed a kiss to the scar on his chest.

"Are you gonna get on your knees for me or what?" There was a playful tone to his voice.

"So fucking bossy," I joked. "Sit on the edge of the bed."

One of his dark brows cocked. "Make me."

Hunger seared through me. I took a step closer to

him and gently pushed him toward the mattress.

"You can do better than that," Callum taunted.

Yeah, yeah I could. My arms went around him. I lifted him, then dropped him on the bed. He bounced there and looked up at me, naked and gorgeous and mine.

Then he was lying down, his ass toward the edge of the mattress, his legs hanging over the side. Slowly, I knelt between his legs. He went to sit, but I put a palm on his chest and held him down. When I was sure he wasn't going to move, I wrapped a hand around his cock. With my index finger, I swiped at the clear bead of precome at the tip and tasted it.

"Oh fuck, that was sexy. I can't believe this is going to happen."

A few months ago I would have thought the same thing, but now it felt inevitable.

Callum was a little longer than me, but not as thick. His balls were tighter, and his hair was shorter, neatly groomed. I leaned in, nerves tickling the base of my spine, but it wasn't as powerful as the want. His scent was heady, masculine. I tested the waters, lashing my tongue over the head of his cock to taste his salty skin.

My eyes met his, Callum leaning up on his elbows, staring down at me. He looked drunk with lust, his blue eyes cloudy. I wanted to be good for him, wanted to make him lose his mind. My gaze didn't leave his as I licked him, got used to what I was doing, as my tongue journeyed up and down his shaft.

His breathing picked up. "Can you, um…lick and suck my balls a little? I like that."

"Oh, yeah. Okay." I should have thought of that, but I did it then, and it was…different, but not bad, feeling the soft skin of his sac against my tongue, pulling his nuts into my mouth.

"Fuck…yeah…God, Knox. My dick now. Shit, I'm literally already trying not to come."

I did as he said, using my hand to help as I stroked and sucked, tasted and teased, learned and enjoyed, sometimes gagged, and thought maybe I liked that a little too.

Each noise he made, each gasp and groan and whimper and plea, fueled me, made me want to give more, earn more from him until he was unraveling and couldn't hold back.

"I love the way your beard feels on my inner thighs."

I made sure to give him that too, rubbing my face against his pale skin, because giving Callum pleasure was the best sort of high.

His hands went into my hair, fisting it, tugging it.

"Knox…fuck, baby. I'm gonna." He was nearly thrashing around on the bed, his term of endearment filling my head. I kept sucking and jacking, and when he made this deep whimper, I knew from experience he was about to come. I pulled off and stroked him through it, watched as he spilled his release all over my hand and his belly.

"Jack off on me," he said, and I wasn't going to say no to that.

I shoved to my feet and fisted my dick. It only took a few strokes before my damn brain melted and I shot ropes of come all over Callum's spent cock.

"Come here," he said, and pulled me on top of him. "That was incredible. Thank you."

"Stay with me," fell out of my mouth.

"What?"

"We can go get your stuff from home. I want to go to bed with you every night over the next two weeks and wake up with you each morning."

Callum paused, his eyes closing longer than they should have when he blinked, making me wonder if I said something wrong.

"Okay," he replied. "I'd love to stay with you for two weeks."

When he kissed me, everything else melted away.

CHAPTER TWENTY-THREE

Callum

KNOX INSISTED ON coming with me to pick up my things. Not that I minded, obviously—it was such a Knox thing to do, wanting to be there and help. But my brain was a little murky, and I felt like I had a whole lot to work through. We'd just been going, the past few weeks, and I hadn't let myself think about much. I was afraid that if I did, I would worry and question and wonder where it would all go and if I'd get hurt.

It was impossible for me to ignore today.

Taking Logan to the airport, Knox and I had felt like such a team. When Logan had joked about having two dads and then the flight attendant had said dads as well, my heart had soared.

I wasn't Logan's parent. He had a great mom and dad who loved him, but...I wanted to be something more than just Callum, his friend.

Then Knox had put his arm around me at the airport, and I'd seen this life I wanted—us being a unit, a family, and people knowing he was mine.

Add the blowjob I wasn't sure I'd survive, having Knox on his knees for me, asking me to stay, saying he wanted to go to sleep with me and wake up with me, and it had almost short-circuited my brain, but then…then all I could focus on was his *two weeks*.

I didn't want a limit to it. Not that I expected him to move me in and discount what was best for his life, for his kids, but…I wanted them to know. I wanted it to be possible to stay over sometimes, or to cuddle with him on the couch, or for him to put his arm around me when we were walking together as a family.

I didn't know if I was being fair or not, if I was expecting too much or not, and I didn't really have anyone to talk to about it.

"Is everything okay?" he asked when we pulled up in front of Mom's house. "You seem a little down. If you don't want to stay with me, please don't feel obligated. I just thought we should take advantage."

"Um…being naked in bed with you every night? Obviously I want that. Sorry. I guess I'm kind of tired."

He nodded, but I wasn't sure he believed me.

I said, "You know when we go in there to get my stuff so I can move in with you for two weeks, my mom is going to know something's going on with us, right?"

"Yeah." He shrugged. "Law knows too, and I was thinking we could tell the rest of the guys if you're okay with it. I know it's not perfect, but—"

"I want," I cut him off. "I really, really want." That helped. It made me feel like it wasn't that Knox wanted to keep me a secret; he truly did have to think of his kids first.

"I want too. I'm not ashamed of you. I hope you don't ever think that. I don't know how you feel or what you want out of this relationship, but I care about you. This is real to me, Cal, and if you feel the same way, if you want to make a real go of this, I do too. I need to tell Carol, and I'll have to talk to the kids. I'm not sure if I should do it before we bring Charlie here or what. I haven't seen her in a while, and I don't know if it's best to tell her as soon as she gets here or let her get to know you first. I don't want to hurt her, but I don't want to hurt you either."

It was that moment when I knew I loved him. That Knox Wheeler was everything I'd never known I wanted and the best man I'd ever met. I was crazy about him, and that would never go away. "I do," I finally said. "Feel the same about you, and you're not hurting me. I trust you, and I trust your judgment where your kids are concerned."

"Thank you." He leaned over and pressed a gentle kiss to my lips. "I didn't mean to have this conversation in my truck in front of your house. Let's go in so I can ask your mom's permission to date her son." He winked.

"I expect you to actually do that," I joked in return. "Seriously, please don't, though."

Mom was sitting in her favorite chair when we went inside. "Hey. How'd it go at the airport—oh, hi, Knox," she said, noticing him behind me. Mom stood.

"Hi, Mary Beth. How are you doing?" Knox shook her hand.

"Not too bad. What are you boys up to?"

I opened my mouth to reply, but Knox beat me to it. "I asked Cal if he'd stay with me until the kids get here. I'm planning on talking to them about us, but I just…"

"Need to do it in your own time," Mom said, this unfamiliar softness to her voice I didn't quite understand.

"I need to consider them, yeah, and Cal too," he replied, and my mushy little heart melted even more.

"Well, he must like you a lot if he doesn't care that you call him Cal," Mom said with a playful smile.

Knox cleared his throat. "I hope so because I care about him a lot."

I basically had the best boyfriend ever.

"He's all right," I teased, leaning in and wrapping my arm around him. Mom's eyes got slightly teary. "Hey. Are you okay?"

"I'm fine." She waved me off. "I'm glad you're here and that I get to see this. I didn't think I'd get to."

"Oh, Mama." I stepped closer and pulled her into a hug. We held each other, and I could tell she was crying. "I love you."

"I love you too." She wiped her face. "Look at me crying like a big baby."

"You should come to dinner at the house sometime, especially when the kids are back. It'd be nice if you got to meet them," Knox told her, and I wanted to kiss him, I was so grateful. Well, I always wanted to kiss him, but even more in that moment.

"I'd like that a lot," she replied.

We chatted for a few minutes before Knox went with me to gather my things. When we were in my bedroom, with the door closed, he said, "You could have told me you didn't like to be called Cal."

I shrugged. "I like it when you use the name."

He pulled me close and kissed the back of my neck. "You're mine. I don't ever wanna let you go."

I leaned back into him. I didn't want him to let me go either.

IT HAD BEEN amazing waking up with Knox the next morning. I'd been an octopus all over him and the bed again, and he'd teased me and laughed about it while he made coffee. We had a quick breakfast together, then left for work at the same time, after chatting about what we'd have for dinner.

I swear we were right out of a gay made-for-TV movie, if they actually had gay made-for-TV movies, which they didn't, and that sucked. But that was what it felt like, and yeah, I was loving it.

After my eight-hour shift at the clinic, I headed to the gym to get a workout in. When I signed up, I thought I needed to give myself a life outside of Knox, and I hadn't really talked to Josh since I'd canceled on him for going to Richmond.

I parked, and as soon as I walked up to the building, Kellan came around the other corner.

"Oh. Hey!" He gave me a wide smile.

"How are you?" I pulled the door open and signaled for him to go inside.

"I'd be better if I wasn't about to exercise."

I laughed. "I hear ya…though it always feels good once I'm here."

"That makes one of us." He bumped my hip with his. "Josh got off work a few minutes ago. I'm working out with him. Wanna join us?"

"Yeah, I'd like that."

Kellan went around the main desk and to the hallway toward Josh's office like he owned the place. No one said anything, so I followed him. Before we got there, Josh walked around the corner.

"What's up?" He kissed Kellan's forehead and then grinned at me. "You joining us?"

"If you've got room for one more."

"Always."

The three of us went for the main part of the gym. They went straight for the treadmills and cardio first. It wasn't incredibly busy at the moment, so we found three machines together. There wasn't anyone else directly around us. Less than a minute later, Kellan said, "I heard through the Havenwood rumor mill that a certain pretty—too pretty—new member in town had a hickey not too long back."

I stumbled over my own feet and almost fell off the treadmill.

"Well, obviously the rumors are true." He winked at me.

"Here we go," Josh said.

"Oh, don't you pretend you don't want to know just as much as I do."

"Yeah, but I don't ask."

"That's because you suck," Kellan countered, and I realized I envied their friendship. I wanted something like that. My friends had known my ex was cheating on me and never told me. "So…"

I paused for a moment, wondering what to say. Knox had said he didn't want us to be a secret around his friends, that he wanted all of us to hang out, but it felt weird being the one to tell them. Still, I wanted people to know. I wanted to be able to say Knox Wheeler was mine. "Maybe." I shrugged playfully and sped up to a slow jog.

"Maybe always means yes," Kellan replied.

"Maybe," I confirmed.

"Oh my God! I'm freaking out here! I mean, this is who I think it is, right? I won't say because I would never out someone like that, but, dude, I didn't know he…well, I don't think he knew he did either. Check you out, you fucking legend. You turned him. That's like the dream."

Both Josh and I laughed, even though that wasn't possible—turning someone bisexual. I didn't believe Kellan thought so either. It was just his personality to be funny.

Josh didn't let it slide, though. "Doesn't work that way."

"Stop ruining my imaginings!" Kellan said dramatically.

"I'm ignoring you, then," Josh said. "And can we acknowledge there's some kind of queer magic at work in Havenwood? Everyone is falling in love and pairing off. I would say it's in the water, but I drink that water, and that sure as shit isn't happening to me."

"Maybe it will," I added.

"If you just cursed me, I'm gonna be pissed," Josh joked.

Kellan looked at me. "They would have to take Josh kicking and screaming."

"I'm young. I like to have fun. There's nothing wrong with that."

"You're not that young." Kellan's voice was more breathless than it had been a moment ago. "You're older than me. Wait…is that a gray hair I see?"

"Oh, fuck you, Kell." I didn't know exactly how old Josh was, but I figured around my age, early thirties. "I like my freedom too much, ya know? Different strokes and all, but we're not talking about me right now; we're talking about Hickey Neck over there and how the first night in Havenwood he zeroed in directly on our boy. He saw something he wanted, and he got it."

"Can you blame me? He's gorgeous." And now I knew he was even more than just sexy. He was kind and funny. He had a big heart, and he was a great friend, father, and ex-husband. "But it's not really like that. I mean, yeah, I noticed him right away, but I never foresaw this…and once I got to know him, he's even better than I could have imagined."

"Uh-oh," Kellan said. "I recognize that tone of voice. This is serious."

I kept jogging, but I was going at a slower pace than I would have if we weren't chatting. "I want it to be. It's difficult, though. He has his kids to think about, so it's not as easy as just jumping in. We have to wade in the shallow end for a while."

"It'll be worth it," Kellan said reassuringly.

I had no doubt. Knox was worth everything.

"Okay, now can you guys stop yapping?" Kellan said. "I'm trying to keep this gorgeous body. After we're done, we'll get smoothies and chat more."

"Such a bossy motherfucker," Josh teased, and I laughed.

I couldn't wait to spend more time with them.

CHAPTER TWENTY-FOUR

Knox

"ARE YOU SURE you're not taking me somewhere to hide my body?" Callum asked as we made our way along the trail through the woods.

I glanced at him over my shoulder. "There are a lot of things I'd like to do to your body, but hiding it isn't one of them."

Cal stopped in his tracks. "Oh my God." He wobbled slightly, and I was afraid he was going to go down.

"Hey, what's wrong?"

"Nothing. That was really hot."

"You brat." Reaching over, I took his hand. We each had a backpack full of supplies for what I was hoping would be a day out of the house, but secluded, just us. I wanted to simply...*be* with him while also sharing one of my favorite places.

"I'm sorry. I didn't mean to scare you." He kissed my shoulder as we walked.

"Nah, it's fine."

"You still won't tell me where we're going?" he asked. I'd packed the bags and hadn't let him look inside them.

"Nope."

"You like to torture me."

"Again, not what I want to do to your body, unless we're talking making you crazy because of how much you want me."

"Um…because that's not already my constant state? Apparently it was obvious from the very beginning. When I was working out with Kellan and Josh yesterday, they thought I staked my claim that first night."

When he'd come home from the gym, he'd told me he hung out with them and they'd talked about us. I appreciated that he made sure it was okay, which it was, and I was also glad he'd connected with them. I wanted Callum to love it here. I wanted it to be his home. "I was so confused."

"You were?" We kept walking along the overgrown trail.

"Yeah. You have to remember, I never really thought about being with a guy before. I didn't know I was bi, and no guy had looked at me like that before, not that I'm aware of, anyway. It threw me for a loop, but I think maybe, if I let myself see it, even then you intrigued me.

I didn't understand why, but I felt…something." I rubbed a hand over my beard, feeling a bit like an idiot. "That sounds dumb."

"No." Cal shook his head, and I noticed he was touching his chest the same way. "It sounds like us."

My heart sped up, swelled until I felt almost too much pressure in my chest. "I like that."

It only took us another ten minutes to get there, and then the thick army of trees opened up, revealing the swimming hole. It was secluded, this little oasis tucked into the forest, too small for most people to consider anything special. It was always quiet, with a shallower side with rocks that was almost a rock slide and then a deeper section.

"Knox…it's beautiful here. Why isn't it busier?" Callum let go of my hand and began to explore.

"Too far out, I guess. And too small. Most people don't bother as there are other areas to swim, but I love it. This is one of my favorite places in Havenwood."

"Thank you for sharing it with me."

I wasn't sure there was anything I didn't want to share with him.

"The waterfall is pretty." Callum pointed. "Can we walk to the other side?"

"Yeah, of course." We took our backpacks off. I

tugged my shirt over my head and dropped it, and we removed our shoes and socks too. "The rocks on the edge go across."

I led him over, and we started to make our trip along the slippery path. I didn't get far before my foot slid and I went down on my ass, jeans getting wet in the water.

"Oh my God. Are you okay?" Callum rushed out.

"Fine. Feeling clumsy, is all."

"Does that mean I get to laugh at you? Because the way your arms flailed…" He laughed, and I looked up at him. "But damn, now I don't feel like laughing anymore. You look really hot."

"Yeah, well, now you're going to be wet and hot." I grabbed his wrist and tugged him, making sure to catch him so he didn't hurt himself.

Callum went down between my legs, his back to my chest and my arms around him. His body vibrated with laughter, from his back through to me.

He cocked his head and looked up at me. My damn breath hitched, and I leaned in and took his mouth. Like always, he tasted both sweet and sassy but mainly just mine. I was falling deep, likely already fell. After Carol, I never saw myself getting serious with anyone again, but now…now, I couldn't imagine my life without Callum. I didn't want him to ever leave it.

"Come on. Let me show you the waterfall."

He nodded, stood carefully, and held his hand out for me. I let him help me up, but then he went back the way we came and began stripping out of his clothes. I followed and did the same, until we were both down to our underwear.

This time we were more careful as we went to the waterfall. There was an open space behind it, where rock naturally formed into what was almost a bench. I sat down, but Callum stood right under the spray, letting the water fall down over his head, face, and chest.

Then he ducked in with me. "I think this is the most amazing thing I've ever seen."

Seeing him there was the most incredible thing I'd ever seen, but I didn't tell him that. Instead I lay down on the rock bed behind the waterfall and pulled him with me. Callum came easily, lying on top of me as our mouths fused together again.

He was hard, his erection thrusting against mine slowly as we lazily kissed like we had all the time in the world.

I dipped my hand down the back of his underwear, squeezed his ass, teased his crack. We hadn't fooled around like that yet, but I had blown him another time.

Cal whimpered when I rubbed my finger along his

hole. He pulled his mouth away from mine, and his eyes rolled. "God, that's good. I miss that. Can you push your finger inside?"

A tremor made my body jolt with want beneath him. "Yeah, fuck yeah, I can do that."

I pulled my hand free and sucked my finger before finding his rim again. I pushed in, and it was so fucking tight, just inching the digit in the ring of muscle. He made a hungry, needy sound again, moving against me, riding my hand.

I didn't understand how it could feel good, because I'd never had something in my ass before, but the bliss was clear on his face. "What do you need?" I was so out of my element, but not embarrassed about wanting to pleasure him. I wanted to give Callum everything he needed.

"Here, let me..." He lifted away from me. I missed the feel of his body instantly, but then Callum tugged his trunks off and lay on his back. His cock was hard, pulsing with veins, and I licked my lips, wanting to taste him again. "Water or saliva isn't the best lube, but we can make it work. If you finger me, about two or so inches in, curl your finger like this." He showed me. "You'll find my prostate. You play with that, and I'll go off like a rocket."

"Okay." I nodded, sucked my finger, and pushed it inside him again. He was tight and hot, and I was sure would feel like heaven wrapped around my cock. I did what he said with my finger, before finding a spongy bump. As soon as I touched it, Callum arched off the rock.

"Yeah...fuck yes. Right there." Precome leaked from his slit, his blue eyes fiery with desire as they held me. I'd never seen anyone so beautiful.

I played with his prostate, fingering him and rubbing it, while I used my other hand to stroke his cock. I kissed his scar, licked his nipples, and swallowed his sounds as he mumbled and moaned and thrashed against the earth.

"Knox...so good. God, it's so good. Add another finger." Leaning over, I spit for more lubrication before doing what he said.

I jacked him and fucked him with my hand while my cock ached and throbbed to be inside him.

"Close...so close," he said breathlessly.

I pushed my fingers deeper, faster, before brushing that spot inside him that made him fly.

Callum's whole body tightened and bowed toward me, his mouth falling open as his cock spurted come on his abs and my hand.

"Jesus, you're gorgeous. The sexiest damn thing I've

ever seen."

I shoved my underwear down and jerked my cock until my own orgasm barreled into me and I spilled my release all over him.

We lay there together, hard rock beneath us, the waterfall in front of us, catching our breath.

"I missed that."

"You could have asked me. I always want to give you what you need."

Callum turned to me, a sweet, almost bashful smile on his lips. "You do."

CHAPTER TWENTY-FIVE

Callum

I WAS RUNNING around like a chicken with my head cut off.

We were having Josh, Natalie, Kellan, Chase, Griffin, Lawson, and Remington—Remy, he said I could call him Remy—to the house today, and for some reason, I was acting like they were royalty or something.

It wasn't as if I hadn't been around all of them; maybe not a lot, but I had. The thing was, I hadn't been around all of them as Knox's guy, which made it different. I really did like being Knox's guy, though. In fact, I liked it so much, I wished I could sing and dance to a song with lyrics about what it was like being Knox's guy...or wear a T-shirt that said it so everyone would know. They'd see me and be like, *Oh, look. There's Knox's guy.* Maybe all that made me a little crazy, but right then I couldn't find it in myself to care.

"Boo!" Strong hands grabbed my waist, and I

258

jumped about ten feet in the air.

"You scared the shit out of me."

"I can see that. I said your name a couple of times, but you were staring into the Tupperware cabinet like it held the meaning of life."

Well, that's because he couldn't hear what had been going on in my head. I was thankful as fuck about that. "We'll just say you don't want to know."

He kissed my nape, tightened his arms around me, and rested his chin on my shoulder. "Is something wrong?"

"Absolutely not, but we do have a lot of work to do before your friends arrive, so chop-chop."

"Our."

"Our what?" I asked.

"Friends."

He kissed me again, and I managed to turn around to face him without melting into a puddle of mush. It wasn't easy. "Okay. Our friends."

"You're nervous." He brushed his thumb over my cheekbone. "You don't have to be."

"It's so weird. I don't know why I'm freaking out. I'm not usually like this, but I think it's just…this is your first time with a man, and we're spending the day with your friends, and I want it to be perfect for you. I don't want you to feel like it's not worth it." Oh, shit. I hadn't even realized that was how I felt until I said it. I'd also called them his friends again, but I wasn't sure he noticed.

"Hey." Knox tilted my head up so I looked at him. "You don't have to try and make anything perfect. The whole point of today is to have fun. To cut loose and be around friends with *you*. The last thing I want is for you to feel like you have something to prove. Nothing that happens today could ever make me feel like you aren't worth it."

"When you say it like that it does sound silly." He was tying me in knots, though. I'd never felt the way I did about Knox, and I wanted to do everything I could to hold on to him.

"It is. I want you, Cal. That's not going to change."

I nodded, feeling a little ridiculous. "Even if I put you to work all day before they arrive?"

"Even then."

I winked. "Remember you said that."

So that's what we spent the morning doing—cleaning a house that didn't really need to be cleaned, marinating meat, cutting vegetables, making potato salad and finger foods for before the meal was ready. We cut a watermelon, cleaned out half of it, and used it as a fruit bowl. I also made this alcoholic punch I loved. Frankie Blue followed us around the house the whole time, like she knew something exciting was happening.

Knox didn't complain, and he did everything. We only took one break to make out when he jokingly rubbed a piece of cantaloupe all over my face to get it sticky and I bit his finger trying to eat it. We laughed, and kissed, and it was great.

We got everything finished with enough time to shower together and get dressed before the first knock came at the door.

"Relax." Knox swatted my ass.

"Oh, I liked that. You should do it more often."

Chuckling, he shook his head and went for the door. I wasn't surprised to see it was Lawson and Remington who arrived first, Bear stumbling in behind them.

"Hey, brother. How's it going?" Lawson said.

"He's been working me like crazy all day, that's how it's going," Knox teased.

"And you listened very well," I joked back. "It's good to see you again, Remington." I still couldn't get over the fact that he was famous.

"Remy," he reminded me.

"And Law," Lawson added.

Remy and Law. I appreciated the fact that they were

trying so hard to pull me into the fold. "Thanks, um…you guys want a drink? There's sweet tea, water, beer, and this fruity vodka punch I love."

"Just sweet tea for me, thanks," Law replied.

"I'll take the fruity vodka punch," Remy said. "Here, I'll help you."

"Thanks." We went into the kitchen together, and I grabbed two glasses from the cabinet.

"This was me last year."

"Huh?" I looked at him.

"Law and I had a barbecue at the house. There's apparently no other way to introduce your boyfriend to your friends in Havenwood," he teased. "I wasn't out. No one knew I was gay except for Law and my friend Brit. My anxiety was really bad back then. I thought I was going to lose my mind, but it was great. They're all really good guys. Knox is one of the best men I know. Even though this is new for him, he'll do right by you. If you're nervous, I thought I'd let you know you don't need to be."

I exhaled a deep breath, one that came from the bottom of my lungs. "Thank you. Sometimes you can know something inside, but you still need to hear it from someone not involved in the situation, ya know? I might have always known I'm gay, but this, what I feel for

Knox, I've never had that before." He was my family. I wanted his kids to be my family too.

"Havenwood has a way of bringing people together."

"I'm seeing that." I smiled, and Remy gave me a kind, somewhat shy one in return, just as we heard more people at the door.

"So like, can I start singing Knoxy and Callum sitting in the tree?" Kellan's voice came from the other room.

"Yes!" I called back playfully, hoping it was okay. A loud round of laughter followed, Knox's the loudest. We grabbed the drinks, I got Knox a beer, then went into the living room. Frankie Blue and Bear were all over a German shepherd. I didn't know who it belonged to, as Kellan, Chase, Griff, Josh, and Natalie all arrived together.

"Hey, Knoxy." I bumped him with my hip.

"Not you too," he said playfully. "I thought I was your lumberjack? I need a tough name like that."

"Oooh, so tough. Hard Knox," Kellan teased.

"Why is it always you causin' trouble?" Chase said to his boyfriend.

"Because I'm more fun than the rest of you?" Kellan looked at me. "Though I have a feeling Callum and I could get into some trouble together."

"Ah, hell, we're screwed," Josh added. "But at the

same time, I want to get into trouble with you guys too."

Another round of laughter followed, and any nerves I had melted away with it. I felt at home, not just with Knox, but with these people.

"Come on. Let's head out back," Knox said. We all started to go, and he wrapped an arm around my shoulders and kissed the top of my head.

"K-I-S-S-I-N-G!" Kellan sang as we went.

First time with a man or not, Knox didn't shy away from touching me, and that meant more than I could ever say.

We'd put extra chairs and tables in the back. The three dogs were running around, poor Frankie Blue the youngest and littlest of the bunch. Our girl held her own with them, though.

We played horseshoes and cornhole, and Kellan and I kept making jokes about the name. At one point, Josh tossed Kellan over his shoulder like a sack of potatoes, and I was struck by how close they were, the bond they had, and that it didn't seem to bother Chase at all. But then, the way Kellan looked at Chase was all it took to know who he loved.

"I'm not sure I've ever seen so many vegetables or fruits at one of your barbecues," Griff said.

"That's him." Knox pointed at me.

"They're good for you! I swear I'm going to start a class on healthy eating in this town. I don't know how all of you look the way you do."

"I know, I'm hot, right?" Josh teased.

"You're conceited is what you are," Griff countered.

"Aw, you like it, Griffy. It's your favorite thing about me. You just don't want to admit it." Josh winked at him.

With a stern, serious look on his face, Griff shook his head. "No. I used to think you were the responsible one out of you three." He pointed to Josh, Kellan, and Natalie. "But now I'm not so sure."

"Hey! I've always been the responsible one!" Natalie countered.

"One can be sensible and fun at the same time," Josh replied. "You should try it sometime."

Griffin flipped him off, but there was a small smile on his face as he did so.

I looked around, trying to figure out if I was the only one who noticed the simmering sexual tension between Josh and Griff, but everyone else was acting business as usual, so maybe I was imagining it. The whole group was close, so I guessed those two would be no different.

A few minutes later Knox got up to go flip the chicken on the grill. I went over with him. Things had been so busy since everyone arrived, we hadn't had any time to check in.

"How are you doing?" I asked softly. The grill was far enough from the group that they couldn't hear us.

"I'm doing great. Happy. Feels good. I didn't...I didn't realize something was missing until I found it," he said without looking at me, as if he hadn't just said the sweetest thing I'd ever heard. God, the things this man did to me. He'd broken my heart open and filled it with him, bigger and more whole than it had been before.

"I kinda wanna drop to my knees for you after that," I said, trying to play it smooth.

Finally, he looked at me. "Maybe not in front of everyone. You're all mine."

"I am. I want to be, for as long as you'll have me."

Knox tugged me to him, pressed a soft kiss to my lips. I loved the feel of his hard body against mine, the contrast between his gentle kisses and the roughness of his beard.

"It's not fair. I want a boyfriend!" Natalie said, while Kellan was singing in the background, "K-I-S-S-I-N-G."

Knox answered by pulling me tighter, taking my mouth again, and doing just as Kellan said.

CHAPTER TWENTY-SIX

Knox

EVERYONE HAD LEFT a while ago. Callum said he was going to shower, but he'd been in there for quite a while. I cleaned up the house a little, then found myself sitting in the backyard again, thinking about the day. It had been... Well, Callum said he wanted it to be perfect, and it had been. It felt good to be with him around my friends, to touch him and kiss him and hold him while we all laughed and chatted.

Something settled inside me since meeting Callum, this restlessness that had become such a part of me, I hadn't realized it wasn't normal, that something was missing, but now it was calm and it felt right.

I didn't know what made me do it, but I pulled my phone out and called Carol.

"Hey, you," she said.

"Hey."

"I have to say, Knox, Logan seems different…happier. It's like my sweet little boy is back. As hard as it is for me to say—and not because of you, but because I'm his mom—I feel like as his mom, he should be better off with me. But he's not. He's happy. You're doing great with him. I wanted to make sure I told you that."

I leaned against the house, appreciation swelling in my chest. "Thanks. That means a lot to me."

"He really likes Callum."

"I do too."

"Romantically?"

"Yes." There was no sense in denying it. I didn't want to deny Callum.

She was quiet for a moment. I'd be lying if I didn't admit my pulse sped up.

"Is that a problem?" I finally asked.

"No. Of course not. You know me better than that. And I had a feeling after the movie night and then hearing Logan talk about how much time you spend together. I'm surprised, but not in a bad way."

"I was surprised too. I never saw it coming. I didn't even realize I was bisexual before him."

"Eh, that's okay. We're human. We're all learning about who we are all the time."

I knew she would understand. "I have to tell the kids.

Logan loves him, so I'm sure he'll be okay. I think Charlie will love him too, but it's one thing to like Dad's friend and another for it to be Dad's boyfriend, ya know? Christ, even saying that word is weird to me."

"If you're okay, they'll be okay. If you're happy, they'll be happy, even if it takes some getting used to. And it might, especially for Charlie. She's a daddy's girl and always has been. Plus, she hasn't been around the two of you the way Logan has. We can talk to them together, if you want."

"Thanks." I was so damn lucky to have her as the mother of my kids. Still, I couldn't stop thinking about what she said about Charlie. Deep down, I figured it was true, but I hadn't wanted to admit it. I really did think she would like Callum, but I wondered if it would take some getting used to. "I don't know when. I don't know if I should do it right away or give Charlie some time to get to know him. Plus, this is her time with me. Does that make me an asshole if it becomes about someone else?"

She chuckled softly. "I don't know. Got me there. I thought we were supposed to have all the answers when we became parents."

"You and me both."

I heard the door open and looked over to see Callum

come out. His hair was wet, and he had on a T-shirt and a pair of boxer trunks.

Heat flooded my body, heading straight for my groin. I wanted him, fuck, I wanted him so bad. "I gotta go."

"We'll talk soon."

I ended the call, and Callum asked, "Is everything okay?"

I went to him, feeling like a lion stalking my prey. There were so many things I wanted to do to him, places I wanted to touch him and taste him. Sounds I wanted to hear from his lips. "Everything is perfect." I pushed my knee between his legs, used my body to press his against the house.

"Mmm. Very okay." He moved his hips so he was damn near riding my leg, just before I crushed his mouth under mine. Callum's arms wrapped around me as I thrust against him. The kiss was wild, turbulent, the perfect storm of want and chaos and raw desire, and maybe that word I hadn't said out loud but felt. *Love.*

Callum surrendered to my touch, lifting his arms over his head as I shoved my hands under his shirt and pulled it off, tossing it to the grass.

I was ravenous, craving him in this way that was almost unbearable. I rutted against him, pushing him tighter between me and the house. My mouth went to his neck again, and I sucked the tender skin between my lips.

"Oh my God. You're killing me. You can't give me a hickey again. I have to work tomorrow."

"Sorry." I flicked the spot with my tongue. "I wish I could mark you all over so everyone knows you're mine."

"Oh fuck," Callum said tightly. "That's so hot. You can be a little rougher with me in other ways. I like that, ya know?"

A growl tore from the back of my throat. I didn't know what got into me. I wanted to claim him. Fuck him. Love him. I felt him in my bones, in every damn part of me. "I want you." I pulled his earlobe between my teeth and tugged.

"Thank God. I was hoping you'd say that. I've been getting ready for you."

"I think it might kill me to finally be inside you." I hooked my hands under his thighs and lifted him. Callum wrapped his legs around my waist as I carried him toward the door. I almost tripped on the stairs, and we laughed as we fumbled to get inside.

Once we were finally there, I kicked the door closed behind us, and he took my mouth. We kissed and stumbled our way to the bedroom, where I pushed him against the wall again. I held Cal up with my body as I claimed his mouth, licked and gently sucked at his neck, though not enough to mark him, all the while thrusting against him like I was fucking him right there.

"I know you said you might die, but I'm feeling that way too," he said when we parted for air.

I felt like a starving man and Callum was my favorite meal. I didn't know what had gotten into me, into us, but I was filled with a constant, powerful need for him. "You make me crazy in the best ways. I want to touch you everywhere. I want to make this good for you." I pulled back so he was on his feet. My forehead was against his as we breathed the same air.

Callum seemed to understand exactly what I meant. I hadn't been with a guy. I knew how much he liked this, and I didn't want to fuck it up. "It's you, so it'll be more than good for me. I just want you." He pulled at my shirt. "Let's get this off. I fucking love your chest."

He took my shirt off, then went for my jeans. Callum went down on his knees to remove them and my underwear, before leaning in to nuzzle my groin. He lapped at my balls and sucked the head of my cock into his mouth. I hissed in pleasure at the hot suction of his mouth on my already tender cock.

When he stood again, he took his trunks off too,

then put his arms over his head, wrists together. Damned if my knees didn't go weak. He stood there in front of me, golden, tight body, hard cock, full balls, flat nipples, the scar I kissed every time we were together, and he was giving himself to me.

Somehow I knew what he wanted. I held his wrists against the wall, like he couldn't get free. Callum moaned as soon as I did, and his eyes fluttered. I cupped his balls, then slid my hand up and stroked his shaft. "You like to be my little prisoner?" I asked into his neck before dragging my teeth along his skin.

"Fuck yes." His legs went around my waist again. I still kept hold of him, pinned him to the wall with my body as we moved together like we were fucking.

"You like to be mine, don't you?"

"God yes." He arched toward me. I licked his scar, then one flat nipple, making it pebble. My free hand was at his hip, holding him, and he begged, "A little tighter," so I listened, gave him more pressure in the two places I held him.

"This is okay?" I asked.

"This is good." His head rolled to the side. "So good. And if you want to give me hickeys, you can on my torso where no one can see."

My cock jerked...throbbed.

"We need to get to the bed so it's easier for me to work."

He laughed and held on tight as I carried him over. I laid Callum down, then went over on top of him. I held his wrists together over his head again while I sucked at one of his pecs.

"Fuck…Knox…please…" I kept drawing his skin into my mouth, making the blood rush to the surface and bruise.

When I pulled off, there was a purple hickey there. I smiled, kissed it, then looked up and saw the raw desire in Callum's eyes. "Stay still so I can mark what's mine."

"Yours."

I sucked numerous spots on his torso, his stomach. Callum writhed and begged and gasped beneath me.

"Since we're here," he said, "do you know what else I love?" He moved his body against mine, his hard cock rubbing against me.

"What?" I asked, wanting to please him, before leaning down and licking and sucking the skin of his stomach into my mouth again.

"I think I made it obvious how much I like to be fingered…and you don't have to if you don't want to, but when you're getting me ready… I'm sure you haven't felt this, but it's about the best thing in the world to have your ass eaten."

I looked up at him. "I want to taste you everywhere."

"Jesus, Knox. You're gonna fucking kill me. That's so hot."

I moved, and Cal turned over to lie on his belly. He spread his legs, and I settled between them, ran my hands over the full mounds of his ass. His skin was so soft, so hot. He rolled his hips, pushed his ass out toward me, then thrust against the bed again. I pulled his cheeks open, saw his tight, pink rim. "Fuck." I rubbed my thumb over it. "Such a pretty little hole." It clinched beneath my ministrations.

"Please, Knox."

"I like to hear you beg." I didn't know where this was coming from. I hadn't been this way with any of my other lovers, but there, in this space that belonged to us, it felt right.

"Please," he asked again.

I rubbed him again, tapped his entrance a few times, then leaned in to taste him. It was a mixture of soap and a heady musk that went straight to my head.

I did it again and again and again, used my tongue on him as Cal moaned and begged and writhed beneath me. I wanted nothing more than to devour him. I could feel him loosening up as I worshipped him. That was exactly what it felt like I was doing—worshipping, praising.

"Oh fuck…Knox…I can't…you…" He was rambling, not making any sense, and I couldn't help smiling against him. I rubbed my beard along his ass, because I knew he liked it in other places. Callum damn near shot off the bed, but I held him down, licked and kissed and teased his hole, loving every second of it. "Lube. Fingers. Fuck." He reached for the nightstand. It was a new purchase I'd made this week.

"My little prisoner has had enough?"

"Your little prisoner wants his lumberjack's cock."

I laughed, flying that I could make him feel this way, that he wanted me that much.

I got my fingers slick and worked him open, the way he'd shown me he liked. It was something else, watching them sink into his ass, feeling him hug them the way he would soon do to my cock.

"I'm good. Fuck me. Please, Knox. I need you."

My dick pulsed, jerked at that. "I need you too."

He handed me the condom. I ripped it open and suited up. He pushed up on his hands and knees. I knelt behind him and just…froze.

Callum looked over his shoulder, eyebrows furrowed and concern on his face. "It's okay if you're not ready. I didn't mean to rush you."

"No." I shook my head. "I…I think I'm in love with you." I probably knew I was and thought about it before, but the truth slammed into me in that moment, and I couldn't hold it back. "I'm in love with you."

Time slowed. Callum turned, crawled toward me, his eyes filled with tears. "I love you too, so much, it's all I can feel or think sometimes."

We smiled, both on our knees in the middle of the bed. I pulled him to me, kissed him, smiled against him, before laying him down on his back. I lubed my cock, and he spread his legs for me.

"I like looking at you." I leaned over, pressed against him, and worked my way inside. I felt his body tighten, then give, but still this hot grip around me.

Callum breathed deep, and when he did, I'd pause. "You're big. I haven't had anything that big inside me for a while. We have to go slow."

So I did. I kissed his temple and eyebrow, the tip of his nose, until his body relaxed and loosened up enough for me to sink all the way in. "Jesus Christ. I've never been inside something so tight." My whole body was trembling.

Cal wrapped his arms around me, moved against me, and that made all the live wires inside me start to work together in unison. I pulled my hips back, then snapped them forward. I fucked him fast, then slow, each stroke of my cock shooting me higher and higher until I wasn't sure I'd find the earth again.

His nails dug into my back, his heels into me as his body moved with each pump of my hips.

"Harder," he begged, and I gave it. Fucked him until I couldn't breathe, until I was sweaty, and our bodies were slapping together, and my world spun too fast for me to hang on.

"What do you need?" I asked. I'd be damned if I came before him.

Callum licked his hand and shoved it between us to jack his cock. I leaned up to give him space and watched as he worked himself, his body still jolting with each of my thrusts until he squeezed his eyes closed tightly and cried out, shooting all over his chest. His ass spasmed around me. My vision went blurry and my body jittery as I came.

I fell on top of him. When I went to move, he wrapped his arms and legs around me, kissing my head and forehead and holding me. "Did you mean it?" Callum finally asked.

"Yes." I looked at him. "I love you."

He smiled like I'd given him the world. "I love you too."

CHAPTER TWENTY-SEVEN

Callum

I WASN'T SURE two weeks had ever gone by faster than the last couple. It had been everything, going to bed with Knox each night and waking up with him every morning. We had meals together and watched TV together and argued about who would get up first to make coffee.

We talked about things we wanted to do with the kids, and I quietly freaked out that Charlie would hate me, or Logan would realize he hated me, and I'd lose this little family I so much wanted to be a part of.

And we fucked.

A lot.

It was awesome.

Knox was very good at what he did, and liked to learn, and when he found something that really got me off, like being a little rough, or holding me down, or making me feel like I belonged to him, he explored it a whole lot.

Maybe it was a good thing that the kids were coming home today because my ass probably needed a break.

He'd also spent quite a lot of time working on his blowjob skills. It wasn't as if I was complaining about any of it.

Now, though, I knew everything was going to change. I'd moved back into Mom's house, and I'd have to get used to sleeping alone again. It was crazy how you could spend your whole life without someone in your arms, but once you had them there, you didn't know how you could survive without them. Okay, not that I thought I was going to die or anything, but I'd miss being an octopus with him while we were sleeping, and I knew it would be hard being alone now.

But I hoped, God, how I hoped the changes would lead to something good. That Charlie would like me the way Logan seemed to so far, and that they would understand and be happy when Knox told them we were together. That the four of us would go to the beach again, and to museums, and we'd play together with Frankie Blue in the yard, and I'd eat dinner with them and be able to spend the night.

I wanted to belong with them more than I'd ever wanted anything in my life.

But I knew that couldn't happen right away. Knox was picking the kids up by himself. Since it was Charlie's first day there, he thought it was important, and I understood. Other than the short visit when he'd picked up Logan, which had been all about her brother, he hadn't seen her since Christmas. She hadn't been to Havenwood since last summer. She needed some time with her dad before it became about the new guy hanging around.

I was sitting at the dining-room table when Mom came home with groceries.

"Oh, hey. Let me help you," I told her, taking the load out of her arms.

"Thanks."

We began putting the food away together. I liked doing things like this with her; so simple, yet they made me feel closer to her.

"What do you want for dinner?" she asked.

"How about we choose and cook together?"

Mom smiled. "I'd like that."

We decided to make black-bean enchiladas. They were one of my favorites, and I wanted Mom to try them. "I think you'll really like it. I hope we have the green sauce," I said, looking through the cabinet before finding a couple of cans. "Can you grab a large bowl?" I washed my hands.

"Sure can."

As we got started, she said, "I bet you're excited to meet Knox's daughter. Charlotte is her name, right?"

"Yeah, but she prefers Charlie. I'm definitely excited. Knox said she's a wild one. She's apparently got very strong feelings and opinions, is outspoken, loves to be in the barn working with him, but also wants her nails perfectly painted while she does it, not that I can blame her. Who doesn't want beautiful nails while building things?"

Mom chuckled softly. "Well, she sounds great. And I know how much Logan means to you. It's okay to be a little nervous too. You know that, right?"

I began opening cans. "Am I that obvious?"

"No, sweetheart. You're just human. Who wouldn't be?"

I paused, looked down at what I was doing as I tried to sort through all the thoughts in my head. "I, um...I love him. Knox, I mean. He says he loves me too, and I believe him, of course. It shocks the hell out of me—"

"Not me. How can someone not love you?"

I smiled. "You have to say that. You're my mom."

We snickered together.

"But yeah, Knox isn't the type of guy to say something he doesn't mean, ya know? Regardless, there's this fear that he's going to change his mind, realize he doesn't love me or decide he doesn't want to be with a man or doesn't want something serious. That the kids won't be on board, or Charlie will hate me, and he'll have to do what's right for them. Of course he would. I expect nothing else, but I...I want them, Mama. I feel like I belong. I never knew I wanted a family, and maybe I only do because it's them, but I want them. I'm so scared it's going to get screwed up and I'm going to lose them."

"Oh, sweetheart. That's a normal, healthy fear. We're all a little afraid of being alone. It's frightening when it matters, and that's part of how you know it really *does* matter."

"Well, that's no fun. Can't there be a better way to be sure than fear?"

"No," she replied seriously. "But the thing is, you're in there, even though you're afraid. It takes a lot of guts to do that. A lot of us walk away, steer clear of stuff we're terrified of. It's easier not to put ourselves out there so we don't have to risk the pain. You've always been braver than me, though."

"What are you afraid of, Mama?"

She waved her hand dismissively, as if I was being foolish. "Nothin'. I'm just an old lady rambling."

"That's not true. You know, trust is a two-way street. Whatever it is, whatever it always has been—and I'm ashamed to admit I didn't realize it was something until moving here—you can tell me."

Mom's chin quivered, but she brushed it off, shook her head like she wasn't close to crying. "You always did have an active imagination. Now, are you going to teach me how to make these enchiladas or what? Then maybe we can watch a movie together."

I was silent a moment, hoping she would look at me, hoping she would open up, but she didn't. And I couldn't push. I was a big believer in letting people talk when they were ready. "Yeah, Mama. I'd like that. And I'm always here for you."

"I know," she said softly, which was the first time she'd admitted in any way that there was something to tell.

CHAPTER TWENTY-EIGHT

Knox

"WHO WANTS PANCAKES for breakfast?" I asked. Logan was sitting in a chair at the table, a book beside him. My Charlie-girl was on her knees on another chair, waving wildly. "I do! I do!"

Logan said, "We should have some kind of protein with it. That's what Callum says, even if it's something like yogurt." He still wasn't big on vegetables, but I loved that he was taking after Callum in some ways and starting to think about eating right.

"Good point. Hmm, let me see what we have." I was hoping this would be a good lead-in for me to start speaking about Callum. The kids had been home a few days now, and we hadn't seen each other. I'd taken some time off work to be with the kids. I wanted to give it a little while just the three of us before I introduced Cal to Charlie.

"You talk about him a lot," she told Logan.

"That's because he's my friend, buttface. He's Dad's friend too."

"Whatever, four eyes!" Charlie countered.

"Hey! Both of you, stop it. It's not okay to name-call." I pointed the spatula at Logan. "And you should know better. You're older and you started it."

"Sorry," Logan grumbled, opening his book.

I went to the fridge and pulled out the turkey bacon, which had taken some getting used to, and set it on the counter. "How about this: since we're adding turkey bacon, that's our healthy, and that means we can put chocolate chips in our pancakes. Is that a good deal?"

"Yes!" they both answered excitedly. Logan might be considering what he ate a little more, but he was still a kid.

I got out a skillet, turned on the stove, and set the bacon in the pan before grabbing the stuff for the pancakes. "So...how would you guys feel if maybe we picked Callum up today and we all went to Pike's State Park? Remember we went there last summer? They have those climbing trees you like, Charlie, and that little petting zoo. We can maybe bring some lunch and rent bikes and spend the day there."

"That'd be awesome! I missed Callum while I was in Colorado," Logan replied.

"He missed you too. He told me." I looked at my daughter. "And he's really excited to officially meet you, Charlie-girl."

"Okay. The park sounds good," she replied but didn't say anything about Callum.

"Good. It's a date, then." We'd planned it two days ago, even though I'd just mentioned it to the kids. I didn't know why. Like they wouldn't want to go to the park? I knew I was being overly cautious about this, but Charlie was so perceptive in ways Logan wasn't, and when she noticed things, she voiced them. It was ridiculous, and I was acting like a damn kid, but I had this fear that she'd look at me and know I was in love with him. What I didn't understand was why it mattered so much if she did.

I picked my phone up off the counter and shot him a quick text. **We'll pick you up at 10:30.**

Can't wait. I miss you.

I couldn't stop the cheesy smile that spread across my face. **Miss you too.**

I finished cooking breakfast, and the three of us ate. Charlie was talkative the whole time, and we laughed together, she and Logan not fighting. It was a good morning, and I couldn't stop thinking about Cal joining us for times like this.

Everyone got ready after that, and before I knew it, we were pulling up in front of Mary Beth's house. He came out instantly with a bag in his hands. He was wearing simple shorts, a T-shirt, and sneakers. He didn't have any eyeliner on today. I could tell from the way he moved that he was a little stiff and nervous.

I wished he hadn't come out so I would have needed to go in to get him.

He opened the passenger door to the truck—Charlie and Logan were in the cab behind us.

The moment he climbed in, Logan said, "Hey! I'm so glad you had the day off and could go with us. I've been bugging Dad every day since we got home. I was gonna tell you about this new game I got."

I noticed Callum didn't make eye contact with me as he replied, "You could have called me. I totally would have wanted to hear about it."

"We'll play it later. It's this sort of escape-room thing. They're harder and harder to get out of."

Callum nodded at Logan.

I turned in the seat. "Charlie, you remember Callum from the video movie night?"

"Yep, I remember. Plus, how could I forget? All you and Logan do is talk about him."

"Charlie," I warned.

"You do. That's not something bad."

"It's okay. She just stated a fact," Callum said before giving her his attention. "I've been super excited to officially meet you. Your dad told me you like nail polish." He dug into his bag and pulled something out. "I got this set, and I thought we can do nails sometime if you wanted. They're all glittery and supposed to be different galaxy kind of colors."

Her eyes glowed at that. "Oh my God! Those are so cool." She took the package he handed her.

"Did you get me something?" Logan asked.

"Of course I did. I know you wanted to go to that Edgar Allan Poe museum in Richmond, so I thought you could read some of these first." Callum handed him a book. "We can read them together if you want, but you might be too cool for that."

"Of course not," Logan replied, and warmth spread through my chest. "We're the founding members of the you-know-what-cool-kids club!"

"Yeah, we are!" Callum said, and Logan gave him a high five.

"You can be a member too," Callum told Charlie.

"That's okay," she replied, making my gut tighten.

"Hey," I said to her, but Callum put a hand on my arm.

"It's fine. She has to get to know me first."

I sighed, hoping he was right. "Did you get *me* something?"

"Nah. I like them more than you," he joked, and damn, I wanted to lean forward and kiss the smile on his face.

"You guys are looking at each other weird," Charlie said, making me jerk my attention away from Callum.

"They're not looking at each other weird," Logan countered. From there the two of them were arguing.

"Okay, guys, cut it out. We're supposed to have a good day. Callum did something really nice for you guys, though I hope he knows he didn't have to buy you anything. He didn't need to do that." I cocked a brow at him.

"Yeah, but I wanted to," Callum replied.

"Yeah, Dad, he wanted to," added Logan.

"Yeah, Dad." Callum smirked.

"Great, I'm back to you two ganging up on me. Put your seat belt on, traitor, so we can go."

"Sooooo bossy." Callum rolled his eyes, and I laughed, before getting on the road.

It was a forty-five-minute ride to the park. We chatted as we drove. Cal tried hard to engage with Charlie, and while she was polite and talkative, it was different than it had been with Logan. He'd connected with Callum instantly, this bond I still couldn't explain, but I knew my daughter. To her, he was a random adult trying too hard to be friends with her, but she wasn't really into it.

I told myself it was the first time they met and it had been less than an hour. I didn't know what I expected, but I knew I'd wished it would be automatic like it had been with Logan.

We got to the park, and everyone climbed out of the truck.

"What do you guys want to do first?" I asked.

"Bikes!" Charlie said as Logan replied with, "Petting zoo!"

Shit. I should have known better than to ask. Even if they wanted to do the same thing, they would always say the opposite as each other.

"We can flip a coin to decide." Callum pulled a quarter out of his pocket and looked at me. "Is that okay?"

"Yeah, yeah of course." I put my hand on the back of his neck and brushed my thumb along the soft skin there. I didn't realize what I was doing until Charlie practically flung herself at me, tugging my arm away.

"Hold my hand, Daddy."

Logan looked at Callum. "Charlie is a daddy's girl.

She wants all his attention when they're together."

"I do not!" she argued, and they were at it again, bickering back and forth.

"Stop it! Both of you. We're trying to have a nice time today."

Logan looked down. "Yes, sir."

"Sorry, Daddy," Charlie replied.

Callum cleared his throat. "Okay, so heads we ride bikes first and tails we go to the petting zoo first." He flipped the coin, looked at it and then us, "Tails." Callum showed it.

Logan cheered.

Charlie grumbled.

Cal looked...sad.

Damned if I didn't feel a little bit that way too.

CHAPTER TWENTY-NINE

Callum

I T WAS ONE hundred percent clear that Charlie hated
me.

Every time I tried to engage with her, it didn't go as
planned. I felt like I always said the wrong thing or did
the wrong thing.

At the petting zoo, I was telling Knox something
when she pulled him away.

We ate lunch outdoors at a small café in the park. He
sat next to me on one side of the picnic table, with Logan
on the other. Instead of sitting by her brother, she
squeezed between the two of us.

Knox looked at me over her head and gave me a
small smile I was pretty sure was meant to be reassuring,
but all it did was make me feel depressed. "Why don't I
sit over here by Logan?" I tried to play it off like it didn't
hurt.

We rode bikes, then went to climb trees. Logan had

no interest in the last one, and honestly, I didn't either, but I asked Charlie, "Can I climb with you?"

"If you want." She shrugged. "I want Daddy too, though."

This sadness crushed my chest. "I'll let you guys do it together, then."

"You can climb with us," Knox said. "We'd love to have you." But I shook my head before walking over and sitting with Logan in the grass.

"It's not your fault," he said.

My brows pulled together. "What?"

"Charlie. It's not your fault, and don't take it personally. Like I said, she's a daddy's girl. She always wants to impress him, and she's used to having a lot of his attention because they like the same things."

I couldn't help wondering how Logan felt about that, about Charlie having all Knox's attention. "Does that bother you?"

"It used to." He shrugged. "Sometimes."

"You know your dad loves you. More than anything."

"I know. I used to wish I was more like her, which you know. I feel better about it now, and it's been awesome, living with Dad and finding our own things, like working on the models, taking the art classes and stuff. I don't feel like Dad wants me to be someone else, like I used to. And technically, I know Charlie doesn't mean anything by it, at least not with me. You, on the other hand, I feel like it might be on purpose."

"Thanks for that," I replied, though I knew he was right. I also knew the kid beside me was pretty great. "You're old beyond your years, you know that? And you're also one of my favorite people in the world. No matter what, you always will be."

"Thanks." Logan nodded. "You're one of mine too…and Dad's."

My eyes shot to his. Was he saying what I thought he was? Did Logan know there was something more going on between Knox and me? "We're, um…good friends. The best."

He didn't reply to that, just said, "Do you wanna start one of the stories? In the book?"

"I'd love to."

We lay in the grass, reading *The Raven*.

Knox called our names and waved to us from the tree. As much as I enjoyed spending time with Logan, I couldn't help the melancholy weighing heavily on me. I'd wanted this day to go so much better than it had, and even though I knew it was likely normal that it hadn't, I couldn't stop myself from being disappointed.

That was why when we were in the truck, almost home, and Knox asked, "Do you want to come to the house for a while to hang out?" I replied, "I'm a little tired. Do you mind taking me home?"

He rubbed a hand over his beard, in that way he did when he was upset or overthinking things. "Of course. Whatever you want."

They dropped me off, and I said my goodbyes.

I showered, put on a pair of pajama bottoms and a T-shirt. Watched a couple of episodes of a TV show, thought about making dinner, but I didn't feel like eating.

Mom was in Richmond at a gardening event and wouldn't be home until late tonight. I thought about calling Josh or Kellan to hang out. I could use a drink or some friends, but I didn't.

My phone buzzed with a text, and I was surprised to see Knox's, **I'm outside. Can I come in?**

My pulse sped up, and I went to the door. Sure enough, he was leaning against his truck in front of the house. "Hey, come on in. Is everything okay? Did something happen?" Was it too much? Was he already going to throw in the towel?

"I just... We're alone?" he asked, coming inside. I closed the door behind him.

"Yeah, Mom's in Richmond."

"I need you." Knox's mouth crushed mine. We kissed and touched and stumbled our way into the bedroom. He shoved the door closed before lifting my arms and tugging my shirt over my head. My cock was hard from the first moment his lips touched mine.

We pulled at each other's clothes with rough, eager hands, our frustration at the day fueling us. I wrapped a hand around Knox's cock and tugged just as he leaned forward and sucked the skin of my right pec into his mouth. Hard.

"Mine," he said before drawing it into his mouth again.

"Yessss," I hissed, pulling at his hair and his cock, one hand on each.

His mouth found mine again, kissing me deep and hard, then nibbling my lip and giving me his tongue again.

I ached with need, this fierce surge of desire flooding me. I wanted him inside me, to feel connected to him, to be reminded I was his. "I need it hard."

Knox growled in response, walking me backward toward the bed.

"No." I shook my head. There were no drawers in the bedside table, so I didn't keep the lube there, plus that wasn't how I wanted him. I pulled him over to the dresser. It was one that was lower and longer instead of tall with a mirror on it. The tree carving he gave me in the beginning sat perched on the side.

I grabbed the lube and condoms from the top drawer, set them down, then bent over. Our eyes met in the mirror, his green gaze intense and fierce, like he was possessed and would soon be possessing me.

"You have no idea what you do to me…the things you make me feel." Knox danced his fingers down my spine, goose bumps chasing after them.

"Tell me."

"Reckless and wild. Free. Like everything suddenly makes sense when I didn't know the world wasn't right before you."

"Oh God." I was trembling.

Knox lubed his fingers, ran his hand over the cheeks of my ass. I spread my legs, and he found my hole, our eyes locked on each other in the mirror as I lay over the dresser for him.

He pushed what felt like two fingers inside me. "Knox…baby, please."

"Lucky," he added. "I feel that too. Possessive. Like I can't be tamed, except by you."

He fucked me with his fingers roughly, the way I

liked from him.

"Loved…in love. Like I belong. Like someone knows me in ways others don't, in ways I didn't before you."

He pulled his fingers out, and immediately I felt empty, alone.

Knox slicked his cock, then pushed in, slow and gentle. Leaned over me and kissed my shoulder, fucked me softly. "I love you."

When you looked at him, he appeared so hard. This rugged, tough man. I adored that he could be hard one moment and tender the next. That he was the most caring man I'd ever known. "I love you too."

He leisurely pulled out before driving back inside again, then froze. "Shit. Condom. I didn't think."

Knox went to pull out, but I said, "Wait," and he did. "I'm negative. I get checked religiously, every three months. I haven't been with anyone in a long time except you. I understand if you don't want to. No obligation, but…"

"I'm negative too. I, um…went in and got tested during a lunch hour at work last week. Just in case." He looked bashful about that.

"Always smart to think ahead. Now are you going to fuck me or not? I'm in the mood to really feel it after you're gone."

Knox grinned, then winked at me in the mirror. Strong hands held my waist as he eased nearly all the way out, then thrust forward again, hard...and kept going.

I held on to the dresser as he pounded my ass. We watched each other the whole time. The dresser shook, hit the wall, my deodorant fell off. My hands slid as he drove into me with powerful, deep strokes. I bumped a knickknack, knocked my face-cleaning products and a pill bottle to the floor, but not the carving; it stayed put. Knox didn't stop, he kept fucking, kept loving, and I was frenzied for it.

Our bodies slapped together. I was sweaty, his hair wet with the same. It hung in his eyes. He looked almost feral...for me. My hole was tender, but I didn't want him to stop. My cock leaked precome, my balls ached for release.

Knox still held my hips, pushed down a little so I arched just right for him. He slowed the pump of his hips, wrapped his arms around me, bent over so his chest was on my back, his mouth close to my ear. We still watched each other, but it had changed. We were still fucking, yeah, but he was also making love to me. All my wires were fried, my body overheating and my heart swelling as he hit all the right places inside me.

Knox wrapped a hand around my cock and stroked.

"Christ, you feel so good. I'm dying to fill you up, to mark you that way too."

"Oh God." My eyes rolled back before zeroing in on him again. Just as they did, he gave a sharp thrust and jerk at the same time. It was all I needed to send me careening over the edge into orgasm. I shot, kept shooting, each drive of his hips pulling another creamy spurt.

"Fuck, Cal. Me too." Knox's cock spasmed inside me, and I felt a hot spurt of come, then another and another.

He didn't move. We stayed there, me leaning over the dresser, Knox mounting me from behind.

He kissed my neck, my sweaty shoulder. His hair tickled my skin.

"I like seeing this there." He pointed to the tree. "Having a part of me in this room with you when I'm not here."

"You're always with me, Knox."

When he went soft, he took my hand and led me to the bed. We lay down, facing each other. "I have to go. I made up a reason to head out, but I don't want to leave them alone too long."

"She hates me," I said with more vulnerability in my voice than I'd meant.

"Cal, she doesn't hate you." He pushed my hair off my forehead. "She's a tough one...protective...possessive. She'll love you just like Logan and I do."

The perfect words, but there was something in his voice that told me Knox wasn't sure he believed them any more than I did.

"Has she ever been like this with your friends before?" She didn't know we were together, so it couldn't even be that.

Knox didn't answer, which was all the reply I needed.

"It'll work out," he said softly.

I hoped he was right.

CHAPTER THIRTY

Knox

ABOUT A WEEK had gone by since our day at the park. Callum had been to the house a few times, and so far, Charlie hadn't been any better with him than that first time. She wasn't outright rude, but she made it clear she didn't want anything to do with him. She was also clingy to me when he was around, doing her best to keep us away from each other, sitting between us, or politely refusing him anytime he tried to actively engage with her.

I wasn't sure what was going on, but something was. I sat down and had a talk with her—without telling her Callum and I were together—trying to see if she would tell me what was wrong, but she played it off as if it was nothing. Obviously, now wasn't the time to tell her about us. That truth sat heavy and aching in my chest. Every time I looked at Callum, I could tell he felt it too. It was wearing on him, and I felt trapped between my child and the man I loved.

It was a Saturday, and Callum was coming over later for dinner and to watch a movie. Dale had stayed over the night before. He and Logan were playing video games while they waited for Amanda to pick him up.

I was in the barn, working on Callum's table—I hadn't had much time lately to finish it—when my daughter came in.

"Hey, Charlie-girl." I smiled, and she returned it.

"Hi, Daddy."

"Do you want to help me with this table I'm working on?"

Her eyes widened with delight. "Yes!" She wandered over. "You're gonna put the epoxy stuff through the middle where it's open, right? And it'll look like a river the way the one in the living room does."

"Exactly. Here, let's get you some gloves." I tugged two out of a box and slipped them on her hands. I kept a package of smalls for when she was here.

"How come you need two of these tables?"

"I don't," I replied, trying to gauge her reactions without making it too obvious. "We're making this one for Callum."

She rolled her eyes.

"Charlie."

"You do everything for Callum. He's always hanging out with us. You and Logan never stop talking about him. Your other friends don't hang out with us all the time, and you don't make them tables, and you and Logan don't always blab about how awesome they are."

My gut twisted uncomfortably. I fought to ignore it and test the waters some. I didn't want to outright lie to her, to either of my kids. "That's because Callum is a little different."

"Whatever. I'm gonna go play with Frankie Blue." She took the gloves off.

"Charlie."

"I don't want to make the table with you."

"Then can I come play with you and Frankie?"

She stopped, looked at me, and shrugged.

While I put my things away, she lingered, waiting. Then we went to the yard and threw the ball for the dog, who never fucking got tired. She could do the same thing all day. Charlie loved it, though. We laughed and played around. Afterward, we went inside and played this board game she liked, where you had to do silly things and the other person had to figure out what your card said. This was Charlie, so she was dramatic about the whole thing, and by the time we finished, my stomach was hurting from laughing so much.

She went to watch TV while I made lunch. I was thinking about her reaction in the barn, then her laughter while playing the game. My cell was heavy in my pocket, this taunt I couldn't get away from. I didn't know what to do here. Did I call Callum and ask him not to come over tonight? That maybe we ease up with spending time together while I worked through whatever was going on with Charlie? But then I thought about him and knew he would be crushed. He would understand; that's how Callum was. But I loved him. I didn't want to hurt him. I didn't want to lose him. What if Charlie didn't come around?

Because sometimes life liked to beat you when you were down, my phone buzzed. I tugged it out of my pocket to see a text from Cal. **What's Charlie's favorite pizza?**

"Fuck." I dropped my head back and looked up at the ceiling, hoping to somehow find answers there. He couldn't bribe her. That wasn't how this worked— maybe temporarily, but that was all. But he was trying so damn hard. Charlie also needed to see she couldn't be rewarded for her behavior. Hell, maybe I should have taken Carol up on her offer to talk to the kids together. I didn't know what to do.

Before I could reply, there was a knock at the door. I

turned the stove off and answered it.

"Hi, Amanda." I smiled.

"Hi. How are you doing? I hope the boys were good."

I nodded. "I'm all right. Just got a lot going on. The boys were good, though."

"Anything I can help with?" she asked kindly. She really was a nice woman.

"Nah, but I appreciate it." I turned and called, "Logan! Dale! Your mom is here."

There was a clatter, and the two boys and Charlie came bounding down the stairs. She must have gone up with them.

"Dad! Does he have to go home? Can't he stay again?" Logan asked, adjusting his glasses. I would never get tired of how that felt, seeing him happy and having a friend, but Callum was supposed to come over. I already had a lot on my plate.

"I don't know, buddy," I replied.

"Please, Dad!" Charlie added. "They let me play with them too. Or can they come back and have dinner with us tonight? We're having pizza!"

The tightness in my gut intensified.

"Yeah, Dad! That'd be fun. Can Dale come have dinner with us and Callum?"

"You can come too, Ms. Amanda," Charlie added. "We're going to make a fire in the pit in the backyard. You always say the more the merrier, Dad."

"I would hate to intrude," Amanda said.

"That'd be so much fun, Dad. Please?" Logan asked.

Dale added, "Mom, you say it's important to have friends and to do more than play games, but you never do anything fun or hang out with friends either."

Fuck. I was so screwed. How in the hell did I get out of this without looking like an asshole? Amanda was new in town. It made sense that she didn't know many people yet. She'd told me as much the first night we met.

"The two of you are welcome to come back for pizza and s'mores tonight," I told Amanda.

"Yesssss!" both boys cheered.

"Sounds fun," she replied. "Are you sure it wouldn't be a bother?"

"Of course. Callum will be here too." Even though she didn't know who he was to me, it felt wrong not to mention him. For all I knew, she caught on that morning when his car was here, so maybe she did know. "The more the merrier," I added.

We discussed details and when they should come back. As soon as they were gone, I turned to Charlie. "That wasn't okay. You know better than to invite people over without asking me in private first."

"I was trying to be nice!" she shouted, then turned and ran for the stairs.

"*Fuck!*" I gritted out again, falling back to lean against the door. This was a disaster. The last thing I wanted to do now was to call Callum and tell him what was happening.

I went straight for my bedroom, closing and locking the door behind me. I'd tell Callum, then go upstairs and try to talk with Charlie again.

"Hey. How's my lumberjack?" he said playfully, and while hearing his voice eased some of the tension in my body, I knew it wouldn't last long.

"Your lumberjack is missing you…but I also have awkward news."

"Okay…"

"Charlie invited Amanda and Dale to dinner and the bonfire tonight. I was backed into a corner and didn't know how to say no."

"Oh." The tentative softness in his voice made my chest ache. "Should I not come?"

"What? No. Absolutely not. I want you here."

"And I want to be there, but this is going to be weird. You know Amanda is attracted to you. And no one can know we're together. Charlie hates me. Oh God.

Do you think she knows? That we're together and that's why she invited Amanda? She wants you with a woman?" His words were coming so fast, I could hardly understand him.

"Hey, no. I think she senses something's going on. I need to tell them. Given the circumstances, I don't think today is the best day, but I'm going to talk to Carol and sit down with the kids on a video-call tomorrow, okay?" It wasn't until I said the words that I knew they were true. Keeping it a secret wasn't making things any easier, and Charlie would feel lied to later. "Even if this is something we have to work through with Charlie, I'm not going anywhere. I don't want Amanda or any other woman. I want you, and I would love for you to be here tonight, but I don't want to push you either." I waited, but only silence greeted me. "I'm sorry, Cal."

"I know."

"I love you."

"I love you too." There was another pause, then, "How many pizzas should I bring? And what kinds?"

Though I didn't know if it was the right decision or not, I breathed easier. Knowing he was there made everything easier.

CHAPTER THIRTY-ONE

Callum

AT FIRST I wasn't sure I was going to go. I went back and forth, even after I confirmed with Knox I'd be there. Finally, there were three things that convinced me to go. First, I loved him. I wanted to be a part of his family. I wasn't giving up that easily. Second, I wanted Charlie to know that she couldn't push me away. That I liked her and I would keep trying to get her to like me, because that's what you did when you loved someone— and I loved Knox, which meant I loved her too. Eventually she would see that, right? She had to see it. And third, no offense to Amanda—because it wasn't her fault and she seemed like a nice woman; the poor thing was dragged into the middle of this—but I sure as shit wanted her to know he was my man.

Not that I could tell her, which okay, yeah, so maybe the last reason didn't make sense, but it would at least feel like I was staking my claim if I was there.

I also wanted to curl into a ball and cry, but I was trying to pretend that wasn't the case.

I picked up dinner at six and made my way to Knox's house. My stomach tumbled with nerves, which it had never done before when it came to a guy. The truth was, no matter how much bravado I showed, I knew that Charlie had to be the most important thing. If she didn't come around, then I couldn't be with Knox. I refused to come between him and his daughter, and no matter how much he loved me, I knew he couldn't allow it either.

Why had I decided to go tonight again?

When I pulled up, Knox was standing on the porch, waiting. He had his hands shoved into his pockets as he leaned against the house. Even seeing him made my heart pump harder and my body feel jittery. He was so fucking gorgeous, sometimes I couldn't believe he was mine. That he was taking a chance, turning his world upside down for me.

My dad hadn't loved me enough to really give a shit about me, to accept me. My ex had cheated on me. But Knox...Knox was choosing me, changing his world for me, loving me.

He came down the porch stairs, opened the passenger door, and slid in. "I feel like I'm fuckin' this up. I should have told Charlie already. I should have told her right away."

Part of me wanted to say he should have, but the other part knew it wasn't true. Plus, what did I know about being a parent? "It wouldn't have made things easier. She loves you. I don't think…I don't think she wants to share you with me, and all that would have done was make things worse."

He gave me a sad smile. "You're good at this, the whole parenting thing. You're a natural, you know that?"

I tried not to get lost in the compliment, in him calling me the very thing I thought I knew nothing about. "I'm trying to bribe your daughter into liking me with nail polish and pizza. I'm not sure how much of a natural I am."

"Well, I'm sure." Knox reached over and cupped my face. I kissed his palm, and he lowered his hand to rest at the back of my neck. The sound of wheels on gravel came from behind us, and he broke the contact. "We doing this?" he asked.

I winked, trying not to let him see how upset I was. "We're doing this, Knoxy."

"Ah, hell, not you too. I'm gonna have to punish you for that later."

"Is there any way you can now?" I teased, and we laughed.

Amanda and Dale got out of the car behind us. She looked at us, likely wondering why in the hell we'd been sitting in my car together. She was a beautiful woman, with perfect strawberry-blonde hair and bright blue eyes. She had a few freckles and a shy smile, and again, I couldn't stop myself from thinking about how much easier Knox's life would be if he were with someone like Amanda. I hadn't doubted myself in a long time. This whole thing was playing tricks with my head.

"I brought some sodas," Amanda said.

"You didn't have to do that, but thanks," Knox told her. "Amanda, this is Callum." He turned to me. "Cal, Amanda." Dale had already run inside to see Logan.

"Nice to meet you." I reached out and shook her hand.

"He's around a lot, so I'm sure Logan has mentioned him."

"He has," Amanda replied. The way her eyes darted between us, it was clear as day she knew. "I, um...I'm feeling a little silly being here, actually. I think maybe there's more going on than I realized at first. I don't want to intrude."

I started, "You don't have to—" but Knox cut me off.

"The kids don't know yet...about us."

My eyes shot to his. "Knox…"

"No, it's fine," he said, then turned to Amanda. "Logan will be fine, I think. He loves Callum. I mean, I've never… He doesn't know I'm… I've never been with a man before, so it will come as a surprise, but it'll be okay, I think. Charlie's struggling a bit, having anyone else in my life, even if she does think he's only a friend. You got dragged into that and I'm sorry, but I—we— would like it if you stayed. You can never have too many friends and all."

Oh, if I hadn't been crazy in love with him already, I would have fallen right then and there. "Yeah, definitely," I added. "I haven't lived here long either. I know how it can be. I'm always looking to connect with new people."

"Thank you. I'd like that." Amanda nodded. She looked to be closer to my age than Knox's. I didn't figure this was easy for her.

I went back to the car for the pizza, and the three of us went inside. The kids were all sitting around the coffee table.

"Callum!" Logan stood. "After dinner, will you play the maze game with us?" He looked at Dale. "He's super good at it. He can power up better than I can and get through that one spot we were having trouble with."

"Yeah, sure. That'd be fun," I told him, before looking at Charlie. "Your dad told me you like Canadian bacon and pineapple, so I got a whole pizza with that on it."

"It's so gross," Logan said. "Fruit doesn't belong on pizza."

"Fruit belongs everywhere, kid," I replied, then turned and went to the kitchen to set the boxes down. I'd decided I would be polite to Charlie, of course, but I wasn't going to push. Where a couple of days ago I likely would have continued to try and engage after telling her about the pizza, I decided to walk away. Everyone followed behind me. "Knox, do we still have those paper plates I bought?" I asked, looking in the cabinet.

"Yeah, I put them in the microwave."

I passed around plates to everyone as Knox opened the boxes. The boys dived in right away, piling their plates with pepperoni pizza.

"Geez, guys. What happened to ladies first?" Knox asked.

"Sorry," Logan replied around a mouthful.

"Go ahead, Charlie and Amanda," Knox added, standing beside me.

"I'll wait for you, Daddy," Charlie replied.

"No, you can go ahead and make your plate," he

countered.

She didn't seem happy with his response, but did so.

Knox and I grabbed our food next. We headed to the table outside, then came back in for drinks. I purposefully sat beside Logan and Dale. Now that Amanda knew, I didn't feel the same need to claim what was mine. I was also hoping to show Charlie I wasn't any kind of competition. She would still have her dad no matter what.

We ate, then played some yard games, like we had when Knox and I had the barbecue. Amanda seemed to be having a good time, and when Charlie forgot she was supposed to hate me, she'd let go and almost act like she liked me.

When it started to get dark, Knox built a fire in the pit. We toasted marshmallows and made s'mores. The kids were laughing, Knox and Amanda chatting, and I stood back a little and let myself take it in.

I couldn't help smiling. This was how it could be— this life, Knox and me; firepits, dinners, laughter and friendships. It was perfect.

I was closer to Logan than Knox was and I suddenly heard the familiar sound of wheezing. I looked over, and noticed something was off with the color of Logan's skin. Dale was rambling to him and acting something out, and

Logan was trying to keep up with him. I could see he was attempting to play it off, that he didn't want his friend to know something was wrong, but it only took me a moment to realize it was.

Logan started coughing, his deep wheeze growing worse. I rushed over to him, felt his pockets for his inhaler that wasn't there.

"Knox!" I shouted. "Watch Logan!" I shot into the house for the other inhaler and the peak flow meter I knew they kept in a bowl on the kitchen counter. My heart was racing. I was sweating and felt like I couldn't breathe myself, fear clawing and ripping at my insides.

I grabbed his medication, and by the time I got out, Knox was calmly trying to calm him down. His breathing was worse, making quick, short panting sounds mingled with his cough. I handed the inhaler over and he sucked the albuterol in, then held his breath before doing it again a minute later. He was still coughing and wheezing, so Knox put the peak flow monitor to his mouth and instructed him. Knox looked at me and shook his head.

"Take him in," I rushed out. "Shh. You've got this, buddy. You're doing good. Try to calm down." Knox's hand was running through Logan's hair as I spoke.

We all rushed to the front of the house. Knox's truck

was blocked in by my car and Amanda's. The fire was still going out back. I didn't know if the grill was on and Frankie Blue was out. Charlie was crying hysterically, so I tossed him my keys. "Take my car."

He looked back and forth between me and Charlie. "Cal," Knox said, panic in his voice.

"I got Charlie. You take care of Logan. We'll meet you there."

"We can drive you and Charlie," Amanda told us.

"Thank you."

"Call Carol," Knox added before he and Logan climbed into my car and drove away.

Amanda added, "I can keep Charlie—"

"No!" Charlie cut her off, crying. "I want to go. Please don't make me stay, Callum. Please let me go with you."

"Shh. Hey, it's okay. You can go with me. Are you kidding me? Logan needs his sister, and your dad needs his girl. Can you get your phone for me? So I can call your mom?"

She ran into the house.

Dale was crying, so I told him, "He's going to be fine. They need to get some oxygen in him, and he'll be just fine."

I went for the backyard, turning on the hose to put

the fire out. I checked the grill and got Frankie Blue in the house.

Amanda was hugging Charlie when I got there again and I tried not to wish that was me. Now wasn't the time.

She pulled away from Amanda and handed me the phone. "Get in the back seat with me, okay, sweetie? Put your seat belt on." She obeyed.

Amanda and Dale got into the front.

I called Carol first and told her what was happening. "I'm sure he's fine. He'll be okay." And while she was appreciative, she still said she was getting a flight out. I figured that was a mom thing. Plus, I wasn't sure if Logan had an attack this bad before. Knox hadn't mentioned emergency room visits.

The drive seemed to take forever. "Thank you," I told Amanda when she let us out at the hospital.

We got to the ER. Charlie held my hand as we rushed to the counter. "Logan Wheeler was brought in with his dad a few minutes ago. I'm..." His dad's boyfriend? I couldn't say that. I wasn't Logan's stepfather or uncle or anything else. "A friend. This is his sister. Can we—Actually..." I turned to Charlie. "Come over here and sit down for me, okay? Let's get you comfortable in the waiting room while I find out what's going on with your brother."

"Sir," the woman at the counter said, "is his mother here?" I shook my head. I worked in the medical field. I understood how all this went. They always limited how many people could go back in the ER and they mostly wanted it to be family. Still, being on the other side of it stung. I suddenly wished I worked there instead of at the Havenwood clinic so maybe they'd make an exception. "We can't tell you anything. Not yet. They're working on him now."

"Okay. We'll wait. We'll be right in the waiting room. If Knox is looking for us, can you let him know Callum and his daughter are here?"

I was trying to hold it together, trying to keep from showing how I was cracking apart inside. I wasn't supposed to be freaking out, but this was…this was Logan. This was too close to my heart.

I sat down with Charlie, who was crying.

"Do you want a hug? Are you okay?" I asked, and she leaned against me, let me wrap my arm around her and hold her while she cried. I didn't move until she fell asleep against me.

Knox still hadn't come out. Still hadn't updated me.

I dialed Mom's number. It was late, and she answered with, "What's wrong?"

I replied softly so as not to wake Charlie. "Mama, I need you."

"Where are you?" I told her, and she said, "I'll be right there."

CHAPTER THIRTY-TWO

Knox

I'D NEVER BEEN so scared in my life.

They had Logan's breathing under control now. He'd had X-rays and a breathing treatment. They wanted to run some tests and keep him at least overnight. They weren't sure exactly why he'd had such a bad asthma attack. It could have been the smoke and the exacerbation of playing the games. He likely felt it coming on but thought he had it under control and didn't want to stop and use his inhaler when he was playing with his friend.

I would never get the sound out of my head, of Callum's voice when he'd said my name. The sharp edge of fear that had sliced through me. I tried not to think about it. Things were better now. Logan was fine. It would be okay. It was hard sometimes, when you could be used to something, can have dealt with it, but for me, it was still hard because it was my son. Plus, we'd had urgent-care trips before and the ER once, but those had always been when it was me and Carol.

He was sleeping now while I waited for them to get him admitted to the floor. We'd been here for hours, and I hadn't left his side. I didn't have my phone on me, but I'd spoken to one of the nurses about letting Callum know Logan was okay. They wouldn't allow him and Charlie into his ER room, because of Charlie's age and they only wanted one person in the room.

A tech stuck his head around the curtain. "They got him a room. He'll probably go up in about thirty minutes."

"Okay." I rubbed a hand over my face. My eyes were scratchy. "I'm gonna head out to the waiting room to talk to my...Callum." My Callum? Christ, I needed to get it together. "Make sure he and Logan's sister know what's going on. Can you tell Logan where I am if he wakes up?"

The man gave me a kind smile. "Yeah, of course. He'll be all right. We're taking good care of him."

"Thank you." Natalie worked in the ER, and I'd been hoping she was here tonight, but she wasn't. Everyone had been great, but it would have been nice to have her there.

My legs were stiff as I stood. I was aching to see Callum. To hold him and have him tell me that everything was going to be okay. I knew it would, but sometimes you needed to hear it from someone you loved, someone you trusted.

I also wanted to hold Charlie, to make sure she was okay. Having something happen to Logan made me want to keep them both a little closer.

I made my way to the waiting room. It was the middle of the night, so it was quiet there. When I walked around the corner, I saw them. Callum with his arm around Charlie, who was asleep against him. Mary Beth sitting on the other side of Cal, then Law and Remy.

Callum's eyes darted up, as if he sensed me, even though I hadn't moved from my spot near the entrance.

"Knox," he said softly, pain in his voice.

I walked over. "He's okay. We aren't sure why things got so bad there. They want to keep him overnight to watch his oxygen levels. We might need to adjust his treatment. He's sleeping now. They had to give him some oxygen. That's never…" That had never happened before.

Charlie rolled over but didn't wake. Her position made it so she wasn't as heavily against Cal as she had been. He was able to slip out from under her, and she didn't move, stayed curled up where she was. I whispered, "How did you all…?"

"Here, let's go around the corner so we don't wake her," Callum said.

We all left the waiting room and went right around the corner, so we could still keep an eye on her and hear her but have some privacy.

"I called Carol. She's on her way. I told her she didn't have to come, but…"

"She's a mom," Knox filled in.

Callum bit his thumbnail nervously. I'd never seen him do that before. "I called my mom. I hope that's okay. I was worried. Jesus, I've never been so scared in my life."

"Hey, come here. I'm sorry I couldn't be out here with you." I pulled him close, my arms around his shoulders, his around my waist. I kissed the top of his head, savored the feel of him against me.

"I called Law," Mary Beth filled me in. Callum had his cheek against my chest. My heart raced, and I wondered if he felt it beat against him, if he knew he'd brought it to life again. "I wanted to tell him I might not be in to work in the morning."

"And there was no way I was going to stay at home," Law added. "We went over and took Frankie Blue out before we got here. What can we do, brother?"

"Coffee," I replied. And time with Callum, but I

think they knew that.

Law nodded. Remy clamped a hand on my shoulder in support.

"I'll head down with them," Mary Beth said, and the three of them walked away, leaving us.

"Christ, I needed this, needed you. I was so scared. I've never seen it come on so hard that fast. I kept thinking, what if something happens? My kids are my world. I…"

"Hey, it's okay. Logan's gonna be fine. Nothing's going to happen to your kids. You're such a good dad, Knox. They're so lucky to have you."

"I'm lucky to have *you*. Just having you against me makes me feel like it's going to be okay."

Callum nuzzled his face into my chest. I squeezed him tighter, didn't care that we were in the hospital where people from Havenwood could see us. He was mine, and I was his. That was all that mattered to me.

"I was so scared too. I've never had this—something like this, ya know? And I never thought I would. I know it's not the same. Logan's not my son, and he never will be, but I love him like he is, and I…"

I could feel the fear in the set of his body. In how tense it was and the way his words broke apart.

"Like I said, I know I'm not his dad, but—"

"Aren't you, though?" I interrupted. "At least in some ways. You're the man I love and want to spend my life with. You're one of the people he trusts most in the world. One of the people he goes to when he needs someone to talk to, or when he needs help with homework, or wants to play video games. I don't think being a dad has a damn bit to do with blood. It has to do with love, and that kid couldn't love you any more than he does."

Callum's whole body went rigid. I wondered if I said something wrong, but then he backed up slightly, looked up at me with watery eyes. His hands were still at my hips, and I raised mine to cup his face.

"Don't cry, Cal. This is a good thing, right?"

"The best," he said, and I wiped his tears away with my thumb. "I love them both. I want to be part of your family. It feels right. And tonight, when Charlie let me comfort her... I've never felt something like it. I want to belong with you guys...so much."

"You belong."

More tears spilled from his eyes. I brushed those too, then used my lips to kiss them away. Callum melted against me as my lips made their way down his face. Our lips touched, a soft yet passionate meeting of mouths, over and over, with no tongue.

I dropped my forehead against his just as I heard,

"Daddy?"

Callum jerked away from me. My pulse shot through the roof, this panic clinging to me.

"I knew it!" she shouted as Law, Remy, and Mary Beth were walking back to us. "I knew you loved him more than us!"

"Charlie, stop it," I warned.

"That's what happens! My best friend's dad met someone else, and he started a new family and didn't love her anymore!" She turned to Callum. "I hate you!"

"Charlotte! That's enough! I'm not going anywhere. I'll always love you. Apologize to Callum right now."

"No!" She turned and ran down the hall and toward the ER doors.

"Charlotte!" I called after her just as the tech came out.

"Mr. Wheeler, they're ready to take Logan up. Room 2026." They were pushing Logan's bed into the hallway.

"Dad?" Logan asked. "What's going on? What's wrong with Charlie?"

"It's fine, buddy. I'll talk to you about it soon." Then to the tech, I said, "This is my partner. He'll go up with Logan." I looked at Cal, and he nodded, his eyes wide and full of pain. "I'm sorry. We'll work it out," I told him. He gave me another nod, and I took off after Charlie.

CHAPTER THIRTY-THREE

Callum

"YOU KNOW SHE didn't mean that, right?" Mom said. "She's young and confused and—"

"I know," I replied, but really I didn't. And I didn't have it in me to talk about it at the moment. "Right now I'm going to do as Knox asked and stay with Logan."

"Only Mr. Wheeler's partner can go up with us right now," the tech said.

"Partner? Wait. What? What does that mean? Callum?" Logan asked, and my heart stumbled in my chest again. What would I do if Logan wasn't okay with it either? All sorts of horror stories played in my head.

"I'll talk to you about it in a minute," I told Logan. "You guys can go. Thanks for coming." I was trying not to sound upset, even though I was broken. I wanted to be strong for Logan, so he'd feel like everything was okay, but the rest of them, they knew.

"You're doing a good job, man. It'll work out," Law

said.

"We'll check on you in the morning and run over and take care of Frankie Blue again," Remy added.

I nodded at them both, hugged Mom, and then we were on our way up to Logan's room. I couldn't stop thinking of the tears in Charlie's eyes, hearing her say she hated me. My chest ached, and I reached over to hold the railing on Logan's bed to feel closer to him.

"I hate you!"

I squeezed tighter as we kept walking.

Logan's room was on the second floor. The tech took us in, locked the bed in place, and said the nurse would be in soon.

The second he left, Logan asked, "What was wrong with Charlie? And why did Dad say you're his partner?"

I adjusted his nasal cannula. "Your dad will talk to you soon." I was pretty sure he already knew. I'd considered that at the park, and he'd seemed okay with it, I thought, so he still would be, right?

"You and Dad are together, aren't you? You're like, boyfriends or whatever?"

"Logan…"

"Oh my God! You are! Are you going to move in with us? I hope you move in with us. I thought maybe you guys were, but I didn't want to get my hopes up and…" He tried to suck in a breath. He was speaking too fast.

There was a part of me that relaxed at what he said, that was even a little giddy that he was so happy. But then I thought about Charlie. I wanted her to like me. I wanted her to be happy too. "You need to calm down, kiddo. You're getting yourself worked up."

"Then tell me, please."

"You're not going to let this go, are you?"

"No."

I sighed. "Your dad and I are together, yes, but it's complicated. You and Charlie have to come first, always. We have to think about what's best for you and—"

"This is best for me! For us. And Dad too. I've never seen him so happy."

I brushed his dark hair back from his forehead. "Thank you. You don't know how much that means to me. And I love you very much. You're so special to me, and no matter what happens with me and your dad, I will always be a part of your life, okay? But there's a lot to consider. It won't always be easy, even if it is at home. Kids at school might—"

"I don't care about kids at school. I already told Dale I hope you moved in with us and married Dad. He said you're cool. Who cares about everyone else?"

My heart thumped excitedly against my chest. "Well, I am pretty cool."

"You're the best." Logan nodded.

"You need to get some rest. We'll talk about this later, okay?"

"Okay." Logan yawned again. "I love you, Callum."

"I love you too, kiddo."

As I looked at him, I knew right then and there that I would fight for them, for my family.

CHAPTER THIRTY-FOUR

Knox

I SAT WITH Charlie at a picnic table outside the ER, in a seating area with lights around it that kept the whole place illuminated.

"I love you. So, so, so much. I will always love you. I'll never start a new family and leave you or your brother behind." I made sure that was the first thing I said to her. I didn't ever want her to think that would change.

I waited a moment for her to reply, but she didn't, wouldn't even look at me.

"It's okay to be surprised at what you saw," I told her. "I understand if you're upset or confused, Charlie-girl, but how you talked to Callum isn't okay. He's...he's very important to me, and he's going to be around from now on. But remember, how I feel about Callum doesn't change how much I love you and your brother. I'll always love you, and you'll always be the most important people in my life."

She kept her arms crossed and still said nothing.

"You're stubborn like me. Your mom used to tell me that all the time when we were married, that I was stubborn. I've gotten better at it over the years, though."

She still didn't talk.

"You're allowed to be mad at me, but I wish you'd at least talk to me so I can understand more."

Charlie sniffed, then finally said, "It's not fair."

"What's not fair? Is it because Callum is a man?"

She shook her head. "Mom isn't going to marry someone else. Mom isn't starting a new family. You and Callum and Logan are starting a whole new family without me! You're going to forget all about me, like Emma's dad did."

My heart shattered, like someone had taken a hammer to it. "No way. Not possible. I love you too much. I could never forget about my Charlie-girl, do you hear me? Never. I love you and your brother more than anything in this world, and I always, always will."

In that moment, I felt like I'd let my little girl down. She had always been so much like me, blunt and strong and fierce. She didn't let people get the best of her, and she stood up for herself, so I assumed she would be okay, that she would understand what was happening. I hadn't seen that no matter what, she was still a kid. We all had so many complicated emotions. I hadn't seen that she could have felt left behind; that the fact that we'd always been so close, so alike, could have made her jealous when Logan moved in with me. That she could have felt like we were starting a different family without her. Then, when you added Callum to the mix, that he and Logan were so close and that neither Carol nor I had been serious about anyone since each other. Callum was the only person she'd been introduced to, because even though we'd said we were only friends, Charlie had obviously seen through it.

"You guys do all sorts of fun stuff without me. When we watched the movie with Mom, we were left out. You have all these fun stories, and this was supposed to be our time, and you kept saying Callum was only your friend, but I knew that wasn't true because you're different with him than your other friends. You're not supposed to lie to me, Daddy. We're a team, that's what you always say."

"Oh, kiddo, come here," I said and breathed more easily when she came. When she wrapped her little arms around me and squeezed tighter than I would have thought she was capable of. "You're right. We are a team. I will never move on without you. No matter what happens, you will always be my girl, my daughter, my building buddy, my stubborn little monster," I teased.

"I'm sorry I lied to you about Callum. I shouldn't have done that, and I'm sorry if you felt like he was taking our time. How about we do something special, just you and me? Maybe we can take an overnight fishing trip or something. Would you like that?"

"Who would keep Logan?"

"Callum," I replied tentatively. "I'm sorry I didn't think about how confusing all this would be for you. You and Logan have always lived together, and first he moves, and then there's someone new in our lives. I let you down and I'm sorry. I'll do better, okay?"

She nodded. "Sometimes I wish I could live with you too, but I don't want to leave Mom. I wish we could all live in Havenwood."

I kissed the top of her head. "Maybe we can find a way for you guys to come out more often. Mom too."

She nodded again, was quiet a moment, then asked, "Are you gonna marry Callum? Have more kids? How does that even work?"

I tried not to chuckle. "It's still very new, so I don't know what the future holds. I haven't talked to him about marriage or anything like that, but I love him very much. I want him to stay in our lives. And I know he loves you very much too. He really wants to be close to you, and I hope you'll give him a chance, but no matter what, you still need to know that you can't treat him the way you did tonight. You can't say things like that to him. I don't have plans for more kids, but if we do get married one day, or if we just stay committed to each other in other ways, it will never, ever, ever change how much I love you." I would tell her that all day every day for the rest of our lives if I had to. I felt my dad's love, but he never said it. That wasn't the kind of father I wanted to be.

"I love you too, Daddy."

We hugged again, and she cried into my chest. When she finished, I didn't rush to go inside. I sat with her, talked with her, enjoyed time with just the two of us, knowing Logan was okay with Callum.

An hour or so passed, when she said, "I, um…I really like Callum. I don't hate him. He's fun. It was really hard to stay mad at him. Sometimes I would forget I wasn't supposed to like him."

I chuckled. "Oh, kiddo. You're gonna be a whole lot of trouble, I think."

"Trouble is fun," she replied.

"Don't tell me that. I'd like to stay in the dark for as long as possible," I teased.

"Can we go inside now? I want to see Logan."

"Yeah, of course we can."

I took her hand, and the two of us went inside.

When we got to Logan's room, Callum was standing outside, leaning against the wall, his arms crossed. "He's, um…he's asleep."

"Thank you for staying with him," I replied. Charlie let go of my hand.

"Of course. Whatever you need. I—*umpf*," he said when Charlie flung herself at him. She encircled his waist with her arms, buried her face in his stomach, and cried.

"I'm sorry for being mean to you. I don't hate you and—" She dissolved into tears again.

Callum hugged her back, smoothed her hair down. "Don't worry. It's fine. It's all scary and new. Please don't cry." He looked over at me like he didn't know what to do, his pupils wide, but a smile stretched across his face.

"I don't care if you're Daddy's boyfriend," she said after she calmed down. "Maybe we can do stuff too? Like you and Logan do?"

Callum knelt and looked her in the face. "I would like that a lot. I think we'd have lots of fun together."

He wiped her tears, and then…then she wiped his. Callum stood up. I took Charlie's hand in one of mine, then wrapped my other arm around him, pulled him close, and kissed him.

The three of us went in to see Logan. All the rooms at the hospital were single, so we didn't have to worry about someone else being in there. There was a small couch, and I managed to get Charlie to lie on it and go to sleep.

Callum and I sat in two hard plastic chairs on the other side of the room. I told him what had happened outside. He told me that Logan knew about us and was ecstatic. Neither thing surprised me.

I reached over, squeezed his hand, and didn't let go. "I love you."

"I love you too."

We sat there the rest of the night, watching the kids sleep.

Around seven the next morning, the nurses had a shift change, the hospital was beginning to wake up, and the kids did too.

"I'm sorry I didn't tell you sooner about me and Callum," I told Logan.

"It's okay. I was wondering...hoping. I think it's awesome."

"Me too, buddy."

"Mommy!" Charlie shrieked suddenly and ran for the door. I turned to see Carol and—

"Mom?" Callum added. "You didn't go home last

night?"

"No way." She shook her head. "I couldn't leave you."

"I found her downstairs," Carol said. "I was trying to see what room Logan was in because someone's phone died." She eyed Knox.

He held his hands up. "I don't have mine. Sorry, but Charlie's died. I should have called you."

"I'm here now. Anyway, Mary Beth heard me and told me. I found out she's Callum's mom. They tried to say we couldn't all come up, but she said she was Logan's grandma. I would have smuggled her in if I had to."

"I'm so sorry. I didn't know you were here all night." Callum went over and hugged her.

"I wanted to be here if you needed me," she replied with more emotion than I knew the meaning of.

"You are, Mama. Always." Callum pulled away.

"Come here." Carol hugged him. "It's so good to meet you in person."

"You too." He looked at me over her shoulder and gave me a shy smile.

"Mom, did you know Callum is Dad's boyfriend?" Logan asked.

"Exciting, right?" Carol replied. "Look how much our family is growing! Families can never be too big, if you ask me." She came to me then, patted my chest, and hugged me.

"Thank you," I whispered in her ear.

"He's soooo hot," she replied softly. I rolled my eyes.

"Now, how's my sweet boy doing?" Carol pushed Logan's hair off his forehead and kissed him.

CHAPTER THIRTY-FIVE

Callum

THEY DISCHARGED LOGAN around ten that morning. He had a new inhaler and directions to see his allergist. They insisted on pushing him out in a wheelchair, and Logan's expression seemed like a cross between him thinking it was kind of cool and annoyance at being babied.

"How about we all head to the house for breakfast?" Knox asked.

"Can we make chocolate-chip pancakes?" Charlie asked him.

"Of course we can." He kissed her head.

"Oh my God. Daddy makes the best chocolate-chip pancakes! I've missed them!" Carol added.

I watched them, loving how much of a unit they were for their kids, how much of a family they all were. It had never been like that in my household, no matter how much I knew my mom loved me.

I hung toward the back a little. Carol had just gotten into town, and I was sure they wanted some time together. I didn't want to intrude, especially since Charlie was still getting used to me being around.

"Callum, you're gonna come too, right?" Charlie surprised me by asking.

"Yes," Carol replied. "You have to. I've heard so much about you. I'd love to have the chance to get to know you more."

My heart did this excited flip-flop in my chest. "Yeah, of course. I'd love to."

I was about to ask if Mom could come too when Knox added, "You too, Mary Beth. The whole family should be there."

"I…" Mom started. I reached over and grabbed her hand.

"It wouldn't be the same without you," I told her, and she nodded.

"Okay, I'd love to go."

Carol had taken a car service to the hospital. My car and Mom's were the only two there. We split up into the two vehicles and drove out to the house.

Frankie Blue was yapping and jumping all over us when we got home.

"I'm starving," Knox said. "Let's get breakfast going.

Wanna help me, Charlie-girl?"

"Yes!"

It was a wild mess after that. Logan contacted Dale to let him know he was okay. We all congregated in the kitchen and dining-room area. Knox and Charlie made pancakes. I didn't mention proteins. Now wasn't the time. There was laughter and stories, family jokes Mom and I weren't in on, but Carol made sure to explain everything.

Knox and I had our own stories too. I really loved Carol. I could tell she genuinely wanted Knox to be happy. I thought she and I could be good friends. She spent a lot of time chatting with Mom too.

We all sat around the table and ate together. They teased me about how healthy I ate, and Carol said, "Oh, bummer. And I thought I liked you," and we all laughed.

I was exhausted, having gotten no sleep the night before, but I didn't want the morning to end. It was...perfect. Almost. After breakfast we went to the living room and started watching a movie together. I realized not long into it that Mom had disappeared.

I was sitting next to Knox, Charlie on the other side of him. "I'll be right back," I whispered before going on a hunt for my mom.

I found her in the backyard, sitting in one of the

chairs there. She was bent over, and her head shot up when she saw me, her eyes ringed red.

"Hey, what's wrong?" I went over and sat next to her.

"Nothing." She wiped her eyes. "It's so good to see you happy...to see you with a family."

"Mama, please tell me. I know there's more to it than that. I know you've been keeping something from me."

"I..." she began, then looked back at the house before turning to me again. "I think...now that you're okay, that you're happy, I realize how much I want that too."

"I want that for you too. No one deserves to be happy as much as you do. I don't think...I don't think you ever have been, have you? Even when I was a kid, you weren't happy. You put on a brave face for me to deal with Dad, but you weren't, were you?"

"I was happy I had you."

"I know, but that's not the same thing."

Mom closed her eyes, and I felt like the whole world stopped, like everyone froze but us. The moment belonged to us, and after everything, we deserved it.

"I'm, um...I'm like you," she finally said.

"Like me?" I frowned. "What do you mean?"

"I'm, well, I knew when I was young that I wasn't

attracted to men."

My breath caught. My chest ached, but I tried to hold it in. She needed to have this, and I wanted her to be able to get this out.

"I thought there was something wrong with me at first. Back then it was different, and of course, where we lived and everything… I knew it wouldn't be accepted." I knelt in the grass in front of her as she continued, "I told myself it wasn't true. That I could change. I married your father, and there was nothing I wanted more than you. I will never regret that decision, Callum. Ever. I hope you know that." She started crying, her words hard to make out through her tears.

"I know that. I would never think anything different. You were the best mom ever."

She huffed. "Thank you, sweetheart, but we both know that isn't true. When you told me, when I found out you were gay, I was so scared. I knew your father wouldn't be okay with it, and I wanted your life to be easy. I didn't want you to have to deal with hate and bigotry. It all collided inside me…what I'd done, what I'd been denying my whole life. I will never forgive myself for what I told you. It is the moment I regret most in my life. That's why I thought I should have known about you, because I'd felt the same things."

"You didn't know because I didn't want you to." I wiped her tears and noticed my hand was shaking. "I can't believe you've been holding this in your whole life. That must have been so hard for you." I'd be lying if I didn't silently acknowledge my hurt at her not telling me. We'd lost all this time. If I'd known, maybe things would have been different, but then I reminded myself that we all have our own journeys. We can't expect other people to follow the path we did. Being human was so fragile and nuanced and beautiful and devastating. How could we expect everyone's stories to be the same?

She cupped my face. "You are the best thing I have ever done."

"You deserve more than that. You deserve your own life too."

"I think...I think I'm ready to try and find it." She had been waiting her whole life for me to be happy, to be whole, to find my place in the world, and now that I had, she was willing to look for her own.

"I love you. So much." I pulled her into a hug, and we cried.

I didn't know how long we were out there, but no one interrupted us. After we both settled down, I smiled and asked, "So, what kind of women do you like? Physically, at least."

"Oh my God!" Mom covered her face and laughed. "I can't believe we're having this conversation."

"I'm glad we are."

She reached over and grabbed my hand. "I am too."

We went back inside not long afterward.

The movie was over. Knox, Charlie, and Carol were playing a board game. Logan was sitting at the table where they kept his model planes.

"These are lovely," Mom told him.

"Thanks! Want me to show you all the parts? My dad and I build them together."

Mom looked at me a little panicked for a moment, I think because they were so open, so willing to accept us into their family. I nodded to tell her to go on, and she said, "I'd really like that."

She joined Logan, and he began rambling about airplane stuff. The kid had so many hobbies and likes, I knew the world was wide open for him.

I watched my mom bond with the sweet boy who had opened his heart to me, who had changed my life, and then I glanced over at Knox and Charlie. They were playing and laughing before Charlie hooted and jumped up, obviously winning.

Knox looked up at me, and smiled.

"I'll be right back," he told them, before coming

over. We sneaked into the kitchen together. Knox wrapped his arms around me. "Is everything okay?"

"Yeah. It's better than okay. It's perfect."

He hooked his finger under my chin, leaned in, and kissed me. "Perfect. Now come play this game with us. We have to find someone who can beat Charlie. She keeps winning."

I nodded. He held my hand as we walked over, and the four of us played.

Charlie won again, but maybe really, all of us did.

EPILOGUE

Knox

Four Months Later

"I CAN'T BELIEVE Griff is here," Kellan said.

"Yeah, me neither. How'd you do it?" I asked Josh.

We were all in Richmond for the weekend, at a gay club. Honestly, I couldn't believe I was there either. It was my first time in a gay club, hell, my first time in any club in a long-ass time. I felt old and out of place, but Cal, Josh, and Kellan had wanted to go for a while now, and we finally made it.

"Because I'm fucking good," Josh replied. "He needs to get out and have more fun."

Griffin and Chase approached us then with a handful of beers for everyone. They passed them around, Remy and Law declining. Lawson, like a fierce protector, hadn't let go of Remy all night. Being here was big for Remy, given his anxiety and all, but he was doing well, laughing and joking with the rest of us. He had his good days and bad, but he was trying to experience life more, and I thought that was because of the man beside him.

The thought made me wrap my arms around Callum and pull him close, his back to my chest.

"What were you guys talking about?" Chase asked.

"How my brother is going to steal my best friend," Kellan teased.

"Hello pot, meet kettle," Griffin said.

"He didn't steal me," Chase replied. "You'll always be my brother, Griff. You know that."

Griffin nodded. "Yeah, but I like to give him shit."

"Aw, does that mean you really do think of me as your bestie?" Josh slung an arm over Griff's shoulders. "I'm touched. And don't worry, boys, there's enough of me to go around. I've always wanted to know what it was like to have a pair of brothers, only it wasn't friendship in my fantasies."

Kellan and Chase laughed.

"You're gross," Griffin told Josh.

"You love me, Griffy. I make your life more interesting." Josh leaned over and gave him a loud, smacking kiss on the cheek, much like he would have done with Kellan, only Griff jerked away.

"I don't know where those lips have been." Griff

wiped his cheek.

"Always busting my balls," Josh replied.

"As fun as this is," Cal said, "I want to go dance with my man." He grabbed my hand and began dragging me.

"Wait. I'm old. I can't dance."

"Just move like you do when you're fucking me, and we'll be good," he teased, and damn it, that easily I started to get hard. We found a spot on the dance floor and began moving together.

It had been a great few months. Charlie had spent some extra time in Havenwood—she and I taking a couple of overnight trips, just the two of us. It didn't take her long at all to love Callum as much as Logan did. I wasn't surprised. It was impossible not to love him.

Logan was back in school. He and Dale were still great friends. He didn't have a lot of other ones, but he was okay with that. He'd grown into a much more confident young man. He didn't feel like he had to be any kind of way. He was comfortable in who he was, and I thought a big part of that was due to the man moving his ass against my groin right then, the man who had moved in with us about six weeks before. Maybe that was fast to some people, but it wasn't to us. It was exactly how it was supposed to be.

Logan was staying with Mary Beth while we were in

Richmond. She loved spending time with the kids. I knew Logan reminded her of Callum in a lot of ways.

The hardest part was being away from Charlie. We'd had more than one talk—her, Carol, Callum, and me. She wanted to be close to us, but she didn't want to leave her mom. We were looking into other options, one being Carol and Charlie moving closer. As much as I missed Charlie, Carol missed Logan. She'd said Havenwood had grown on her and maybe I was right about living in the boonies after all.

Callum and I danced for a while. I couldn't keep my eyes or hands off him. He was wearing eyeliner and a tight shirt that showed off his abs. I ran my hands up and down his back, his ass, savoring what was mine.

He pushed up on his toes, mouth close to my ear. "I want you."

I practically growled in response before taking his hand and going back to our friends.

It was only Law, Remy, Griff, and Josh there, Kellan and Chase having disappeared, likely to dance.

"You gonna dance with me or what?" Josh asked Griff, who shook his head. "Friends can dance with each other, you know."

"What? It's not that. I don't give a shit about that. It's just not my thing," Griff replied.

I had no idea what was up with the two of them. There was some weird energy in the air when they were around each other.

A guy walked up to Josh. "You here with anyone?"

I couldn't help noticing Josh's eyes darting toward Griff, who said, "You should go have fun. That's what we're here for, right?"

"You can come along," the newcomer said, and Griff looked scandalized as hell.

"What? No," he replied, then said to Josh, "Go have fun. You don't have to babysit me all night."

Josh looked at him once more, shrugged, and grabbed the guy's hand.

"That your boyfriend?" I heard the guy ask.

"No, just a friend and a pain in my ass," Josh replied.

"We're going to head out," I told them. We'd all gotten rooms at the same hotel. It wasn't far away, so after we said our goodbyes, Callum and I made the quick walk there.

The second we were in our room, our mouths clashed together and we were ripping each other's clothes off. I picked Callum up, dropped him on the bed, then held his hands over his head, wrists in my grip. I kissed his scar, then sucked the skin of his pec into my mouth, making the blood rush to the surface. Christ, I loved marking him this way.

"Fuck yes." Callum arched toward me. "Yours."

"Mine," I replied, before giving him a few more hickeys on his chest and stomach. I lowered myself, licked the precome on his slit, then took him into my mouth. Callum thrust, and I took it. I was a whole lot better at blowjobs than I'd been in the beginning.

He was writhing and whimpering, and I could tell he was already close to coming, when he said, "No, don't. I want to come with you inside me, and I want to play too."

I let him go. Callum flipped me onto my back, knelt beside me, and began sucking me off. "Fuck," I groaned. I loved the feel of his hot, wet mouth.

The lube was on the nightstand, and I grabbed it and slicked up my finger. He was bent over me, on his knees, his ass out to the side, so I could play with his hole while he blew me. I circled the rim, tapped it, pushed a finger inside just as I thrust. He made a quick choking sound, then moaned and pulled off. "So good. Fuck, that's so good."

Callum grabbed the lube from beside me and wet his fingers. I knew what he wanted, so I spread my legs for him. He hadn't fucked me yet, but I knew at some point we would try it. I wanted to. He'd started fingering me, showing me how fucking incredible it was to have your prostate stimulated, and I cursed myself for missing out on that all my life.

On reflex, I tightened a moment when he went to push his finger inside. "It's just me, baby. Let me in," Callum said, and I relaxed, felt the familiar fullness as he pushed one finger, then two inside my hole.

We played like that for a while, fingering each other while Callum lapped at my balls and my cock. I was on a hair trigger, my nuts full and ready to spill, when he trembled and said, "Fuck me."

I tugged him over so he straddled me. He sank down on my cock, and we both breathed together. Then I sat up, and he wrapped his legs around me. I tugged his hair and bit his chest, and he cried out.

"Fuck me. Please, Knox. Own me."

I thrust up. He arched backward, and his mouth opened on a cry as I pumped into him. Callum wrapped a hand around his cock and stroked. I licked the sweat off his neck, fucking him, loving him until we both unraveled, Callum shooting between us as I filled his ass.

I pulled him with me as I lay down, my cock pulling from his ass. "God, I love you. So much."

Callum and the kids were my whole damn world. He'd given me something I hadn't known I needed, completed me in a way I hadn't known I needed either.

"I love you too."

We were quiet for a moment, him lying on top of me as my fingers skated up and down his back.

"Who would have thought, huh?" I asked. "When I saw this new guy walk into Griff's, looking like no one I'd ever seen before, I was so fucking confused, but I couldn't look away either. Who would have thought we'd end up here?"

"I don't know how everyone doesn't always look at you the way I did when I walked into Griff's, my sexy lumberjack." Callum kissed my chest. "I never thought I'd get so lucky, but there is nowhere else I want to be. You're stuck with me now."

I rolled over, pinned him down. "Mine," I said again.

"Always," Callum replied.

Join Riley's Newsletter

Find Riley:
Reader's Group: facebook.com/groups/RileysRebels2.0
Facebook: rileyhartwrites
Twitter: @RileyHart5
Goodreads:
goodreads.com/author/show/7013384.Riley_Hart
Instagram: rileyhartwrites

THE HAVENWOOD SERIES

Want more Havenwood? We have one more story to go! There's no way I could leave my favorite little town without making sure Griffin and Josh got their happily ever after too!

Other Books by Riley Hart

Standalone titles with Devon McCormack:
Beautiful Chaos
Weight of the World
Up For The Challenge

Standalone titles with Christina Lee:
Of Starlight and Stardust
Science and Jockstraps

Stumbling into Love
Stupid Love

Boys in Makeup Series with Christina Lee:
Pretty Perfect
Pretty Sweet

Havenwood
Giving Chase
Murphy's Law

Fever Falls
Fired Up
#Burn by Devon McCormack
Whiskey Throttle
#Royal by Devon McCormack
Game On co-authored with Devon McCormack
Boyfriend 101

Saint and Lucky
Something About You
Something About Us

Standalone
His Truth
Looking for Trouble
Endless Stretch of Blue
Love Always
Finding Finley

Jared and Kieran
Jared's Evolution
Jared's Fulfillment

Metropolis Series: With Devon McCormack
Faking It
Working It
Owning It
Finding It
Trying It
Hitching It

Last Chance Series:
Depth of Field
Color Me In

Wild Side Series:
Dare You To
Gone For You
Tied to You

Crossroads Series:
Crossroads
Shifting Gears
Test Drive
Jumpstart

Rock Solid Construction Series:
Rock Solid

Broken Pieces Series:
Broken Pieces
Full Circle
Losing Control

Blackcreek Series:
Collide
Stay
Pretend
Return to Blackcreek

Forbidden Love Series with Christina Lee:
Ever After: A Gay Fairy Tale
Forever Moore: A Gay Fairy Tale

About the Author

Riley Hart has always been known as the girl who wears her heart on her sleeve. She won her first writing contest in elementary school, and although she primarily focuses on male/male romance, under her various pen names, she's written a little bit of everything. Regardless of the sub-genre, there's always one common theme and that's...romance! No surprise seeing as she's a hopeless romantic herself. Riley's a lover of character-driven plots, flawed characters, and always tries to write stories and characters people can relate to. She believes everyone deserves to see themselves in the books they read. When she's not writing, you'll find her reading or enjoying time with her awesome family in their home in North Carolina.

Riley Hart is represented by Jane Dystel at Dystel, Goderich & Bourret Literary Management. She's a 2019 Lambda Literary Award Finalist for *Of Sunlight and Stardust*. Under her pen name, her young adult novel, *The History of Us* is an ALA Rainbow Booklist Recommended Read and *Turn the World Upside Down* is a Florida Authors and Publishers President's Book Award Winner.

Find Riley:
Reader's Group: facebook.com/groups/RileysRebels2.0
Facebook: rileyhartwrites
Twitter: @RileyHart5
Goodreads:
goodreads.com/author/show/7013384.Riley_Hart

Printed in Great Britain
by Amazon

65764056R00220